### *"I'm impressed."*

"Well, then, I must be doing well," Celie said. "From what I hear, impressing you isn't easy."

"Sounds like people have been doing way too much talking altogether," was Jacob's comment.

"Don't worry. I'm a scientist. I prefer to collect data on my own."

"Are you planning to collect data on me?" Jacob asked.

Celie glanced laughingly back over her shoulder at him. "I don't know. Do you mind?" She reached over to shut off the lights.

Their hands landed on the switch at the same time.

It was just a touch, hand to hand, but the effects ricocheted through his system. Her eyes were shadowed as she looked back at him. He could see her profile, her generous mouth. "Time to go," she said softly.

It might, Jacob thought uneasily, be long past time.

Dear Reader,

Well, if there were ever a month that screamed for a good love story—make that six!—February would be it. So here are our Valentine's Day gifts to you from Silhouette Special Edition. Let's start with *The Road to Reunion* by Gina Wilkins, next up in her FAMILY FOUND series. When the beautiful daughter of the couple who raised him tries to get a taciturn cowboy to come home for a family reunion, Kyle Reeves is determined to turn her down. But try getting Molly Walker to take no for an answer! In Marie Ferrarella's *Husbands and Other Strangers,* a woman in a boating accident finds her head injury left her with no permanent effects—except for the fact that she can't seem to recall her husband. In the next installment of our FAMILY BUSINESS continuity, *The Boss and Miss Baxter* by Wendy Warren, an unemployed single mother is offered a job—not to mention a place to live for her and her children—with the grumpy, if gorgeous, man who fired her!

"Who's Your Daddy?" is a question that takes on new meaning when a young woman learns that a rock star is her biological father, that her mother is really in love with his brother—and that she herself can't resist her new father's protégé. Read all about it in *It Runs in the Family* by Patricia Kay, the second in her CALLIE'S CORNER CAFÉ miniseries. *Vermont Valentine,* the conclusion to Kristin Hardy's HOLIDAY HEARTS miniseries, tells the story of the last single Trask brother, Jacob—he's been alone for thirty-six years. But that's about to change, courtesy of the beautiful scientist now doing research on his property. And in Teresa Hill's *A Little Bit Engaged,* a woman who's been a bride-to-be for five years yet never saw fit to actually set a wedding date finds true love where she least expects it—with a pastor.

So keep warm, stay romantic, and we'll see you next month....

Gail Chasan
Senior Editor

Please address questions and book requests to:
Silhouette Reader Service
U.S.: 3010 Walden Ave., P.O. Box 1325, Buffalo, NY 14269
Canadian: P.O. Box 609, Fort Erie, Ont. L2A 5X3

# VERMONT VALENTINE

## KRISTIN HARDY

Published by Silhouette Books

America's Publisher of Contemporary Romance

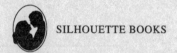

SILHOUETTE BOOKS

ISBN 0-373-24739-7

VERMONT VALENTINE

Copyright © 2006 by Chez Hardy LLC

All rights reserved. Except for use in any review, the reproduction
or utilization of this work in whole or in part in any form by any
electronic, mechanical or other means, now known or hereafter
invented, including xerography, photocopying and recording, or in
any information storage or retrieval system, is forbidden without
the written permission of the editorial office, Silhouette Books,
233 Broadway, New York, NY 10279 U.S.A.

All characters in this book have no existence outside the imagination of
the author and have no relation whatsoever to anyone bearing the same
name or names. They are not even distantly inspired by any individual
known or unknown to the author, and all incidents are pure invention.

This edition published by arrangement with Harlequin Books S.A.

® and TM are trademarks of Harlequin Books S.A., used under license.
Trademarks indicated with ® are registered in the United States Patent
and Trademark Office, the Canadian Trade Marks Office and in other
countries.

Visit Silhouette Books at www.eHarlequin.com

**Printed in U.S.A.**

**Books by Kristin Hardy**

Silhouette Special Edition

*Where There's Smoke* #1720
*Under the Mistletoe* #1725
*Vermont Valentine* #1739

Harlequin Blaze

*My Sexiest Mistake* #44
\*Scoring #78
\*As Bad as Can Be #86
\*Slippery When Wet #94
†Turn Me On #148
†Cutting Loose #156
†Nothing but the Best #164
§Certified Male #187
§U.S. Male #199

\*Under the Covers
†Sex & the Supper Club
§Sealed with a Kiss

---

# KRISTIN HARDY

has always wanted to write, starting her first novel while still in grade school. Although she became a laser engineer by training, she never gave up her dream of being an author. In 2002, her first completed manuscript, *My Sexiest Mistake,* debuted in Harlequin's Blaze line; it was subsequently made into a movie by the Oxygen network. The author of twelve books to date, Kristin lives in New Hampshire with her husband and collaborator. Check out her Web site at www.kristinhardy.com.

Thanks go to Dennis Souto, Mark Twery and
Kathleen Shields, of the USDA Forest Service;
George Cook of the University of Vermont; Joe Doccola
of Arborjet Inc.; and to Doug and Barbara Bragg of the
Bragg Farm (www.braggfarm.com), the inspiration
for the Trask Family Farm.

And as always, to Stephen,
a fine ambassador for the human race.

# *Prologue*

*Vermont, November 2005*

"You want me to do *what?*" Jacob Trask stared at Kelly Christiansen, the teenaged cashier of the Trask Family Farm gift shop.

Kelly shifted and pushed a lock of her blond hair behind her ear. "You know, help out with our fundraiser. Our cheerleading squad qualified for the national championships in February but we need money for our travel. We need your help."

Jacob reached back for his wallet, relieved. "I think I can see my way clear to—"

"No, I'm not asking for money. It's like…" She stood hipshot and stared at the ceiling. "…have you ever seen that cable show where those five stylists fix up a clueless straight guy?"

"No." And he wasn't at all sure he was following.

"Well, we're going to do a hometown version called *Teen Eye for the Eastmont Guy.* Except we put up five possible makeover victims and invite everyone to vote for the one that they'd most like to see made over by donating."

He was beginning to get it. "And?"

"And we want to get you."

"Clueless straight guy?" he repeated dangerously.

She turned beet-red, all the way to the roots of her pale hair. "No, um, you look great, Mr. Trask. We just need someone with…" She flapped her hands at his thick beard and black ponytail. "You know, someone who'll look really different when we cut everything off. The town paper's going to put the before and after of the winner on the front page."

Just what he needed, to be the town entertainment.

Kelly's embarrassment was fading as she warmed to her subject. "We're going to put jars with the candidates' pictures on them in every store in town. It runs through New Year's Day and then we count the money and announce the winner."

Perfect. "When's the makeover?"

"A week later. Don't worry, we won't do it ourselves. We've got stylists all set up in Montpelier. You'll be in good hands. It'd just be some of your time."

Time, something that was at a premium on this, the first year he was working the maple sugar farm after the death of his father. Every hourcounted and so did every dollar. "I don't think—"

"We really want to get to the championships," she pleaded. "This is the only way we can think of to get the money. Won't you help us, Mr. Trask? Please?" Kelly risked another glance. Over her shoulder, Jacob's mother, Molly Trask, watched him from the gift shop's café, her arms crossed.

"Can't I just donate a hundred bucks and call it good?" Jacob asked with a tinge of desperation.

"Oh, with your help we can raise a lot more than that," Kelly said in a tone that suggested she knew she had him beat. "We polled the local storekeepers to see who they wanted to see done over and your name came up most often. You'll get us lots of votes."

And he could just imagine the amusement it would stir up in the maple-sugaring community.

"I think it sounds like an excellent idea," Molly put in briskly. "It's been almost fifteen years since I last saw your face, Jacob. It'll be a nice change of pace."

He didn't need a change of pace. Steady and predictable, that was what Jacob wanted. He didn't need one more thing to worry about.

He liked things just the way they were.

## Chapter One

*Vermont, January 2006*

Celie Favreau muttered an impatient curse and dragged her fingers through her short brown hair. Trees, trees and more trees: beech, ash, birch, the occasional startling green of a pine, and maples, always maples, as far as the eye could see. Sugar maples, Vermont's state tree.

She'd always adored maples. Too bad she hadn't come to the state in the autumn, in time to see the legendary wash of glorious color. Instead, she saw the flat brown and white of a dormant winter landscape. Of course, she knew it wasn't really dormant at all, not in late January. Already the drumbeat of spring was beginning to pulse in the trees as the sap gathered for the rise that triggered rebirth.

And already the threat was stirring.

Celie squinted at the page of directions in her hand and

checked her odometer again. When she'd fled Montreal for a career in forestry, she'd done it partly out of a desire for open space and a conspicuous absence of concrete.

She hadn't thought about the conspicuous absence of road signs.

Of course, she should have been used to it by now. In the past four years she'd been sent to hot spots in seven different states, always moving around. Living somewhere new every few months wasn't a hardship—generally, she enjoyed the variety, she enjoyed a chance to get out of the same old rut.

These days, though, a rut didn't seem like such a bad thing.

The sign by the building up ahead read Ray's Feed 'n' Read. It made her grin. She couldn't pass that one up without a look. With luck, she could also get directions to the Institute.

When she opened the front door, the blast of heat made her forget the winter chill outside. To the left of the door stood a checkout counter, the wall behind it decorated with a lighted Napa sign and a calendar advertising cattle cake. The smile of the balding man at the register faded as he pegged her as a stranger. He gave her a sharp nod.

"Good morning," Celie said. Beyond him lay the swept concrete floor and pallets of goods of a standard seed and grain store. To the right, she saw an incongruously cozy book nook with a dozen shelves and a few comfortable, overstuffed chairs. It called to her irresistibly. "Nice place you've got here."

He grunted.

"Is this Eastmont?" she asked, drifting to a stop in front of a display of lurid thrillers.

"Last time I checked."

Celie fought a smile. "Is this the part where I ask directions and you say 'Cahn't get theah from heah?'"

His lips twitched. "Well, if it's Eastmont, Maine you're

asking about, that's different. We have a translation book for Mainers," he added.

"So I see. No translation book for Vermonters?"

"None needed. We don't have any accent. Now you, you're not from around these parts. What's that I hear in your voice?"

Even after all these years, the whisper of a French accent still lingered. "Canada. I grew up in Montreal."

"Ah. The wife and I went up there about twenty years ago for an anniversary. Nice town, especially the old part."

"My parents own a bookstore in Vieux Montréal."

"Do tell? I thought you looked like a book person when you walked in."

She couldn't tell him that she'd moved away because the bookstore had suffocated her. Instead, she picked up a thriller and headed to the counter. "So what's more popular, the feed or the read?"

"Oh, you'd be surprised. Folks around here will pick up a book, especially in winter. Shoot, we've got one guy buys so many books I don't know how he gets any sugaring done." He passed the book over the bar-code scanner.

"Maybe he's trying to improve himself."

He snorted. "I think Jacob would say he's as improved as he needs to be. That'll be $6.25," he added, slipping the book into a plain brown bag.

Celie passed him a twenty. "I wonder if you could help me out. I'm looking for the Woodward Maple Research Institute. It's around here, right?"

"Close enough."

"I don't suppose you'd be willing to tell me how close?"

He considered, making an effort to look crusty. "Oh, a couple miles as the crow flies."

"Any chance I could get there if I weren't a crow?" she asked, reaching out for her change.

"Oh, you're wanting directions."

"Assuming you can get theah from heah."

The smile was full-fledged this time. "Well, you'll want Bixley Road." He rested his hands on the counter. "Turn right out of the parking lot and go until you see a sign that says Trask Farm. The second left after that is Bixley Road. You'll know it because it heads uphill at first. You'll pass maybe three roads and you'll see the signs for the Institute. If you see the covered bridge, you'll know you've gone too far."

"Thank you kindly," she said.

"You working at the Institute?"

"That depends."

"On what?"

She grinned. "Whether I find it."

"Well, Jacob Trask, who would have thought you were such a good-looking boy under all that hair?" Muriel Anderson, the comfortable-looking clerk at Washington County Maple Supplies gave him a long look up and down. "I almost didn't recognize you. I see those Eastmont girls took you to task."

Those Eastmont girls had trimmed and tidied and upholstered him until he could hardly stand it. In the first stunned moments when he'd stared at his newly shorn face in the salon mirror, all he'd been able to do was calculate feverishly how long it would take to grow back. He'd been shocked at how naked being clean-shaven made him feel.

He'd grown the beard at twenty and left it on. Without it, he almost hadn't recognized himself. In the intervening sixteen years, his face had grown more angular, the chin more stubborn, the bones pressed more tightly against the skin.

It was the face of someone else, not him. A week, he'd figured, a week to get covered up.

He hadn't figured on noticing the mix of gray hairs among

the black in the new beard as it sprouted. More, far more than he'd recalled before. There certainly weren't any on his head. He could do without the ones down below. After all, a man was entitled to some vanity, wasn't he? The beard, he'd decided, would stay gone.

"Hi, Jacob," purred Eliza, Muriel's twenty-year-old daughter, as she walked past.

Or maybe it wouldn't, he thought uneasily, taking the fifty-pound bag of diatomaceous earth off his shoulder and setting it down on the counter. He was all for having a personal life, but the non-stop scrutiny he'd begun attracting from women felt a little weird. He liked cruising along below the radar; he had from the time he'd looked around in third grade and realized he was a head taller than any of his classmates. Cruising below the radar had gotten hard, though, all of a sudden.

"Did you hear they found some cases of maple borer over in New York?" Muriel asked as she started ringing up Jacob's order. "They had to take down 423 trees from the heart of a sugarbush to get it all. Sixteen-inchers, most of them."

Four-hundred-some-odd trees? Nearly ten acres, maybe more. That would be a financial hit, and one that would persist for decades. After all, sugar maples didn't grow old enough to tap for thirty or forty years. "Are you sure they're not exaggerating?"

"Tom Bollinger said it, and he can be trusted." Muriel shook her head. "You should spend less time looking at books in Ray's and more time around the stove talking to people, Jacob. You might find out something you can use."

"I'd rather hear it from you." He winked at her, as he had so many times over the years. And to his everlasting shock, she blushed.

"Oh, you." She shook her head at him. "Talking isn't nearly as hard as chopping brush."

For Jacob talking was harder, except in the case of a handful of people, such as Muriel.

"Everything I hear tells me we've got something to worry about here," Muriel continued. "Some of those Institute fellows were over at Willoughby's sugarbush a couple of weeks ago, poking at his trees and muttering."

Concern was immediate. Willoughby's property adjoined his own. Like most sugar-makers, Jacob found solvency a delicate balancing act, especially now that he was the one running the farm to support his mother and himself. The prospect of losing five or ten percent of his revenue-producing trees was a sobering one. "Do they think his trees are infested?"

"They don't know. Took some samples, said they'd get back to him."

Jacob stuffed his change in his pocket distractedly. "If you see him, tell him I wish him luck."

"You can tell him yourself at the county growers' meeting tomorrow." His noise of disgust earned a click of the tongue from Muriel. "You've got to show up at these things, Jacob," she chided.

"I do show up, Muriel."

"It's not enough to show. You need to talk. You can't just sit through the program. That's not where you learn the important things."

It was where he learned all he needed to know, Jacob thought, that and the Internet. He'd never understood people's obsession with sitting around and yapping their fool heads off about nothing. Working he understood, and he was happy to do it. Standing around and chewing the fat in hopes he might get something more than idle speculation was a waste of time.

A couple of miles from the Feed 'n' Read, Celie began wondering if she'd somehow missed a turn again. It wasn't

that the directions were difficult but that the term "road" was
a vague one. To her, it meant pavement and a sign. To the clerk
at the feed store, who knew? She'd passed several things that
looked more like gravel drives. They could be part of a sugarbush access system, assuming the maples she was driving
through belonged to a sugarbush, or they could lead to someone's house.

Or they could be her landmarks.

She was reasonably confident she'd gotten onto Bixley
Road all right. She hadn't seen a covered bridge, though, and
by the directions her contact had sent her, she should have
found the Institute long since. Wrong turn? Possible, but she
might also have been close because she was clearly driving
through tended maples, and the Institute was located in the
middle of a sugarbush. More than likely, she was on the property already.

She scanned the trees automatically as she drove, a habit
so established she wasn't even aware of it.

Suddenly she saw something that had her swerving to the
side of the road, pulse speeding up. It was almost too subtle
to be seen, the striations of the trunk, the slight thickening at
the base of the tree that set off warning bells. A closer look,
she thought, hoping to God it wasn't what it appeared to be.

Turning off the engine was barely a decision at all. This
was more important than what time she arrived at the Institute. After all, she was already late enough that it wouldn't
matter one way or another.

This would.

Reaching behind the front seat of her truck, Celie pulled
out her field kit.

She wore hiking boots, as was her habit. It paid to be prepared. With a job like hers, you could be tramping around a
stand of trees at a moment's notice. It was one of the things

she loved about it. Oh, growing up in Montreal had been exciting, but it had been too confined, too structured. And it was too associated with the dusty, musty demands of the Cité de L'Ile, the bookstore that was her family's legacy. Her family's, not hers. Hers was going to be eliminating the insatiable pest that had the power to destroy the maple forests of North America.

In warmer weather, the dip she crossed to get to the trees was probably a drainage ditch. Now, it was just a running depression in the snow. Celie walked back parallel to the road. Sixteen- to eighteen-inch trunks, she estimated, moving among them. A mature, tended stand with only a handful of non-maple species. She was unfortunately going to show up at the Institute with some unwelcome news about what had every appearance of being their sugarbush.

The laughter was gone from her eyes now, replaced by focus as she knelt to inspect first one tree, then another. Up close, it was harder to identify the one that had caught her eye. She went through half a dozen before she found it and dug out her loupe. Crouched in the snow, she ignored the sound of passing vehicles on the road, ignored the cold spreading up through her toes. What mattered was the puzzle in front of her. What mattered was finding the evidence.

There were holes, though not the characteristic round holes of the maple borer but something more irregular. Were they signs of the beetle or just normal bark disturbances? Unzipping a pocket of her field kit, she pulled out a wire-thin metal spatula.

Scraping the side of the hole yielded a crumbly, dark residue. Rotted bark or the fungus that the beetle carried from tree to tree? She rubbed a bit thoughtfully between her fingers and tipped the spatula into a glass sample vial. A laboratory analysis would show.

The sudden barking of a dog made her jump and drop the vial. When she turned, shock took her breath. A man stalked toward her, looking as if he'd walked out of another century with his buckskin jacket and his coal-dark hair brushing his shoulders, a black hound at his heels. Way over six feet tall, with shoulders a couple feet wide. The bones of his face stood out strongly, as though pressed there by sheer force of personality. The dark stubble on his jaw only made him look dangerous. But it was his eyes that caught and held her attention, startlingly blue and narrowed now at her in irritation.

"You mind telling me what you're doing in my trees?"

Jacob usually came across trespassers in the fall, when the leaf peepers were out in force. People figured that if there weren't fences, they were free to just walk all over the place, not understanding that they compacted the soil, compressed the roots and generally compromised the health of the trees every time they walked near them.

The battered, rust-streaked mini truck he'd stopped behind boasted out-of-state plates. And the intruder crouched in front of the tree was not just looking at it but messing with it. Sightseers were damaging enough. Those, he usually chatted with and pointed toward the Trask gift shop. A kid vandalizing his trees, though, earned a different treatment. Jacob strode over with the intent of summarily tossing him off the property.

But then the kid looked up and Jacob realized the him was a her, a bright-eyed pixie of a her with a cap of curly dark hair.

Murphy barked his way up in his usual fearsome guard-dog act. It *was* just an act—the minute she began talking to him and rubbing his ears, he began wagging his tail, the traitor.

Of course, if she petted Jacob the way she was currently stroking Murphy, his tail might start wagging, too. "Hi, sweetie," she crooned. "Aren't you gorgeous? And you like that, don't you?" She scratched Murphy's chest until he sank down on the snow and rolled over for her to rub his belly. No dignity at all.

She offered Jacob a disarming smile. "I'm so sorry. I didn't mean to trespass. I thought this was Institute property. Your forestry techniques are top, really top. That's why I thought I was on Institute land," she chattered. And the whole while she was swiftly putting her tools away and zipping up her field kit.

A very professional-looking field kit, he realized with a frown.

"That's why I got confused," she continued. "I wasn't expecting a private grower to be doing such a good job and I—"

"Who are you?" he interrupted. "What were you doing?"

"Just looking at trees. It was an honest mistake." She stood. Propping one fist on her hip, she stared up at him. "Well, you are a big one, aren't you?"

His impression of a pixie had been accurate, Jacob thought—she was easily a foot shorter than he was, and tiny, even wearing her bulky parka. The cold had reddened her cheeks. The humor dancing now in her sherry-brown eyes didn't entirely hide the sharp intelligence—or purpose—that lurked there. Mostly, though, in her red jacket, she was a welcome flash of color in the drab winter backdrop, sloe-eyed, lush-mouthed and far too tempting for the middle of a work day.

She leaned down to give Murphy a last pat. "Anyway, I apologize. I didn't intend to trespass." Nimbly, she stepped around him and walked across the drainage ditch toward the battered red truck. "I tend to get excited about trees and sometimes I don't think, I just stop and take a look. But I'll get out of your way now." She was opening the door and inside almost before he realized she was really going.

And then she was gone and only small footprints in the snow gave any evidence that she'd ever been there at all.

* * *

How was someone that beautiful allowed to just walk around in the woods sneaking up on women? Celie wondered feverishly as she drove away. Good lord, the man made her palms sweat. Not to mention the fact that he'd come across her on his land without permission. Strictly against the policy and procedure manual her boss loved to wave in front of her face. You were required to get permission from property owners before venturing in, and mistakes—however well-intentioned—weren't allowed. Oh yes, Gavin Masterson would have a field day with the incident. Shoot, it would give him fodder for a whole week of lectures.

Assuming he found out.

She breathed a silent prayer that the hunk of a property owner—the very large hunk of a property owner—would just let the incident go. Then again, there wasn't much she could do about it if he didn't. He'd do what he was going to do. All she could do in return was roll with the changes, something she'd always been good at.

"Thank God," she muttered at the sight of the Woodward Institute sign at the side of the road. At least something was finally going right.

The Institute occupied an unprepossessing two-story building faced with biscuit-colored vinyl siding and roofed in pale brown. Rising behind it she saw the high venting peak of a sugarhouse. In all directions stretched different varieties of maples.

The inhabitants of the facility didn't stand on ceremony. When she walked through the doors, she stepped into an empty reception area separated from the central room beyond by a waist-high wooden barrier fitted with a gate and a bell. To get someone's attention, presumably, you rang, although she supposed yelling was always an option. The central area held a few cubicles inside the perimeter of offices.

A number of the doors were open, letting winter sunlight stream through.

A bearded man in a flannel shirt and jeans stood in front of a copy machine. He glanced up at her, the light glinting off his gold-rimmed glasses. "Can I help you?"

"I'm looking for Bob Ford."

"You've found him." He collected his copies and took the original off the glass plate. "Are you Celie?"

She nodded. "Sorry I'm late. I had some adventures finding the place."

"I'm not surprised. We really need to sit down and redo our directions. Come on in." He waved her through the barrier and put his hand out to shake. "Pleasure to meet you. Come on, my office is over here."

She followed him along the aisle to where he turned in a door. "Wow." She stopped short, staring through the wide band of windows at the sugarbush beyond. "Quite a view you've got here."

"A corner office." His teeth gleamed against his neatly trimmed silver beard. "The perks of command."

At his gesture, she sat in the client chair. "It's gorgeous up here."

"We like to think so. It won't be for long if your bug gets loose, though."

*Her* bug. Celie had studied the scarlet-horned maple borer since undergraduate school, shocked by the toll it had exacted in Asia. Finding a way to destroy it became a personal mission, not just the subject of her doctorate. When the beetle had emerged as a threat to the northern forests of the United States, she and her advisor, Jack Benchley, had been recruited for the science advisory panel that determined a plan of action. From there, it had been only a short step to taking the job heading up the eradication program.

And there she'd been ever since, her name synonymous with a predator of increasing destructiveness.

"Do you think you've got things under control in New York?"

That was the question, wasn't it. She moved her shoulders. "We took down a lot of trees. Will it help? I don't know. I suppose in our own way we're just as bad as the borer."

"You don't destroy trees for the sake of destruction," Ford said quietly.

"Neither do they. They're just going about the business of life." But they were relentless, implacable, and every time she had to take out an acre of century-old trees it made her soul sick. "Do the sugar-makers around here know that you've discovered evidence of the borer?"

"We've done some inspections but I haven't said anything. I thought you ought to get a look around. There's a county growers' meeting tomorrow night. You can fill them in on the details then, let them know what to expect."

"When I figure that out, I'll let you know." Through the open door, she heard the sudden sound of voices as a group of people came in from outside.

Ford glanced out toward the central room and his jaw set a fraction. "You should be aware, we've also got an…official from the Vermont Division of Forestry to oversee the project."

Hairs prickled on the back of her neck. "To oversee the project? This is a federal program. I'm running it."

"Not in my state," said a voice from the door.

Without turning, Celie knew who it was. Dick Rumson, the old guard head of forest resource protection for the state. Undereducated and overprotected, he was a political appointee who ran roughshod over far-more-qualified people by virtue of his connections. He'd wangled a spot on the science advisory panel for the maple borer and obdurately contested the findings put forth by Celie and Benchley. Fortunately, they'd had the data to back up every assertion, whereas he'd had only bluster. Ultimately, she and Benchley had carried all the votes, with Rumson as the lone holdout. That he still bitterly resented being shown up was obvious by the set of his beaky mouth.

"Dick," she said smoothly, rising to put out her hand. "Good to see you again."

"We can handle this ourselves," Rumson said brusquely, ignoring Celie to aim a stare at Bob Ford. "We don't need federal folks in here."

"I think it's too early to assume that," Celie countered, jamming her hands in her pockets. "The staff here has reason to suspect an infestation, and I think they might be right." Calm, she reminded herself. Calmness was the best way to get to him. He wasn't a threat, only an irritant. Everything would be twice as hard and take twice as long with him around, but it would get done. "I'll know more about the situation after I've had a chance to do some inspections." She toyed with the items in her pocket: a coin, a paperclip, a hard cylinder she didn't remember putting in there.

"We've already inspected and we haven't found anything. You might as well save your time."

"Now, Dick," Ford began, "you know we've found—"

"You university types jump to conclusions," Rumson said contemptuously. "I've got a staff of experienced forestry specialists and we haven't found anything."

Celie touched the hard cylinder again. The sample vial, she realized. "Really?" She brought it out. "You want to tell me what this is, then?"

Rumson squinted over at it. "What's that?"

"A sample from a bore hole."

Rumson gave a contemptuous snort. "That's bark."

"Look closer," she invited. "That greenish powder on the top might be maple-borer fungi."

"Or it could just be bark dust."

"You want to come into the lab with me and find out?"

"I don't have time for this load of time-wasting horse hockey," he barked, a sure sign he was feeling on unsteady ground.

"I'll be happy to call you with the results," Celie said silkily. "I'm not doing this for entertainment, Dick. If the maple borer is in your woods, we've got to find it and act quickly. Unless you want to lose your entire maple syrup industry and all those tourist dollars the leaf peepers bring in the fall. How many billion dollars does that add up to again?"

Rumson's face turned a dull red. "Now just a minute here. Don't you think you can come in and just start clearing acres. How do I know you didn't bring that in?"

"Careful, Dick." Somehow, Ford's voice managed to be both mild and steely with warning.

Rumson worked his jaw a moment in silence. "I want to talk with your supervisor."

"I'll be happy to give you his number. We need to work together on this."

"I saw how you cooperated at the advisory panel meeting," he said, his expression sullen. "I want my team overseeing everything you do."

"I'll go you one better. Once I've trained them, your team can be involved in every inspection. We've got a lot of ground to cover and very little time to do it in. We're going to need every pair of eyeballs we can get."

"If you think that—"

"What I *think* is that as head of resource protection you want what's best for your forests, Dick. I've always thought that. How we work out the specifics is just details." She gave him a friendly, open smile.

It stopped him for a long moment while he tried to work out a response. "Don't think this is over," he said finally, turning toward the door.

Celie resisted the urge to roll her eyes. "Trust me, Dick, I know it's only the start."

## Chapter Two

"Sorry you had to deal with that," Ford said as Rumson slammed out. "I was going to warn you but there wasn't time."

Celie shrugged. "I should have expected it. Dick and I go back a ways." And little of their history was pleasant.

Ford studied her. "Is he going to get in the way of you getting the job done?"

"I'm sure he'll try, but he's never managed to be more than an annoyance so far."

"Let me see that sample." He reached out a hand and she passed over the glass cylinder.

Ford studied it, turning it over in his hands. "You really think this is the fungus?"

"I don't know. It's not as green as it usually is but the trunk showed the typical thickening of the bark, and holes, although they looked like a bird had been at them. Hard to say if they were made by our boy or not."

"Where'd you see it?"

"A sugarbush on the way here. I'm not sure where. I ran into the owner while I was out there—a big, tall guy with black hair." And shoulders to die for but she didn't figure he wanted to hear that.

"Jacob Trask," Ford said. "He's got about a hundred acres of maples adjoining the Institute." He shook his head. "Let's hope this is just bark in here. He lost his father last spring. That family doesn't need any more bad news."

He hadn't looked like someone's son but like some woodmaster sprung out of the earth to walk the forest, with his black hair and those cheekbones and those eyes, those impossibly blue eyes. And he'd stood there staring at her until all she'd been able to do was babble like an idiot and scramble away before she just started whimpering and salivating right there in front of him.

"Well, there's nothing for it," Ford said, handing the sample vial back and rising. "You've got to do your job. Come on, I'll show you the cube and the lab you can use."

The cubicle was small but more than adequate for her purposes. The lab facilities were what counted. It was there that the major detective work went on, there that the test she'd developed could confirm or deny the presence of the maple borer.

Setting down her computer bag, Celie began to pull out files and hook up her computer to the network.

"About damned time you showed up to do some work," said a voice from the doorway.

Celie whipped around to stare at the rangy blonde who leaned against the cubicle entrance. "Marce!" She jumped up and threw her arms around the newcomer. "It's so good to see you."

"You, too." Marce gave her another squeeze and released her. "I thought you were coming in last night."

"I left you a message. I got a late start yesterday so I just stopped somewhere overnight and finished up this morning."

Marce eyed her. "Tell me it wasn't some rest stop."

"Why do you think I got the camper shell put on?" Celie said reasonably.

"It was one thing when we were in grad school," Marce protested. "You've got a job now. You can afford to stay in a real hotel with real locks and a real bed."

"On a government travel stipend?" Celie snorted. "Anyway, I'm going to be staying in a real bed while I'm here, aren't I? Didn't you tell me you got rid of your futon in the guest room?"

"Yeah."

"Well, it's already a step up from my camper shell and what I've got back in Maryland."

"You're still sleeping on a futon? Celie, you're practically thirty."

"And I spend a day or two there a month if I'm lucky. I ought just to rent a storage unit and bunk there."

Marce rolled her eyes. "You're no better than you were in grad school."

"Hey, your average storage facility is miles better than that pit we all lived in during grad school."

"Agreed." Marce grinned. "Anyway, it's almost the end of the day. Why don't we knock off early and get you settled? I made a pot of barley soup last night."

"Still into the junk food, I see."

"I don't consider burgers and potato chips two of the major food groups, if that's what you mean."

"Well I do. So I've got a better idea: let's knock off early, get me settled and scare up a pizza."

"All right," Marce sighed, "I can tell when I'm beat."


"I can't believe you. I live here for three years and I barely see anyone human. You stop in the woods to sample a tree and you stumble across a god?" Marce shook her head and bit into a slice of pepperoni pizza.

"It's not like he was falling at my feet or anything," Celie pointed out. "In fact, I think he was pretty pissed that I was in his trees. All I wanted to do was get out of there."

"Before or after you decided to have his baby?"

"His baby? Maybe in a parallel universe."

"Are you sure you didn't see him in a parallel universe? I can't think of anyone around here who looks like that. Trust me, I'd have remembered."

"Bob Ford said it was someone named Jacob Trask."

"Jacob Trask?" Marce almost dropped her pizza. "Wait a minute, the Jacob Trask I know looks like the kind of guy who trapped beaver during the Gold Rush. We can't be talking about the same person. I mean, he's big enough but…"

"Well, I didn't describe him in exhaustive detail to Bob. Maybe he had it wrong." Celie raised her beer bottle.

"Let's hope so. Jacob Trask is not the friendliest guy around, I'll warn you. I had to go out and help him thin his sugarbush last year. I think I got two words out of him the whole time. Of course," she said thoughtfully, "that's not exactly going to be a problem for you."

Celie froze with the bottle at her lips. "Are you suggesting I talk too much?"

"Far be it from me to suggest. I mean, I do use semaphore with you when you get on a roll, but I'm sure there are times when you're merely voluble rather than garrulous."

"I just talk a lot when I'm nervous," Celie protested.

"I guess you spend all your time nervous, then," Marce replied, ducking when Celie tossed a wadded-up napkin at her.

"Serve you right if I never talk again."

Marce snorted. "That'll be the day."

\* \* \*

Jacob walked the hall of the James Woodward Elementary School, remembering the days he'd run down the tile floors to the playground at recess. He'd always hated being cooped up inside; he didn't fit. He fitted outdoors, in the sugarbush. Going into class was something to put off until the last minute.

The passage of years had made it no different, even if he was going to a growers' meeting now instead of a class. It still meant a room full of people and making conversation. Granted, the talk was mostly about sugaring, but still, he'd rather be at home with a book or playing guitar than standing about searching for things to say.

The auditorium echoed with the voices of sugar-makers, louder than usual. When he saw the cluster of people crowded around the coffee machine, he wondered if some kind soul had brought in free food. And then the crowd parted enough for him to see what was attracting all the attention.

Or who.

It was the pixie he'd stumbled over in his maples. She wasn't enveloped in a parka now but stood in narrow red trousers and a shiny white blouse with a little black and white checked sweater over the top. She looked impossibly lively and bright against the muted tones of the clothing around her, seeming to take up more room than just her body would explain, as though her energy occupied physical space.

She'd stuck in his mind after he'd seen her the day before. At odd moments he'd thought of those laughing eyes, that soft, tempting mouth. And when he'd closed his own eyes and fallen into sleep, she'd drifted through his dreams, leaving him to wake feeling vaguely restless.

Now, he watched her amid the crowd, animated and quick as a butterfly. And he heard her laughter, spilling out across the room in a bubbly arpeggio that invited everyone around to join in. For a moment, he was tempted to go over. Only to find out who she was, he told himself, not to get a better look. Then again, given the fact that she'd shown up in his trees one day and at the growers' meeting the next, it was pretty obvious she had something to do with the Institute.

And if he'd figured that out, there was no point in fighting his way through the crowd to talk with her. Not his style, first of all. Second, he had more important things to focus on than a pretty face and an inviting laugh. Like finding out the status of the situation and what, if anything, his exposure was. He'd done his Internet research, he knew the enormous risk posed by the maple borer. Now he had to find out what that meant for him, personally.

At the front of the room, Bob Ford from the Institute tapped the mike. "Okay, everybody, let's get started." He waited a few minutes as people drifted toward the rows of seats. "There are some contact sheets being circulated. Please fill them out and hand them in as you leave. We need to update our roster."

Someone handed Jacob a clipboard. He pulled out a pen and bent over the form, filling out the top. When he looked at the questions, though, he frowned. Number of taps? Monoculture or mixed population forest? What the hell?

Then a scent drifted over to him, something tempting and subtle and essentially female. Something immediately distracting. He glanced up to see her sitting beside him.

And all his senses vaulted to the alert.

"Hi," she whispered. "Is this seat taken?"

Low and quiet, with a little husk of promise beneath it. The way she might sound over drinks, in some dark, quiet bar.

Or in a bedroom, late at night.

"All yours," he said, fighting the image.

Her smile bloomed like a summer flower.

At the podium, Ford cleared his throat. "Since I know everyone here, I'm going to skip introducing myself and get to business. As some of you may have heard, there have been scarlet-horned maple borer outbreaks in New York. It's something we need to be concerned about here. Understand, if this thing gets a chance to spread it can take down entire forests. Entire forests, people. No maple syrup, no fall foliage, no tourist dollars, nothing." He cleared his throat. "We've invited Celie Favreau of APHIS, the USDA's Animal and Plant Health Inspection Service, to come to the Woodward Institute to take a look around the area. She's going to tell you a little more about what we're up against and what happens next. Celie?"

"Wish me luck," Celie murmured, squaring her shoulders and rising to walk to the front of the room. From a distance, she looked even smaller than she had in the woods. She didn't stand behind the podium but leaned against the table next to it, microphone in hand.

"Good evening. I'm Celie Favreau with APHIS. I head up the program to eradicate the scarlet-horned maple borer. How many know something about the beetle?" Only a sprinkling of hands went up, including Jacob's, and she nodded. "All right, let me give you a quick rundown. The scarlet-horned maple borer is a nasty customer. It's about half an inch long and is often mistaken for a benign bark beetle unless you look closely at the horns. Unlike the bark beetle, though, the maple borer targets live wood, not dead. And it's particularly fond of maples.

"It bores through the bark down near the root collar and lays its eggs at the cambium, where the bark and wood interface. Over the course of a few weeks, a fertilized female can lay several dozen eggs in galleries in the first few rings of wood. When the eggs hatch, the larvae live on the cambium. I don't need to tell any of you what that means."

No indeed. A few dozen larvae merrily eating their way into maturity could easily girdle a tree. No fluids could travel from root to leaf. Presto, instant death. Jacob could hear the rustling around him as his fellow sugar-makers took it all in. It wasn't news to him but he still felt the hot press of anxiety.

"Of course," Celie continued, "there's a bigger problem than just girdling. The maple borer carries a fungus that's deadly to maples. Each time a borer works its way into the tree, the fungus spores rub off on the sides of the hole. At that point, the tree is both infected and infested and it's just a matter of time. Our trap tests have shown that the mature beetle will range up to a hundred yards in search of a suitable host tree."

There was some shifting and muttering at this. Celie scanned the room, making eye contact with each of them in turn. "So you see what we're up against. We can't take chances with this one. If one adult gets loose, population growth is exponential. And that means if we find any infestations, we have to take radical action to control them."

In the audience, a craggy-faced man with a lantern jaw raised a hand. "Just how radical do you mean?"

"It's pointless to talk about action until we've investigated the scope of the problem. I'll be teaming up with forestry specialists from the Institute and the state to cover as much territory as possible before the days warm up. We can't afford to play wait and see. The maple borer hatches early, so we've got to find any infestation pronto and take measures."

"And they are?" the sugar-maker persisted.

Celie took a breath. "We have to take down any infested trees we find, plus a buffer circle of at least a hundred and fifty yards in radius around that host tree. The felled trees have to be cut up, chipped and burned immediately, and the stumps ground down to eight inches below ground level."

An angry buzz erupted in the room. The men who'd been charmed by her weren't charmed any more. "You're talking about clearing acres," a burly redhead protested.

"Let's not get ahead of things," she said calmly. "We don't even know what we're dealing with, yet. In Michigan, they called me in and I didn't find a sign of infestation."

"And in New York, you cut down half the state," the craggy-faced man retorted.

For an instant, Jacob thought, she looked like she didn't know whether to sigh or laugh. Instead, she merely shook her head. "We took out a total of twelve hundred trees, spread across three different sugarbushes and a town common. I don't take felling trees lightly." She looked around the room. "But I've seen what the maple borer can do and I'm ready to do everything in my power to stop it. If there's infestation here, all of your trees are at risk. All of them. I hope you'll cooperate with me to stop it."

"You're not here for your health. You're here because you know there's a problem," the redhead accused.

She hesitated and locked eyes with Jacob. She'd been crouched at the foot of his tree, he remembered, and felt the clutch of foreboding in his gut. "I've seen early signs that might be cause for concern. If we take care of things quickly, before the weather warms up, we can get a handle on it. If anything slows that down, well, this time next year your sugarbushes are going to look very different." She let out a breath. "Next question?"

The session dragged on nearly an hour before Celie finally passed around handouts on the maple borer. Jacob waited impatiently for the meeting to end. He didn't need handouts. He didn't need to hear any more questions. What he needed was to talk to Celie Favreau.

Alone.

The knot around her was as thick as it had been before the meeting. But Jacob was nothing if not patient. One by one, the sugar-makers drifted off, and finally she stood on the low stage, stacking up the last of the literature she'd brought along.

"I thought it went well," Bob Ford was saying as Jacob walked up.

"We got the information out there, anyway. What happens now will depend on what we find."

"And how the lab tests turn out."

Lab tests? Jacob's eyes narrowed. He stepped forward to stop just below the steps. "May I speak with you a moment?"

Celie glanced over at him, then at Bob Ford. "Why don't you go on ahead, Bob? I'll take care of this."

"You want me to take that back to the Institute?" He nodded at the box of remaining leaflets and flyers.

"I'll do it," Celie said.

He nodded "I'll lock the doors on my way out. Just make sure the lights are off and things are shut up when you leave." He shook hands with them both and headed up the aisle.

Jacob looked at Celie. For the first time, they were eye to eye. Her gaze was speculative. She studied him, in fact, as though he were a puzzle that interested her.

Jacob shifted and nodded at the box of literature. "I can get that for you." Action always came more easily to him than standing around. Or speaking.

"Thanks." Celie watched him climb onto the low stage and pick up the heavy box. "So what do you think?"

"Of the talk?" Or of her? There was something about her, he thought, something appealing, maybe irresistible.

But that wasn't why he was here.

"You were in my trees yesterday," he said abruptly, knowing no other way than to be direct. "Were you inspecting them?"

The glint of humor in her eyes disappeared. "Not officially, no. I thought I was on Institute property. Something just caught my eye and I wanted a better look."

"At what?"

Her pause was too deliberate. It made him uneasy. "Something interesting about the trunk."

He felt the flare of impatience. "Don't dance around the question. You were bent over one of my maples with a field kit when I walked up. What was that about?"

"Maybe nothing. I noticed the tree as I was driving by. Some things that are characteristic of an infested tree," she elaborated. "I just wanted to take a closer look, but I didn't realize it was your land."

"I don't give a damn about trespassing. I want to know what you saw."

"I'm not sure." She looked at him, her eyes troubled. "The bore holes were the right size but the wrong shape. I thought the sample I got out of the hole contained fungus but the test I did showed up negative."

"Negative?" Relief made him lightheaded. "So it's clear?"

"I'll do a more comprehensive test tomorrow, once I get my lab set up. Of course, your dog knocked my vial into the snow before I got the top on, so the results aren't iron-clad."

"Murph can be a little overenthusiastic sometimes."

"I'll say. What is he, the love child of a lab and a Shetland pony?"

Jacob grinned. "Lab, great Dane and a little bloodhound thrown in for good measure, or so the vet tells me."

"An interesting background beats a pedigree any time."

"We're nothing if not interesting around here."

"I bet you are." Killer smile, Celie thought as they stepped off the stage. A mouth that begged to be nibbled on and she was just the nibbler to do it. But it was the smile that light-

ened up that sober face, that made him approachable. His nose
looked as though it had lost a battle once with something bigger or harder, but the resultant bump only made him look more
interestingly rugged.

There was a strength to him, not just height and width of
shoulder but some quality she couldn't name. Certainty of
self, perhaps. It was what had driven her to seek him out
when she could have wandered to a seat by any of the men
she'd been chatting with. They didn't intrigue her.

Jacob Trask did.

They started up the aisle. "Speaking of interesting," she
said, "I've never seen a Feed 'n' Read before."

"I guess you've been by Ray's. One of my favorite places."

"So he was telling me."

"He was telling you?" Jacob watched her walk ahead of
him, the red trousers shifting in some very intriguing ways.

"He mentioned you."

"If you got Ray talking, you're good." Then again, she'd
somehow managed to get him talking, too.

"I got the impression he likes to do nothing but."

"Not to strangers. Ray usually barks at strangers, if he
talks to them at all.

"I guess I charmed him."

Like she was charming him, Jacob thought. "I'm impressed."

"Well, then I must be doing well. From what I hear, impressing you isn't easy."

"Sounds like people have been doing way too much talking, altogether."

"Don't worry," she said as they neared the open doorway.
"I'm a scientist. I prefer to collect data on my own."

"Are you planning to collect data on me?" he asked, amused.

She glanced laughingly back over her shoulder at him. "I

don't know. Do you mind?" She started out the open door and then reached back in to shut off the lights.

Their hands landed on the switch at the same time.

It was just a touch, hand to hand, but the effects ricocheted crazily through his system. Vivid awareness of her fingers, cool and soft and tangled with his. For an instant, he felt her tense in reaction, then relax. It took him a moment longer than it should have to move his hand.

When he snapped the switch down, it enveloped them in a darkness broken only by the hallway light coming through the open door.

Her eyes were shadowed as she looked back in at him. He could see her profile, the quick tilt of her nose, the generous mouth. "Time to go."

It might, **Jacob** thought uneasily, be long past time.

## Chapter Three

Painted maple leaves in a blaze of autumn colors adorned the white sign at the side of the road. "Trask Family Farm and Sugarhouse," read the forest-green letters. The long, low clapboard building beyond was presumably the gift shop; at the far end, the shingled roof jumped up abruptly to the sugarhouse vent.

Celie turned into the parking lot, navigating the mixture of rolled gravel and snow to nose her truck against the post-and-rail perimeter fence. She'd come on a whim, driven by the impulse to see Jacob Trask again. And Celie generally went with her impulses. Granted, it was a Saturday morning, a time most people took off, but she had a feeling Jacob Trask didn't.

She already knew he wasn't like most people.

At the start of the gravel path that led from parking lot to gift shop stood a tall, thick post with a galvanized sap bucket hanging from it, a little peaked hood snapped in place. Smart people, the Trasks. A person could make a living from selling maple syrup purely to distributors but a business that catered to both the wholesale and retail trade benefited from higher margins and greater diversity. Little touches like the bucket gave the feel of sap collecting. People would stop out of curiosity, stop for the novelty. They'd stay around to buy.

Besides, it was charming.

She climbed the steps to the broad veranda that ran along the front of the building. Of course, the incongruous part of the setup was the idea of gruff Jacob Trask at a cash register selling maple syrup in little metal log-cabin-shaped containers. Or serving up maple ice cream, she thought with a smile as she glanced at the cone-shaped sign beside the door.

Then she stepped inside and all she could think was that it was a shame she hadn't been in the store a few weeks before when she'd been feverishly trying to finish her Christmas shopping. Her mother would have loved the quilted potholders and matching dish towels. Her sister the gourmet would have been even happier with the jars of lemon curd. She could have given her little nephew a plush stuffed moose and her father the illustrated history of the Green Mountains. And maybe bought one of the gilded maple leaf Christmas ornaments for herself.

The shop itself was a delight with walls and shelves of pine, floors of wide-planked hardwood, polished until they gleamed. Through an archway, Celie could see a bright room furnished with picnic tables. There, presumably, the currently absent staff served up maple ice cream and other snacks.

A hollow-sounding thump had her jumping. She turned to look around the deserted shop. "Hello?" She stepped forward and glanced into the café. Nope, no one there, either. Which was strange. Granted, it was just opening time and hers was the only car in the lot, but still…

The thump sounded again, this time, closer at hand. Scanning the shop, Celie suddenly saw what looked like a closet door shake in time with another thump. Before her astounded eyes, the doorknob rattled and rotated just a bit. It was either a poltergeist or…

A very human voice spat out a succinct curse. "Where the hell is a third hand when you need one?" someone demanded.

Fighting a smile, Celie reached out for the handle.

And opened the door, only to see a stack of teetering cardboard boxes, and stairs leading down into what was, presumably, a basement. "Bless your heart," a voice said from behind the stack and stepped forward.

The cardboard ziggurat wavered, in imminent peril of falling. Celie reached out a hand. "If you don't stop, you're going to lose them." Reaching out, she took the top two cases—foam cups and paper napkins, if the labels were to be believed— and like magic, the head and shoulders of a silver-haired woman appeared from behind them. A woman with a vaguely familiar face.

"Just set them on the floor there," she directed.

"No way. Let's just take them in where they go. The café?"

"Good guess."

Celie headed across the gift shop and under the arch to the cheerful café with its red-and-white-covered picnic tables. At the entrance to the ice-cream counter, she set down her load. "Here all right?"

"More than. You're a dear." The woman set down the boxes. "I'm Molly Trask," she said, holding out her hand.

Of course. Celie could see the resemblance now that she looked, the high cheekbones, the arch of the eyes. Instead of black, Molly Trask's hair was silver, a chin-length bob that curved along her jaw and made her eyes look even bluer.

"Celie Favreau, at your service."

"More than you know. One of these days I'm going to get that door fixed. It was supposed to stay ajar."

"It probably got sucked shut when I came in," Celie said apologetically.

"Not your fault. I should learn to take more than one trip. I just hate taking the time."

Celie winked. "I'm the same way. You know those plastic grocery bags with the looped handles? I've been known to hang five or six of them on each hand just to get everything in the house all at once."

Molly laughed. "Separated at birth?"

"Could be."

They grinned at each other.

"Can I help you with anything?" Molly asked.

"Actually, that was going to be my question to you. Need anything else brought up?"

"Nothing I can't get later."

Celie shook her head. "Separated at birth, remember?"

"Customers aren't supposed to help out."

"Well, here's the thing. I'm not a customer. I actually work for the government, so I really work for you."

"Ah, so *you're* the one."

The one? "What do you mean?"

"The one who spoke at the meeting last night. Jacob filled me in a little. He left a few things out, though," she said, looking Celie up and down.

Celie stared at her, nonplussed. Somehow, she had a feeling Molly wasn't talking about the maple borer. "Well, I don't…I'd be happy to send you some information."

"Clearly I'm missing out on all kinds of interesting information at these meetings," Molly said, with what might just have been speculative amusement.

Before Celie could decide, the door to the sugarhouse opened abruptly and she heard Jacob's voice. "Hey Ma, did you still want me to bring up—" He stopped short, staring at Celie.

He wore jeans and a blue plaid shirt hanging open over a gray T-shirt. His hair was tousled, as though he'd had his hands in it, his jaw dark with the previous day's growth of beard.

Jesus, he was a gorgeous man.

Celie smiled at him. "Hello."

Jacob didn't like being caught flatfooted. He liked things to be predictable, consistent. So why was it that the first emotion he felt after surprise at seeing Celie was pleasure? That, and the desire to be able one of these days to look his fill at her. "What brings you here?"

Celie rummaged in her pocket. "Is that dog of yours around?"

"Murph?"

"The Shetland pony."

Molly smothered a snort of laughter.

"He's at my house. We don't let him in the sugarhouse, and it's too cold for him to be out back this time of year."

Celie looked disappointed. "I brought him some cookies."

"Cookies?"

"Doggy biscuits. I stopped by Ray's this morning and he was running a special."

"Well, you've just earned Murphy's lifetime devotion," Molly observed.

It was a small thing, a goofy thing, but Jacob found himself charmed. They always said the first way to a woman's heart was through her children. What did it say about him that he was so ridiculously tickled at her kindness to his dog?

"Why don't you take her back to the house so she can give them to Murphy herself?" Molly asked casually.

Jacob blinked. "What about those boxes?"

"Oh, I got the important ones. Celie helped me."

He shouldn't have been surprised. She had that way about her. Two seconds after 'hello,' she somehow seemed to become everyone's best friend.

The front door opened and a trio of women came in, chattering and unbuttoning their coats. "Okay, out." Molly made shooing motions. "I've got customers. Take Celie to see the Shetland pony. Unless you want to start giving tours," she added.

One of the women turned to him. "Oh! You offer tours?"

"Let's go say hi to Murph," Jacob said hastily.

"I was wondering how you fitted into the gift-shop thing," Celie said as they stepped out into the crisp January air.

"I don't. That's Ma's territory. My job is sugar-making."

"Selling potholders not your thing?"

Jacob slipped on his buckskin jacket. "Buddying up to anyone who walks through the door isn't my thing."

"Ah. Doesn't work with your image."

He gave her a narrow-eyed glance. "I don't have an image."

"Sure you do. Town curmudgeon, everybody tells me. I think you like it. Of course, you're not very good at staying in character, it seems to me. So I'm thinking maybe it's actually all just a put-on for the gullible."

He glowered at her. "Maybe I should just take those biscuits myself."

"No way." She shoved the bag deep into her pocket. "I bought them, I get the doggy devotion. So where's your house?"

"Oh, a half mile or so away, down that road." He gestured toward a curving path that led through the trees. "Close enough to walk, if you don't mind the cold."

Celie slipped on her gloves. "I like being outside. Besides, I get to look at trees."

"For signs of the scarlet-horned maple borer?"

"No, I just like looking at trees."

"Do you ever stop?"

She gave him a sidelong glance. "No. Do you?"

"Got me there," he admitted.

The dry snow squeaked under their boots as they walked. There was something timeless and calm about the columns of the trees rising around them, sugar maples, red maples, the occasional ash, birch or beech. A light dusting of snow the night before had frosted all the branches so that the whole world felt wrapped in a white muffler.

"So why do you live out on your own in the woods instead of in that big farmhouse? Does your aversion to people extend to your mother?" She gestured at the three-story white clapboard house with its curving porch and carved posts.

"That's the Trask family house."

"Home to millions of Trasks everywhere?"

"Enough of them," he said shortly.

"Relax, I was only teasing." She pushed at his shoulder a little. "I think it sounds nice."

"It's where I grew up but I wanted my own space. Ma's the only one living there now."

"So what do you have, a hermit's cave in the woods?"

He gave her an amused look. "See? My reputation's useful."

"Like I said, I think your reputation is a pose. You've got everyone fooled into thinking you're this crusty fellow, when all you really want is not to be bugged by boring people. Isn't that right? Not that I blame you, of course."

He blinked at her. "Shouldn't I be on the couch for this, doctor?"

Celie laughed. "Sorry. I talk too much sometimes. And it's not always what people want to hear."

"It's easy to tell people what they want to hear. Being straight takes something more."

"I'm so glad you approve." Her lips twitched. "So you don't live in a hermit's hut. Just where do you live?"

"There's another place out here. My great grandfather's brother wanted to get away from the family house, too. He built a home of his own."

Celie stared at him. "Your great grandfather's brother? How long have you people owned this place, anyway?"

"Since 1870. My great-great-grandfather, Hiram Trask, bought it when he came home from the Civil War."

"What did he do, pick up a few souvenirs on his way home?"

"He went to war in the place of a mill-owner's son from Burlington. In trade, he got a nice chunk of change. He'd planned to go to Europe on it, or maybe South America."

"But he didn't."

"Little jaunts like Antietam kind of take it out of a man. Hiram came home, bought up as many acres of maples as he could and just hunkered down. I guess he figured he'd seen as much of the outside world as he needed."

"So you come by it honestly," she commented, straying to the edge of the road to brush her fingers over the smooth, bright trunk of a birch.

"I suppose. In every generation there's been a Trask who keeps to himself."

"And in every generation has there been a Trask who's known as the town grump?"

His lips twitched. "Maybe."

"Then I guess you fit right in. So how do you know so much about them?"

"We've got all their journals in the main house. I went through them the year I was sixteen."

"Summer reading project?"

He shrugged. "I thought I should know more about where I came from."

She could imagine them coming to life on pages covered in painstaking copperplate. Not distant ancestors but sons and brothers, fathers and uncles, real men with real desires and torments. Somehow, it didn't seem stifling the way her family's dusty history did. It felt warm, grounded. Maybe it was part of what made Jacob seem so sure of who he was. "So was the land already in sugar maples when Hiram bought the place?"

"Some. He bought sections of two or three different sugarbushes and tied them all together with open land that he planted himself. He kind of made a life's work of it."

She could imagine him, coming back from chaos and carnage to patiently build an ordered retreat from the world, a place of safety and security, a place where knowledge and planning could take the place of luck and survival.

"The trees look like they were laid out by someone who knew what he was doing."

"Hiram had a whole journal just on maple-farming techniques. Pages of it. He read everything he could get his hands on. Sent his son, Ethan, to school for it."

"The one who built your house?"

"No, that was his brother, Isaac, who stayed on the farm."

"By choice or because he had to?"

"A little of both. Education wasn't cheap back then but his journals sound like he was happiest keeping to himself. He courted a woman for years but she wound up marrying a guy from Boston. Didn't like the idea of living out in the middle of nowhere, I guess."

"I imagine it's an acquired taste," Celie agreed.

He turned to look at her and his deep-blue gaze jolted her system. "I don't know that you can acquire the ability to be happy in yourself. You've either got it or you don't." They rounded a curve and started into a long avenue of oak trees that led to Jacob's home.

And Celie caught her breath.

She'd expected a small clapboard farmhouse, not this three story Victorian edifice, all gables and gingerbread and carved pillars and railings. The paint job alone was a work of art, a half dozen tones of umber and green and gold that both stood out and melded with the landscape around it. "My God, he built this himself?"

Jacob nodded. "It took him eight years, working on it every minute he wasn't in the sugarbush. He built it for the woman he hoped would be his wife. She was from Montpelier." They started down the tree-lined drive.

Celie's brow furrowed. "Montpelier? That was a long way to go back then. How did they meet?"

"She came to a maple-sugar-on-snow party at the farm. Isaac fell for her hard. Sarah Jane Embree. I think she was fifteen, he was twenty-four. Her father was a lawyer, big in the Montpelier social set."

The oaks rose to either side, the bare branches curving over their heads. In summer, she thought, they would make a full canopy, leafy-green and glorious. "How could he have courted her? I'd think the father would have kept a farmer as far away from his daughter as possible."

"Don't forget, though, Isaac had half of a very prosperous farm coming to him. Embree hedged his bets. He told Isaac he could court Sarah Jane with the intention of marriage, but that her husband had to be able to keep her in the style she deserved as an Embree. Isaac underlined that part in his journal. The style she deserved. The best of everything."

"Including a mansion."

Jacob nodded. "That didn't stop Isaac, though. He just put his head down and started building. Spent every penny he had on materials—marble sinks, crystal door knobs, Tiffany stained-glass windows. He even sold off some of his part of the sugarbush to finance it. He figured if he just worked hard enough, just persisted, he'd win her hand."

"It didn't work, though."

"No. He had it just about finished by 1906—mahogany furniture, running water, even electrical power from a generator out back. She'd gotten engaged by then to her brother's school friend. No way a house in the woods could compete with Beacon Hill. I still have the ring he bought her."

"It must have shattered him," Celie murmured, looking up at the house, lonely even in its splendor.

"He never got over it. Never looked at another woman."

"She didn't care for him at all, did she?"

Jacob shook his head. "Isaac thought they had an understanding. The Embrees were just hedging their bets. I tracked down their papers the summer I read the journals. Edwin didn't even mention Isaac. Sarah Jane's had a few entries, mostly about how he was always pestering her with plans for the house when all she cared about was the social scene. I don't think she ever even saw the place."

"It was a quest. Slay the dragon and you get the maiden."

"Kind of like that. But when he completed his task, the maiden was gone. Not even his family knew what he was building out here. He kept it a secret."

"He was obsessed."

"He was in love," Jacob said simply.

It seemed unbearably sad to her. "She wasn't for him."

"Didn't matter. He really believed if he just worked hard enough, offered her enough, he could win her."

"But a house can't do that. Things can't do that. All it takes is the right person, if they really love you." She glanced at Jacob. And she felt a sudden dizziness, as though the world had tilted on its axis. Their gazes met and tangled and then his eyes were all she could see, endlessly blue, endlessly deep, like pools she might fall into, sinking forever into him.

A furious barking broke the spell. With a shake of her head, Celie turned to see Murphy barreling toward them down the aisle of trees. She fell upon him in relief, the strange moment ended. "Who's this? Who's this? Who's this doggie?" she asked, ruffling his neck fur while he leapt around her deliriously.

"Down, Murph," Jacob said and Murphy subsided, tail wagging so furiously his whole body shook with it.

"Look, Murph, it's a cookie. I've brought you a cookie." Celie brought the baggie of dog biscuits out of her pocket. "Here's a cookie for you, here's a cookie for this good dog." She held it up. "Do you think if I give it to you your dad will let me look at the inside of the house?"

Murphy barked.

Celie looked at Jacob, laughter in her eyes. "I'd say that's a yes. What do you say, daddio?"

And he, this generation's Trask loner, merely nodded.

Isaac Trask had been far more than just a maple-sugar-maker, Celie thought in the glorious entrance hall of the house. He'd had an architect's sense of design combined with a builder's meticulousness. The golden oak floors gleamed, the ceilings soared a good ten feet overhead. Sunlight streamed in through the beveled glass oval that lay in the center of the front door.

"My God, this is gorgeous," she murmured.

"Isaac went ahead and lived in it even without Sarah Jane. He died pretty young—basically drank himself to death."

How could something so beautiful come from tragedy? "It's incredible, like something you'd see in Newport, Rhode Island. Tell me it didn't just stay vacant."

"Oh, different people from the family lived in it for a few years here and there. Never for long, though."

"Bad karma?" she asked, but it didn't feel forbidding. It seemed like a house that would welcome life and warmth.

"It was too remote, I think, even when we tried to rent it. Hard to find people who want to be so isolated."

"So what happened?" She trailed her fingers over the antique wallpaper and turned to him. "Did it just sit empty?"

"More or less. My dad and my grandfather did enough to keep it from falling apart, anyway. You know, replacing windows and that. When I read Isaac's journals, it really got to me. After that, I did some stuff here and there when I got the chance. I started in earnest when I moved in."

"When was that?"

"About seventeen years ago. My parents wouldn't let me until I'd turned eighteen, and then I wound up spending about a year working on major structural stuff first. Some of the subflooring had rotted out, and the porch pillars. Once I got that out of the way, it just came down to a lot of interior detail work."

"Which you excel at," she murmured, trailing her fingers over the gleaming moldings around the French doors leading to the living room. "May I?" she asked, tipping her head.

"Sure."

The carpet was Persian and swirled in a complicated pattern of geometric wines and blues. An ornate plaster ceiling medallion surrounded the chain that held up the bronze-and-crystal light fixture. And the walls were almost entirely lined in bookshelves, bookshelves groaning with books. Some were leather-bound and perhaps dated back to Isaac's time; mostly, the shelves were filled with the splashy color of paperbacks. She'd understood from Ray that Jacob read; she'd had no idea how much.

"Were the bookshelves Isaac's idea?"

Jacob shifted his feet a little. "No, those were mine."

"A house like this ought to have a library."

"Yeah, but I like my books close at hand."

Actually, the room felt like a library with its shelves and green lamps and its leather couches and chairs. And then she was surprised again, because next to the chair that faced the fireplace and sat under a brass floor lamp, the chair that was obviously Jacob's favorite sat…

"You play guitar?" She sat down to admire the satiny wood of the well-worn and perfectly cared for acoustic.

He looked suddenly trapped. "Yeah, some."

"How long have you played?"

"Oh, I don't know, since I was about eleven, I think."

She looked at him in amusement. "A little, he says? Twenty-five years? What do you play?"

"Oh, different stuff," he said, drifting toward the door. "Old Creedence, roots music, some classical, some blues."

He was uncomfortable, she realized. Solid, certain Jacob Trask was embarrassed. There was something about it that tugged at her heart. "Well, don't walk away, play something for me."

He stopped and stared at her. "I don't play for people."

"You must have played for your family, at least."

He shifted uneasily. "It's mostly just for me."

"So Murph's the only one who's gotten a concert?"

Hearing his name, Murphy raised his head and rose from his cushion in the corner.

Jacob played with the dog's ears absently. "Playing for other people turns it into something else. It's not about impressing people for me. It's just something I like to do."

"How about if I promise not to be impressed?" Celie offered.

That had him fighting a smile. "Later," he said, walking to the door.

"Is there going to be a later?"

His glance brought warmth to her cheeks. "We'll see."

\* \* \*

The light was fading to dusk. The living room was empty but for Jacob and Murphy. The soft and somehow plaintive strains of an Appalachian finger-picking piece he'd found sounded through the room. He stopped and frowned. *Play for me,* she'd said. It was absurd for him to feel bashful at the idea. He'd probably sounded more than a little eccentric when he'd told her he hadn't even played for his family. Not that he should care what Celie Favreau thought of him.

But he was lying to himself if he tried to pretend he didn't.

Only two days had passed since he'd found her crouched at the base of one of his maples. Only two days that she'd been lurking in his mind, dancing through his thoughts. Somehow it felt as though it had been much longer. It wasn't as though he'd never been with a woman. He knew what it was to want, he knew what it was to bury himself in the warmth and softness of a woman he cared about.

And he knew what it was to watch them leave. There was little to keep a woman in Eastmont. Most of them wanted more, most of them wanted more of him than he was willing to give. Somehow, he was never ready, perhaps because he always saw them walking away, just as Sarah Jane had walked away from Isaac.

Idly, he began playing a slow blues riff.

It was the tag end of January and the pace of his life was beginning to pick up. Winter might be the dormant season for most, but for a sugar-maker, it was when things got exciting. Suddenly, there was more work to be done than hours to do it. He didn't have time for a bright-eyed woman with a disconcerting tendency to get him talking. So what if she made him laugh? So what if she crept into his dreams?

He knew how it went, get involved, see a woman a few times and suddenly there were obligations. Suddenly he'd find himself defending the way he lived, defending who he was. Living with Murph, he didn't have that problem. Alone was the way he was comfortable. Alone was the way he wanted to be.

Especially this year, of all years, when it felt as if everything was piled high on his shoulders. He'd always figured he was strong enough to take on anything that came along, but he was beginning to wonder. There was so much at stake, so much to lose if he screwed up. And now with this maple borer thing, who knew what the future might look like?

Without realizing it, he slipped into a slow, mournful gospel song. When the phone rang, he let it. The answering machine clicked and he heard himself. "It's me. Leave a message."

"It's Gabe. Pick up the phone." He heard his youngest brother's voice. "Don't think I don't know you're there. Hey Murph, you there?" Murphy gave a low whine. "Pick up the phone, will ya?"

Murphy barked and with a grin, Jacob reached out for the receiver. "What do you want?"

"I knew you were there."

"So why are you bugging me?"

"I didn't have anything better to do."

"You get in a fight with Hadley?"

"Naw, she adores me. Can't stop hanging all over me an— ow," he complained to someone in the background. "That hurt."

"Sounds like some pretty energetic hanging," Jacob observed.

"Don't let it fool you, she's crazy about me," Gabe confided. "So what's going on out there? You left a message?"

Jacob's grin faded. "Some things you ought to know about. We might have trouble."

"Trouble how?" Gabe asked sharply.

"Some USDA plant health people are poking around looking for a bug that targets maple trees."

"Targets as in kills them?"

"Yep. Hides in the bark, girdles them and transmits a fungus so that if the chewing doesn't kill them, the fungus will. Reproduces quickly."

"Sounds like a nasty customer."

Jacob reached for his coffee. "It is."

"Has it got any of ours?"

"They don't know. They'll be looking." And Celie popped immediately to mind. He frowned. "If they find it, they could wind up taking down a lot of trees."

"How many, a lot?"

"Like acres."

Gabe digested this for a moment. "That would suck. What would that do to your income?"

"Do the math. We've got a hundred acres right now, forty-five-hundred-some-odd taps. Knock that down by ten percent, it's going to hurt."

"Will you and Ma still be okay?"

"I assume so." Though the uncertainty had been a constant, nagging worry ever since the maple borer situation had turned serious. "It'll cut the shares for you and Nick, though."

Gabe snorted. "Like we care. I've got a job, Jacob, and so does Nick. You're the one working your ass off on the farm. You're the one who should get any money, you and Ma."

"But it's your land, too." And he felt the responsibility every single day.

"As long as I can come and go to the farm as I please, I've got what I want. So with this bug thing, you worried?"

"I don't know. I'm not sure what to think yet."

There was a pause. "You feeling all right?"

"Yeah, fine. Why?"

"Because you've never in your life been short of an opinion. I thought maybe you were sick or something."

"You're a regular laugh riot, you know that?"

"Yeah," Gabe said modestly. "Seriously, though, what's up?"

"Don't know yet. Celie's coming out on Monday with her team to look the place over. I assume we'll know more once we see what they find."

"And then you'll know if you're going to lose trees?"

"I'll know if *we're* going to lose trees. They belong to all of us, Gabe. I don't forget that."

"And we appreciate it," Gabe said. "So how's Ma taking all this?"

"She seems okay. I haven't gone into huge detail just because we don't know enough yet and I don't see the point in getting panicked. Anyway, I think she's distracted right now."

"Yeah," Gabe said quietly. "We're getting close to a year."

"Month after next." This time a year before, Adam Trask had still been around, striding through the maples with his rogue's grin. This time a year before, Jacob had still had a father and business partner, and Molly had had a husband. And then one morning, out in the sugarbush, everything had changed….

"How's she doing?"

"A little rocky, when she thinks no one's looking." He stared moodily at his coffee. "I caught her crying one day."

"Crying?" Gabe echoed uneasily.

"Yeah." Easily one of the most unsettling experiences of his life. "You know Ma, she was fine two minutes later but things are hard for her right now."

"She needs us around," Gabe said, in answer to his brother's unspoken comment.

"Yeah."

"Listen, I've got business in Montpelier next week. I figured I'd drop in at the end of the day, maybe for dinner."

Trust Gabe to come through. "I think she'd like that. Bring Hadley, if you can."

"She won't be around. She's got to go to New York for the week to close on some corporate business and see about her condo."

"Oh yeah? She selling?"

"The place in New York, anyway. She's got a flat out here in the manager's house at the hotel."

"The same manager's house you live in?" Jacob asked innocently.

"Might be."

"So what's hotel ownership going to say to the two of you shacking up together?"

"Considering she's hotel ownership, not a whole lot. Besides, we're not shacking up."

"No?"

"Nope. She's still got her flat, I've still got mine."

Jacob stretched, amused. "You losing your moves, little brother?"

"I've learned to be patient. When it's right, we'll know."

"Good luck on that."

"Yeah." Gabe paused a moment. "So who's this Celie?"

## Chapter Four

"Okay, let's get started." Celie looked across the Institute conference room at the team of foresters who'd been recruited for the inspections. A half dozen of them were from the Institute—not just Marce but Bob Ford and several others. The rest were either from APHIS and the forest service or the state. Nearer at hand, Dick Rumson glowered at her from a ringside seat, arms folded over his chest.

"Good morning, everyone," she began. "First of all, thanks in advance for your help. We've got a lot of work ahead of us. It's essential that we get through the inspections by the end of March, before the borers hatch. If the situation's not under control by then, we'll have worse trouble on our hands." She picked up a stack of sheets and handed them out. "This is a summary of the project to give you an idea of how we'll be dividing up the acreage for maximum efficiency."

Rumson looked up from the summary sheet she'd handed out. "Says here you see this going on for six or seven weeks."

"That's roughly how long it should take the sixteen of us to cover the county," Celie said calmly. "We'll start at the areas of concern and work our way out."

"That's a long time to have a full team inspecting. I don't think I can spare my specialists for that long, especially if you're not finding anything. If we don't see any sign of your bug in the first two weeks, I'm pulling my team back."

Celie gave him a level look. "We're not going to make any decisions about early termination until we've been out in the sugarbushes." *And you're not going to undermine my authority.*

"But if—"

"We're not going to make any decisions about early termination until we've been out in the sugarbushes," she repeated, keeping her voice even. "We've got a job to do. Let's focus on that. The data will tell us what comes next."

Rumson subsided with a glare.

Celie gestured to the wood sitting on the table before her. "For those of you who haven't seen what we're looking for, I've got some show and tell. First, Mr. Scarlet-Horned Maple Borer himself." She passed around a clear sample case with a small beetle inside. It was mostly brown with gaily striped red and brown feelers. "Big things come in small packages, as the saying goes. It doesn't look like it could decimate the hardwood forests of the northeast, but there you are. Now, it's unlikely in the extreme you're going to see one of these beetles. They spend most of their life in the wood of the tree and right now they're at the tail end of their dormancy period. What we want to look for are signs of incursion."

She lifted the section of wood off the table. "See the light-ish streaks and the way the bark has thickened? That's a response to the fungus the maple borer carries. Most trees also release a chemical to combat the beetle. If you find a tree that looks suspicious, mark it and scrape the inside of the bore holes to obtain a sample. Detecting the fungus, or better yet, the inhibitor chemical is the most conclusive method we have for confirming the presence of the beetle."

Ford stirred. "I thought I read somewhere that certain trees are resistant."

"They are. The borer doesn't like ash or black oak, for example. It's not just a taste thing. Those trees have high levels of the inhibitor chemical—if he keeps eating, he dies. Unfortunately, in the sugar maple it's not sufficiently strong for protection."

"Aren't there any insecticides we can use?" asked one of the state forestry specialists.

"None of the insecticides currently approved for use in the U.S. are effective against the maple borer."

Ford looked at her keenly. "So there is something, just not for us?"

"Sort of. I was part of a team that isolated the inhibitor chemical and concentrated it into an insecticide called SMB-17. It was commercially released last year in Canada and in Japan." She waited a beat. "The trade name is Beetlejuice."

That got a round of laughter from all except Rumson.

"What about here?"

She tamped down all frustration so that none would sound in her voice. "U.S. agencies appear to require a little more time and data." And meanwhile, trees by the thousands came down. "We have hopes the red tape part will be done soon."

"Soon enough to help us?" asked Marce.

"I wouldn't hold my breath, although I'm told the regulatory action leader has been reviewing data and should make a decision soon."

"That's encouraging, isn't it?"

"The RAL's *been* reviewing the data for about six months." And ordering more tests, and stalling and stalling and stalling…

"You ask me, they're being responsible," Rumson said heavily. "Just because you think it's hot stuff doesn't mean we can just start spraying it around."

"You don't spray it, you inject it." Her voice was curt.

"There's more involved here than just your program. Maples produce a food product and if you think that you can just whip up something in your lab and expect us to take your word on it, well, you don't know how things work. Taking the time to do it right is the responsible thing to do," he added pompously.

Good old Dick, she reflected, always most patronizing when he didn't have a clue what he was talking about. "Well, they have five years of data from three independent sources, all of it submitted two years ago, to work with. I'd hope they could make a decision based on that in less than a year."

Several of the state specialists looked amused, she noticed. Interesting. It appeared that Rumson wasn't any better liked by his staff than he was by her.

"At any rate, that's the future. It doesn't change what we do today," she said briskly, moving on. "Right now, our only weapon is removal of the infested and high-risk trees, the sooner the better. The inspection process might be hard work, but it's critical to the future of this area, so stay alert. If you find a suspicious candidate, mark the tree, log it, take a sample. I'll collect them from you at the end of the day and follow up from there." She passed out a stack of maps. "Here's where I want you deployed."

Rumson intercepted one of them. "I think I can direct my own people. We'll work the southern half of the county."

"No, Dick, you won't."

His brows lowered. "Don't you tell me—"

Calm, Celie reminded herself. Calm was the way to prevail. "How about if you and Bob and I have a quick confab, Dick? Everybody else, go out to the lobby. We'll be with you shortly."

In a few moments, they were alone.

Rumson rounded on her. "Don't you think you can tell me what's what in front of my people."

"You can't run this, Dick, I'm sorry. For the search to remain focused and effective, it needs central direction."

Rumson bristled. "Are you telling me I don't know how to manage my own staff?"

"I'm telling you it's irrelevant. We need to be organized if we're going to get done on time. I've been running these types of search operations for going on three years. I know how to work them efficiently. We'll get the inspections done quickly and I'll be out of your hair that much sooner."

"You're not going to come in here and take over my people."

Celie searched for patience. "I don't care about your territory, Dick. Trust me, I don't want it. What I want is to get rid of the maple borer. The faster I can do that, the better off we'll all be. People need a single source of information, and I'm in the best position to offer it."

"As head of state forest resource protection, I need to know what's going on here."

"And I'll be happy to keep you informed. Hell, I'll give you a daily report if you like," she snapped, finally worn down. "I don't want to control your people, Dick. I recognize your authority. This is a special project. My experience is that this is the best way to get in, get the job done and leave."

Rumson stared at her.

Celie did her best to look reasonable and unthreatening.

Finally, mollified, he nodded. "All right, but I want those reports."

"Fine."

*"Daily."*

"You'll get them." She rose. "I think we've settled this. Now let's go get the teams out in the field."

Jacob had always loved the winter forest best. There was a stark beauty to the leafless trees, an openness with the thin, winter sunlight shining down. Somehow, though, this time he didn't see the beauty. This time, as he moved through with the inspection team, the trees just looked naked and exposed.

They reached the creek that bordered one side of his property. Celie stopped and raised her voice. "All right, everyone, let's get started. Spread out in a line and move from here to the road, marking as you go."

They were here to help, Jacob reminded himself as he walked behind Celie. They wanted what was best for his trees. So why was it that he felt as though he were letting a pack of strangers paw through his private belongings? They were, after all, just woods.

But they were *his* woods.

"So tell me again why I can't help?" Even as he followed her to her starting point, he assessed each tree from force of habit; he'd known some of them by sight for most of his life.

"This is an official eradication action. We can't have the property owners involved."

"I'd say the property owners are pretty definitely involved if you're talking about clearing acres of trees," he said, an edge to his voice.

She flicked him a glance and then went back to scrutinizing the tree she was circling. "If trees need to come down, they need to come down. I'm not afraid to do what needs to be done, but I'm not the enemy here." Briskly, she dabbed on a spot of yellow paint and walked on.

Jacob made himself release a breath. The fact that the tree she'd marked was safe made it easier. "I know."

"It might be better if you just wait until we're done."

Impossible. There was no way he could stay away while they were out in his trees, no way he could stop himself from wondering where she was, what she was doing, what she was looking at.

What she was thinking?

"Just go on with it. I want to be here for now." He let out a sigh. "You'd better take a look at a couple of the trees down here at the bottom of this hill. One of them looked pretty stressed last summer. It could be the borer."

"I'll check it. There are other kinds of blight. You might be okay." Celie walked forward to stop in front of a tree he'd have been hard-pressed to get his arms around. Slowly, thoughtfully, she circled it.

"So you really do have to look at each and every tree?"

"Each and every one." She dabbed yellow paint and went on to a sapling not much more than two inches in diameter, one he'd been planning to transplant to a new area. "We can ignore ash and black oak—we know they don't like it. Just about all the other hardwoods are fair game, though. That's why we use the paint. It's the only way to be sure."

"Hard on the feet."

She gave him an amused look. "It keeps me in shape."

And he was pathetic because even with his gut tied up in knots he couldn't help but look at her in her parka and remember how she'd looked the other night.

"Speaking of in shape," Celie continued, oblivious, "you've done a really good job with your sugarbush. I haven't seen a single tree I'd thin so far."

"I try to stay on top of it. This red maple over here might have to come out. It's been a slow grower. I don't think it's got your bug, but it's got some kind of a canker at the root line and it would release the others around it." Celie frowned at a sugar maple directly ahead of them. "Not that one," Jacob corrected, "that one's healthy. I mean the red maple over here."

But she ignored him, smile fading, walking forward to the sugar maple.

And a ball of ice formed in his gut. "These trees are healthy," he said, keeping his voice calm. "Most of them took two taps last season." A bucket a day of sap off each tap, ten or fifteen gallons of syrup per tree over the course of the season. Thousands of dollars worth of revenue within a stone's throw of where he stood.

"They're not healthy, Jacob. They're hosts."

"You won't know that until you test," he said, a thread of desperation in his voice.

"That'll confirm it but this one has all the classic signs. I suspect it's infested. We'll have to take it and the trees around it." She must have seen something in his face because her voice softened. "Jacob, we don't have any choice. I know they all look fine but we've got to catch it before it becomes obvious. We've got to be aggressive. We've got no choice—if it spreads, we're looking at losing trees all over the county, maybe the state. The government will cover the cost of removal and replanting."

"Replanting? So that, what, I can start tapping them when I'm seventy?"

"Trees can grow to tappable size in as little as twenty years under the right conditions," she countered.

"Under the right conditions. In the meantime, what about my income? Will the government cover the loss of that?" How would he support his mother? he wondered desperately. How would he support himself?

Celie didn't answer, just looked down to unzip her field kit. Focused on the tree, she scraped at the hole with her little spatula and put the material in a sample vial.

Impotent fury washed through him as he watched her mark the tree with a large *X*.

*X* marked the spot. No more trees, no more sugarbush. "So if your tests prove positive?"

"The tree comes out, along with the buffer circle."

"How far again?" he asked, keeping his voice steady.

Celie glanced at him and began to pace away from the tree, counting he strides. And Jacob followed her, laying a hand on the trunks of the trees as he passed, trying to ignore the sudden pressure in his chest as they moved further and further away. So many. So far.

"Isn't this enough?" he asked, when the sounds of the other inspectors had died away behind them. "These are healthy trees." They'd gone over a low hill and dropped down again.

Celie stopped counting and turned to look at him. "You know how this works. All these trees are within the flight range of the maple borer. If adults emerged from that tree last summer, they could have infested any of these."

He looked ahead of them to where the ground sloped up again to a south-facing slope, the most productive slope of his entire sugarbush. "So are we at the edge of the circle?"

Celie shook her head and stepped forward.

He wanted to grab her and make her stop. Each footfall that sounded made him tighten up inside, like a clock spring wound a bit tighter, and a bit more.

"This is a hundred yards," she told him. "Current protocol calls for a hundred-and-fifty-yard clearance zone around each infested tree."

"A hundred and fifty yards? That's fifteen acres of trees.

How'd you decide that, by licking your finger and holding it to the wind?"

She gave him a sharp look. "No," she said slowly, "we put out traps and release a clutch of marked, sterilized beetles. We take the flight distance of the farthest beetle and add a safety margin to it."

"So this is all based on the physical abilities of a handful of beetles?"

"No, it's based on the physical abilities of an entire species. An entire very destructive species."

"And do you ever wonder if the beetle you catch in your little experiments is just a genetic freak who can go farther than the rest?"

Her eyes narrowed. "Sure, I worry that it's not representative. I worry that we're underestimating their range or that they only fly as far as they need to and if there weren't any maples around they could fly clear to the next county. I worry that I'm taking down trees needlessly precisely because I'm not taking down enough."

She took a few steps, brushing against some branches with a crackle and then swung around to face him, eyes bright with frustration and something more. "You think I take it lightly? They've been here a hundred years, some of the trees I've had felled. And they'd be around long after I'm dust except I'm taking them down to try to save the forests. You think I don't appreciate the irony?" Her voice rose. "I'm taking away people's livelihoods and I hate it. I *hate* it," she said fiercely, eyes swimming with misery, defiance, regret. "But it's got to be done, and at least if I'm doing it I know that it's being done right. Count yourself lucky. You could be in the hands of Dick Rumson."

She turned and began stalking away.

"Wait," Jacob said.

"For what?" she snapped.

He took a couple of steps after her, touching her shoulder. "Hold on, okay?"

She stopped.

"I owe you an apology and I can't give it to your back."

Slowly, she turned to face him. Her face was pale and pinched with unhappiness.

Unhappiness he had put there. Jacob exhaled. "Look, I'm sorry. I shouldn't have said those things. It's just…hard to look around and know all these trees will be gone." He gave a help-less shrug. "They're part of my world." The one place he'd always fitted into.

She bit her lip. "I wish I was here for some other reason."

He wished it, too. "We're lucky to have you here at all." His world was changing and she was helping make it happen, and yet she seemed like one of the few stable things in the middle of the madness.

He found himself reaching out to brush her cheek before he quite realized it. He stopped himself before he could. Then he frowned and touched her arm. "You tore your parka."

"What?" She blinked, then looked down where he pointed. "Oh that. That's a couple years old."

"Ever think about getting a new one?" He fingered a small tuft of fiber sticking out.

"It's a perfectly good parka otherwise. It's warm, it just looks messy." She looked at his expression. "What?"

"There's something to be said for loyalty," he murmured. And somehow, obscurely, it made him feel better. "Come on, let's get back to your inspecting."

## *Chapter Five*

Celie straightened up from her microscope and rubbed her eyes wearily. Dawn had found her back in the sugarbush, tramping from tree to tree, struggling to remain fresh. At least the scarlet-horned maple borer did its business close to the ground rather than in the upper branches or the crown of the tree, where they'd have to use tree-climbers. With the maple borer, she could inspect a tree a minute, counting the walking time.

Assuming there was no need for samples.

The upside was that they could go quickly. The downside was that after an hour or so of it, even she got blurry-eyed. That meant taking frequent breaks. Much as she begrudged the time, though, it was necessary, as were the eight-hour days. Sure, they had another hour of daylight but the last thing she wanted to do was push too hard and risk missing something.

So she tried not to resent the fact that she was back in the lab by late afternoon and instead made use of the time.

Picking up a carefully marked sample vial, she studied the material inside. Greenish-brown, with bits of bark intermixed. Unscrewing the lid, she used a narrow spatula to remove some of the sample. The process was as familiar to her as brushing her teeth: dissolve, filter, separate, then add two drops of re-actant and there it was, the distinctive pale red that indicated the presence of the inhibitor chemical.

She didn't bother to check the petri dish she'd touched with the sample the day before. She already knew it would be covered with a gaudy green carpet of fungus.

With a sigh, she looked at the markings on the vial. Jacob…

When she'd arrived, she'd hoped against hope, the way she always did, that maybe it would be a false alarm. But there would be trees felled this time. Lots of them.

More quickly, now, she finished testing the samples, marking the tree locations on a blown-up topographic map of the area. Taking out her protractor, she drew trios of circles and swallowed. Nineteen acres, give or take. Right out of the oldest, most productive trees, trees that could easily support two taps apiece, maybe three, trees twenty inches in diameter.

Trees that were coming down, and she was the one who had to tell him. She'd could think of a few hundred things she'd prefer to be doing. Getting a root canal, say, or juggling wolverines. Unfortunately, delivering bad news went with her particular territory. She had to do it. She didn't have a choice.

Rubbing at her temple to forestall a rapidly forming headache, Celie picked up the telephone and dialed.

"Pesticides lab, Pete Craven."

"Pete, it's Celie."

"Celie," he said in an overly hearty voice. She could picture him, her grad-school housemate, slight and stoop-shouldered in a white lab coat, black Buddy Holly glasses reflecting the light. He cleared his throat. "You, uh, aren't calling me from inside the building, are you?"

"Why?" she asked sweetly. "Just because last time we talked you told me Beetlejuice would be available by now and it's not?"

"Look, I'm a lab manager, that's all. I got nothing to do with the approval chain. All I do is supply data."

"And information. Hopefully *accurate* information."

"No more, Celie."

"Come on, I bought you rounds at quarter beer night," she wheedled. "Doesn't that count for anything?"

"If anyone found out I was talking to you, I'd be screwed."

"Petey. I'm looking at giving the order to take out nineteen acres of trees, maybe more. I need to know what's going on."

There was a short silence and he sighed. "Okay, okay. Look, the RAL gave it the thumbs-up. A draft of the approval paperwork went by my desk."

She couldn't stop the buzz of excitement. "The approval paperwork? That's—"

"A *draft*," he interrupted. "It didn't have a date. It wasn't stamped Final. You can't put any stock in it, Celie."

"But they're planning to release it?"

"They're *talking* about it. And until the release is out, they can put the brakes on at any time. You can be a little encouraged about it but that's about it. You hear me?"

She nibbled on the inside of her lip. "I'm looking at taking down a lot of trees here, Pete. Should I stall?"

"At this point I've stopped guessing. This baby isn't going by the rules."

"If you had to?" she persisted. "If your feet were in the fire?"

"Guess only? Two, three weeks, call it a month. Or six, if you want to be safe."

"Six? Even one month takes me into hatching season."

"I'm sorry I can't be more specific. Ordinarily, the draft would mean the pesticide would be officially registered any day but nothing about this one has followed plan."

Celie let out a quiet, defeated breath. "Okay. Thanks for the information, anyway."

"Sure. The minute I know something for sure I'll call you, I swear."

"This is driving me nuts here, Pete. It's almost worse having it be so close."

"Not much longer. Look, Celie, you and Benchley did something important here, developing Beetlejuice. A little more patience isn't too much to ask for, is it?"

It was when she was going to have to tell a man the heart of his sugarbush was coming down, Celie thought as she set the receiver in the cradle and stared at the wall of her cubicle.

She had to tell him. A quick phone call, just to say the necessary words and then she could hang up. At least then she wouldn't have to see his face when she delivered the news. It wasn't like any of Gavin's protocols said it had to be done in person. Calling would save her the trip. It would be quicker.

And it would be easier.

It was that, finally, that had her reaching for her keys. He didn't deserve to have her take the easy way out. He deserved to hear it from her in person.

A hollow thunk sounded as Jacob set down an armload of split oak. Four-foot lengths, just right for stuffing into the firebox of the evaporator. He'd walked the sugarbush with Celie and her team until he couldn't stand it any more. He'd walked until he'd had to stop, finally, had to stop because it was too wrenching every time he saw her reach for her field kit. Every time she hesitated in front of a tree, he'd wondered if she'd found another one, another host that would take acres down with it.

And how much that could repeat before the life he knew was gone.

The looks she sent him made it almost harder. That humming sense of something between them, something unfinished and unspoken, something that couldn't coexist with the havoc she was wreaking on his life, and yet something that stubbornly refused to go away.

Even in the midst of the uncertainty, the loss, he couldn't stop wanting her and it made him want to hit something, because everything he was about was at stake, and yet he kept watching those dark eyes, studying that soft mouth, wondering, wondering if she ever lay awake at night, staring at the ceiling and thinking about him as he thought about her.

And so he'd come back and stacked wood, the wood he'd sectioned the previous summer, cutting the beeches and oaks and maples he'd culled into lengths, then cutting the lengths in halves, then quarters, then eighths. He'd hauled the laden utility cart to the sugarhouse to unload it armload by armload, heavy leather gloves protecting his hands. The wood went down in the shape of a square butted up against the door at the end of the sugarhouse. When he was boiling sap, standing by the firebox of the evaporator with that door open wide, all he'd have to do would be reach out to find fuel within arm's reach.

It was hard, mindless work. He didn't think about pushing himself, he simply did it. He'd long since stripped off his coat, tossed aside his faded green flannel shirt. The thermal undershirt underneath was enough to keep him warm.

Lift and stack, turn and lift. Jacob didn't mind working hard. He liked it, feeling the machinery of the body do what it was designed to do. Gradually, the cart emptied, the stacks of wood rising ever taller. And he felt the anticipation. In a few weeks, it would be time to spark up the fire and get sap boiling in the broad, shallow pans of the evaporator. There'd be the scent of woodsmoke, the scent of slightly woody sweetness. The scent of sugaring season.

His favorite time of year.

Lift and turn, step and stack. Moving smoothly, easily, he emptied the cart for the fourth time that day. Already, the wood was chest-high under the eaves of the open roof, the next best thing to walls. He didn't need real ones—once he'd fired up the evaporator, the sugarhouse would stay quite warm enough, even with the doors open to the elements in the wee, frigid hours of the night.

Once the sap started running, the world would really come to life. For now, he labored and tried not to think about Celie.

Which worked about as well as not thinking of elephants.

He hadn't even known her a week and he could summon a picture of her instantly in his mind. Actually, he didn't have to summon because it was pretty well there all the time. Celie was a taste that lingered. Contrary, focused, opinionated. Perhaps a match for him in drive. Certainly a match for him in stubbornness.

And that was saying a lot.

He reached for wood and spun to the sound of crunching footsteps behind him.

"Hey."

And she was there, standing in the little yard behind the sugarhouse, staring at him.

Jacob gave himself a minute to look, just look. There was something in her face, some look of strain that hadn't been there before. Slowly, he set down the wood he held and dusted his hands off on his jeans. "Hey yourself."

"Working hard?"

He shrugged. "I'm playing catch-up after yesterday. The

sugaring season's coming. Lot to get done before then. What about you?" He watched her as she walked restlessly over to the cart to touch the lengths of wood, then turned to the sugarhouse, all without looking at him. And he waited because he knew there was a reason she was here. She just had to get to it.

"You ever heard of quitting time?"

"It doesn't really apply on a farm. The wood's got to get moved."

"Tonight?"

He looked up and realized that the sun was going down. "Hadn't thought about it, really. I was just working."

"In the zone."

"I suppose. How about you? You get in the zone today?"

She looked at him now, her eyes very large and dark. "Yes. We finished your inspection this afternoon. I just left the lab."

He didn't have to ask what the verdict was. He saw it in her eyes. "Dammit," he said softly. "You found them, didn't you?"

"Only three trees," she said quickly, "and they're fairly close together."

He pressed his hands against the wood on the cart, clenching his fingers around the bark as though he could drive them into it, staring blindly down at the ground beneath his feet. The Trask sugarbush had been in his family for generations. He'd been responsible for it for a year. And now they were going to lose Christ knew how much of it.

Celie's feet crunched on the snow and he saw her boots appear next to his. "Jacob, there was nothing you could do. You couldn't have stopped it."

Knowing that didn't help. Hearing her say it did. Finally, he turned his head to look at her. "So how many have to come out?"

"I don't know for sure."

"You know."

"I don't think we need to talk about it—"

"I do." His gaze was unflinching. "Tell me."

She hesitated. "Nineteen acres, maybe a little more. The section off Bixley Road, where we were yesterday."

The most productive section. Some of the oldest—and some of the newest. He closed his eyes.

And felt her hand touch his shoulder.

It didn't matter that she wore gloves, that he wore a shirt. For a moment, the reality of the contact was all that mattered. For a moment, they were connected.

"Jacob." Her voice was soft. "We're going to replant. I know it's not much but we'll do everything we can to get those trees producing in twenty years. I tested the soils while we were out there. The mix is right. You can make it happen if you want to. *We* can make it happen." She bit her lip. "I'm so sorry. I hate having to give you this news."

"Don't be. You're doing the right thing."

"I wish I could fix it."

"So do I." He straightened, trying to get his mind around it. "Nineteen acres, huh?"

She nodded. "How hard is it going to hit?"

They might make it, he thought, provided they didn't have too many bad years in a row. There wouldn't be a lot of extras for a while. His truck would have to last a little longer and he could forget about that new guitar. But they'd find a way to get by. He had some trees on the back side of the sugarbush that would be ready to tap in eight, maybe ten years. All they had to do was get through until then. He gave a short laugh. "If you see me working the counter at Ray's, you'll know."

"Don't joke about it," she said, her voice cracking.

"Ah, hell, Celie, why not? The worst that'll happen is I wind up having to take an outside job for five or ten years. It's not like I've never worked before."

"How can you take it so lightly?"

"I don't know." He leaned one hip against the utility cart and sobered. "This has been the big scary monster in the closet for almost a year, ever since I first read about it on the Internet. And especially since you've been here. At least now I know how bad it is and that we can live with it. Thanks for getting me off the hook." He gave her a serious look. "I mean it."

Celie studied him. No sarcasm lurked in his eyes. He meant it, she realized. "Well, I could have guessed a few hundred other reactions before I hit this one."

"What, did you think I was going to take your head off?"

"That would have been one of them."

"It's not like it's your fault."

"It doesn't matter. It's never easy news to hear. I'd give anything if it weren't true."

He looked at her for a long minute. "Me too."

And even in the gathering dusk she could see the deep, addictive blue of his eyes. She had a sudden impulse to reach out and slide her arms around him. To comfort, she told herself, but she knew that wasn't it. Something pulled her closer to him, like the gravitational pull of planets. How would it feel to touch him, really touch him?

And how would his mouth taste under hers?

As though he could hear her thoughts, his eyes darkened and he leaned toward her.

Only to be interrupted by the sound of a door opening at the back of the farmhouse. "Jeez, Jacob, you going to be out there forever?" said a man's voice. "Dinner's almost ready."

"Go back inside," Jacob replied without shifting his gaze away from Celie.

Celie leaned past him to see a dark-haired man in a suit standing on the back porch of the Trask house.

"Now is that any way to—oh, hello," he said as he caught sight of her.

"Hi," she replied.

"I'm Jacob's brother, Gabe."

"I'm Celie."

"Well how about that." Gabe's smile gleamed in the dusk. "It's really nice to meet you."

And just what was that all about? she wondered.

"Don't you have things to do?" Jacob called. "Why don't you go back inside where it's warm? I'll be there in a sec."

"Aye aye, captain." Gabe closed the door and Jacob turned back to Celie.

"Now where were we?"

She put her hands on her hips and turned to the utility cart. "Looks like you've got a lot to do quickly. Let me help."

"I don't need—"

"Your mom's making dinner, and you'll save time if you're not walking to and from the cart. Come on, they're not that heavy." She lifted a few pieces to demonstrate. Awkward, yes, and she'd never lift a handful the way Jacob could, but she could manage.

He studied her a moment and then walked to the wood stack. "All right."

Celie picked up three of the logs and swiveled to hand them to Jacob. Behind her, he thumped them onto the woodpile. When she turned around with another armload, he was looking at her, waiting for another load. Within minutes, they'd established a working rhythm and with surprising speed the pile of wood in the cart began to diminish.

Then Celie reached for another slab and dropped it, cursing.

"What did you do?" Jacob demanded.

"The wood got me." She pulled her glove off and tugged out the fearsome-looking splinter that had stabbed her forefinger.

Jacob bent to pick up her discarded glove. "I suppose you know you've got a hole in the finger, here."

"They're my work gloves," she said, by way of explanation.

"All the more reason they shouldn't be perforated. Work gloves are supposed to protect."

"So?"

"They don't cost much. You ever think of getting new ones?"

"I don't usually load wood with them. They're fine for inspecting trees. They're perfectly—"

"Yeah, I know, perfectly good gloves. Don't ever let 'em say you're not loyal, Celie." He put down the glove and stripped off his own. "Give me your hand."

"What?"

"Let me look at it."

She gave him a suspicious stare. "What are you, a trained EMT?"

"I am, as a matter of fact," he said mildly. "Now hush and cooperate." He bent over her hand like a palm reader, smoothing the fingers flat.

And heat bloomed through her. Forget about the pain from the splinter. It was every other nerve that she was thinking about. Celie tensed as he brushed her fingertip with the edge of his nail, seeking out the splinter. The little twinge she felt when he hit it was nothing compared to the rush of sensation she felt from his hand holding hers. And it made her want more, much more. It made her want those hands on her, and just her, sliding over her bare skin, touching her everywhere.

And inside her tension began to build.

"Got it," Jacob said as sharp pain flashed through her. He flicked the splinter away and glanced at her, still holding on to her hand. "Better?"

Better? Better would be his mouth on hers, the final discovery of just how that temptation felt. She moistened her lips. "Maybe we—"

The door to the farmhouse opened again and this time

Gabe walked down the path, stepping gingerly on the snow in his street shoes. "Celie? Ma says for you to come to dinner, too." He walked up. "Palm-reading, Jacob?"

Celie pulled her hand back hastily. "He was helping me out with a splinter."

Gabe's teeth shone white in his face. "I'll spare you the obvious lame doctor jokes and just tell you that if I don't go back inside with a yes, I'll never hear the end of it."

She looked at Jacob. "I don't want to intrude."

"You won't," Gabe told her before Jacob could speak. He grinned. "Hell, it'll be the most excitement we've had in years."

"So here I am, ready to go down the hill, trusting my big brother to take care of me."

"And instead you got closely acquainted with a tree?"

"Black maple." Gabe grimaced.

"Wait a minute," Jacob interrupted. "Who got acquainted with the maple tree?"

"Was that my fault?" Gabe demanded. "You were the one who threw yourself between me and the trunk."

"The way I remember it, you insisted on steering and then when things got rough, you bailed and I went into the tree."

"And showed up here covered in blood," Molly added. "Having you three made me old before my time."

"You should thank me," Gabe told Jacob. "Lots of people pay for nose reconstruction. You got it for free. It suits you."

It did, Celie thought. The little lump in his nose kept him from being too perfect, gave him that little bit of graininess to offset that impossibly square chin, that mouth that was just a little bit too pretty.

Gabe was good-looking in an effortlessly stylish way that made her think of fine wines and fancy dinners. Jacob? Jacob was simply himself, so solidly and completely there that there was no room for any polishing, and none needed. What would it be like to be so at home in her own skin, in her own life? Celie wondered.

"More potatoes, Celie?" Molly Trask lifted a big red-patterned ceramic bowl that Celie could have sworn she'd seen at the Trask Farm gift shop.

"No thanks, I'm stuffed." Roast pork, garlic mashed potatoes—Molly Trask had chosen deceptively simple fare that was fiendishly difficult to pull off well. And pull it off, she had, Celie thought, stifling the urge to loosen her belt. "This was excellent. I haven't had a dinner like this since I left home."

"So where's home for you?" Molly asked, handing the potatoes to Gabe, who took a second helping enthusiastically.

"Montreal, I suppose, though I've basically been on the move since I left for college."

"That sounds exciting, seeing lots of different places."

"That was the idea," Celie said, wondering why now, as she sat amid the warmth of the Trask family, it didn't seem so appealing. She'd been on the run from being tied down for so long. On the run from the dusty bookshop in Vieux Montréal. Now, though, as she looked across the table at Jacob, she wondered if she'd lost a piece of herself somewhere along the way.

"Your parents must miss you." Molly raised her water glass. "Do you get to see them much?"

"I get up to Montreal most years," Celie said, realizing as she said the words that they sounded woefully inadequate. "My job's pretty crazy," she added lamely. "And my family's got a bookstore that keeps them all busy."

"Owning a small business usually means it winds up owning you," Molly said ruefully. "I can testify to that."

"So what about you, did you grow up in a sugar-making family, Molly?"

"Heavens no." Molly Trask laughed. "My parents ran a gas station on the other side of town."

"Eastmont?"

"Yep. A small-town girl from day one."

"Did you ever think about leaving?"

"Oh, I went off to college for a few years. The University of Vermont. I thought I might be a teacher. But every time I came home, there would be that pesky Adam Trask asking me out. I kept telling him no, but he didn't seem much of a mind to take no for an answer." Her lips curved. "After a while, it got so I was looking forward to being back home more than I was looking forward to being gone." And then the smile slipped a notch.

Celie caught the glance of concern that flashed between Jacob and Gabe. "You don't need to talk about—"

"Of course I do," Molly said fiercely. "I miss talking about him. That's what happens when people go. Everyone gets so worried you're going to get upset that they try to keep the subject away from the person you've lost. And the less you talk about them, the more they fade away." She swallowed and blinked. "I don't want Adam to fade away."

"He won't," Gabe said. "Not as long as we're around."

"He's in the sugarbush." Jacob's voice was soft, certain. "And he's in the sugarhouse and this house and anywhere on the farm. He's there and so is everyone who ever ran the place. As long as it's still around, so are they."

Legacy, Celie thought. It wasn't always a millstone. Sometimes it was an anchor, something that helped you stay steady in a turbulent world. Sometimes it was the thing that helped you know who you were.

## Chapter Six

The shrieking growl of chain saws shattered the morning quiet. Jacob stood amid his trees and watched the removal crews go to work. At this moment, the sugarbush looked as it always had. And in twenty-four hours, he'd stand in this same spot staring across a bare expanse of ground.

He couldn't get his head around it.

It was too sudden, too easy. In the old days felling trees had been heavy labor, men wielding axes, pulling band saws back and forth to sever trunks slowly and finally, letting them fall with a cry of "Timber!" Now, the chain saws with their voracious chorus collapsed the labor of hours down to minutes. The crews didn't even have to section each tree, taking it apart from the top down as they would in an urban area. In the woods, all it required was a single mercilessly efficient cut to make an end to a hundred years of slow growth.

Laughing at a companion's joke, the arborist for the lead

crew approached his first target, a sugar maple with a trunk as broad as the pillars that held up the State House in Montpelier. Trees weren't sentient creatures, Jacob reminded himself. They couldn't feel pain. Why, then, did it look like the crown was trembling, quaking as the chain saws bit into the trunk, sending woodchips and fragments of bark flying? Why did it fall with such heavy finality?

He squeezed his eyes closed at the thud.

"You don't have to be here," said a voice beside him.

Celie.

"Of course I do. They're my trees. I…" He stopped, about to say "I need to be here for them." Ridiculous but somehow still true. He'd been up before the sun that day, walking through the ranks of maples in the silence of the dawn, trying to accept what he knew was inevitable. "I need to be here."

"You're putting yourself through torture."

But somehow watching the process would make it less shockingly abrupt than arriving a day or two later to see it all gone. He knew that.

It was just making himself endure it that was the hard part.

Celie walked over to supervise the men grinding down the stump. The others briskly sectioned the maple and loaded it into the growling chipper that spat it into the waiting trailer in a hail of wood fragments.

Less than five minutes. It had taken less than five minutes to bring down a tree that had probably spent the better part of a century and a half growing. A tree that his great-grandfather had probably tapped when he'd first owned the property.

A tree that was now only a memory.

Someone whistled. "I'm gonna have to get me one of those chain saws. I bet they have this whole area cleared by sunset."

Jacob turned to see a vaguely familiar man in a green twill

shirt. The crew put their chain saws to the trunk of the next tree and in less than a minute it toppled to the ground.

The man shook his head and spat. "Well that's the sound of a few hundred bucks a year disappearing. The poor son of a bitch who owns this place is going to be in the unemployment line come summer. Then again, looks like he just rolled over for these federal idiots."

Jacob's jaw tightened. "Who are you?"

"Dick Rumson, head of forest resource protection with the Vermont Division of Forestry. Who are you?"

"I'm the owner."

Rumson tucked a toothpick in his mouth and began to chew it. "Ain't going to be the owner of much by nightfall. Hell, they could at least leave you some to use for fuel wood." His words were ripe with disgust. "They're taking them down for no reason. If I was the one running things, I'd at least let you burn them."

"Which is exactly how the maple borer's been transferred in Minnesota and Wisconsin," Celie said as she walked up. "It doesn't matter if the tree's dead. If the eggs or larvae are in the wood, they can emerge as adults. You've got to completely destroy the trees to eliminate all possibility of spread."

"You say." Rumson's voice was contemptuous.

"I say and I'm running the operation. You've gotten your reports, Dick. Is there a reason you're here?"

"Just wanted to see what it looks like when you take away a man's livelihood." He glanced at Jacob. "I'll get going now." He trudged away through the sugarbush toward his green Division of Forestry truck.

"I'm sorry," Celie said in a low voice. "I didn't know he was going to be here."

"He's quite a prize. Is he right?"

"About the eradication? Program policy was decided by a

science advisory panel of the USDA. Fifteen specialists. It was a consensus decision, not just mine."

"In other words, our Mr. Rumson is just a garden variety jackass?"

"No comment."

The roar of additional chain saws added to the noise as the second crew got to work on the other side of the dell, focusing on a strip of smaller trees that bordered the old growth. The chain saws tore into the wood.

It was the same sort of horrified fascination that made people stare as they drove by the scene of an accident, Celie thought. There was damage and wanton destruction and it was impossible to look away. The trees going down were young, only just mature enough for tapping.

She heard an oath and turned to see Jacob, his face drawn taut.

"Are you okay?"

A muscle jumped in his jaw. "I planted those trees with my father," he said. "I was about six. He told me that one of these days I'd be tapping them."

And now his father was gone. She ached for him. "Go away, Jacob, please. Don't watch this."

"I have to."

She wished she could comfort him, but she knew he wouldn't accept it. Not here, not now. She glanced back to his truck to see Murphy in the cab. Without a word, she walked over and opened the door. In an instant, the dog was out and running over to jump around Jacob, leaping up to lick his face.

And Jacob, with a zone of isolation around him a mile wide knelt down to put his arms around the wriggling dog.

Celie walked up and rubbed Murph's ears. "I thought you could use your buddy."

Without turning away from the tree cutting, Jacob laid his hand over hers. "Thanks," he said softly.

And in that moment, she knew she'd take any risk necessary to keep from doing further damage to this man.

The best way to battle rumors was information, Bob Ford said, and Celie agreed. Only a week had passed since the first growers' meeting, only a day since they'd started the removal operation at Jacob's, but the mood at the elementary-school auditorium was decidedly different. It had been since she'd walked in.

There had been no joking around the coffee urn this time, no smiles or flirtations. This time, everyone gave her a wide berth. This time, the stares ranged from skeptical to outright hostile.

It was nothing new to her. Trees coming down changed the atmosphere. She understood it, but understanding didn't keep it from cutting. Understanding didn't take away the sense of isolation. For a brief time, Eastmont had felt like a home. Now, it was anything but.

Celie picked up the microphone. "I asked Bob to call the meeting so I could update you on the situation. I realize that everyone is concerned." She took a long look at the growers. "So far, we've found three infested maples. We're currently taking steps to remove trees at risk in those locations."

"You're taking out maples we need to make a living," somebody protested from the back of the room.

"If we get an infestation, your trees are going to die anyway," she returned. "This is the only chance to save them."

"How do you know it even works?" The gray-haired sugarmaker with the lantern jaw shot to his feet. "You've been taking out trees all over the northeast, but the problem still keeps spreading. Sugar maples don't grow overnight, you know.

You come in here and take them down, we can kiss that part of the sugarbush goodbye for as long as we're around."

"Yeah," echoed the pugnacious redhead. "Clayton's right. How do we know you're not making a mistake?"

"I've spent the last ten years of my life studying the maple borer. We've come closer to controlling it here than anyone has done worldwide."

"Closer," the redhead repeated, his voice rich with contempt. "What does that mean? Do you have it under control or don't you?"

"What we're doing is working," she said.

"If it's working so all fired well, then how did the bug get here at all?" Clayton demanded.

"Yeah," someone else echoed.

The angry muttering grew until Bob Ford rose. "All right, people, getting ticked off about the situation isn't going to change things. We've got a problem and we're dealing with it the best way we know how."

"Sure, by taking away our crop trees."

"Now take it easy," Ford said.

"You take it easy," the redhead retorted. "This is our income we're talking about. She's wading in here clearing out entire acres. It says right here that there's no proof it even works." He waved a newspaper in the air.

"It says so where?" Celie asked.

"The Montpelier paper. A state forestry guy named Dick Rumson. He's the—"

"I'm well aware of who Dick Rumson is." Celie ruthlessly squashed down the surge of anger.

"He says he was on your fancy science panel and voted not to take out such a wide buffer layer of trees."

"And the other fourteen panel members disagreed."

"Are you going to stand there and tell me he's lying?"

Calm, she reminded herself. Stay calm. "I have data to support our control measures."

"Yeah, well, I don't give a crap about your data. I'm watching trees on my neighbor's property coming down and you're coming to me next. Are we going to get any money for this?"

"What's your name?" asked Celie.

"Paul Durkin."

"Don't get ahead of things, Mr. Durkin. Let's go through the inspections before you go borrowing trouble."

"I don't have to borrow trouble," he said hotly. "It's finding me whether I want it to or not."

"And we may have gotten all the infested trees, in which case you're getting bent out of shape unnecessarily. Let us finish our inspections, then we'll know what we're dealing with."

"What if we don't let you on our land?" Durkin demanded.

Celie's gaze chilled. "The eradication of the scarlet-horned maple borer is a federal priority. If anyone refuses to grant me access to their property, I'll get a court order. We've got to get any host trees out now, before adults start emerging in a few weeks. Any delays and we've got a population explosion, and that'll hurt not just the people here but the whole northeast." Her voice hardened. "I've been to Asia, I've seen what the borer can do if left unchecked. And it's not going to happen here."

"What are you going to do to stop us?"

"Whatever it takes, Mr. Durkin. I hope it won't come to that, because I think once you think about the big picture you'll realize the importance of what we're doing here."

"You're just guessing. You could take out all our trees for nothing."

She stared at him steadily. "The eradication program will proceed. Now if there are no more questions, you can get a copy of the inspection schedule up front before you leave."

\* \* \*

The last stragglers were leaving the auditorium as Celie stood in the back, pulling on her coat.

"You okay?" Bob Ford asked, coming up behind her.

Was she ever okay after these sessions? "Yeah, sure. It went better than some."

He gave her a steady look. "They're good people who want to do the right thing. They're just scared right now."

"I know."

"I'll walk you out," he said.

"No, you go ahead. I need to stop in the ladies' room." And she really needed a few minutes alone because she felt way too fragile just then.

She believed in what she was doing, Celie thought after as she stared at her reflection in the low mirror of the girls' room. She'd always believed in it. After four years in the trenches, though, she was getting weary of it all, the debates, the battles, the suspicion, the hostility. That she could understand it didn't make it any easier. She was sick of always being the enemy when she was doing her damnedest to help, sick of knowing what a toll her attempts took on people's lives. She remembered the look on Jacob Trask's face as they'd cut down his father's trees. It didn't matter that it was the only accepted way, it wasn't good enough.

What she needed was Beetlejuice.

Outside, the cold bit at her cheeks and numbed her fingertips even through her down-filled gloves. She plodded to her truck. The cab was little warmer, but at least there was the promise of heat soon to come. She started to fit her key into the ignition. And stopped. Something was wrong, she could feel it. There was a tilt to the vehicle, a tilt that hadn't been apparent when she'd driven in.

And she cursed as she got out in the icy wind and walked

around to find her right rear tire flat. Things hadn't gone as well as she'd thought, apparently. She was familiar with this, oh, she was familiar with it. They were scared and defensive, sure. And ready to strike out, just as others in different towns had struck out, over and over again.

Sighing, she walked back toward the cab of the truck.

"Need a hand?"

She turned to see Jacob standing under the light. In the wash of harsh illumination, his eyes were shadowed, his cheeks hollow.

"Just a flat. I can get it, thanks."

"You'll mess up your clothes. Let me take care of it."

It was on the tip of her tongue to say no, but she was suddenly just too tired to deal with it. "That would be really nice of you. Let me open up the shell so we can lower the tire."

"I'll get that. You get the jack."

By the time she'd managed to undo the toggle bolt and get the jack out, Jacob was sitting on his heels in front of the flat, running his fingers over the slit in the rubber. "Someone slashed your tire," he said blankly.

Celie gave a ghost of a smile. "Not everyone appreciates what I do."

He frowned. "You think it was someone here at the meeting?"

"All I know is that I had four good tires when I got here. I suppose Eastmont could be a hotbed of youth violence but I doubt it. I think someone wanted to vent their frustration."

"You don't sound surprised."

"You get used to it after a while. There's a reason I drive a clunker. If I got a new truck, I'd only be paying money to present a nice, shiny target, and you can bet it would just tick them off all the more."

Before, he'd assumed she drove the old, battered truck for

the same reason he did—frugality and because it was less of a hassle than actually going to a dealership. It never occurred to him that she was a target.

He reached out and ran his fingers over the grooved paint on the side of the truck bed and turned to her, eyes sober. "I guess this wasn't a drunk keying your car in a parking lot."

"It could have been, I suppose. But when the dents and scratches keep showing up, you start to see a pattern."

And a cold anger awoke in him. "You don't deserve this."

"I don't think it's a matter of deserving. I think it's just people."

Because he had to move, he slammed his hand down on the tire iron to crack loose the lug nuts. "Are you telling me it doesn't get to you?"

"Of course it gets to me, especially on a night like tonight. I just don't know anything else to do but put my head down and keep going."

He understood because that was like him. But it wasn't enough. "Next time we have one of these meetings, you should drive in with me." He didn't look at her but jacked up the truck.

"Jacob Trask, escort?"

"If you like. Save you money on new tires."

"What happens if they come after yours?"

His smile was quick and feral. "They won't." He pulled off the flat tire and put on the spare, the heavy tire looking like a toy in his big hands.

When he'd lowered the truck again, he turned to her. "This isn't all sugar-makers, or even most of us. Most of the folks who showed up are decent people. They don't do this kind of thing, no matter how angry or scared they are."

"I know."

"I just want you to—" Suddenly, he stopped, head cocked.

"What?" Celie asked.

He let the tire slip to the ground and walked over to her front wheel. A wheel that was already sagging, she realized with a sinking heart. Dropping to his heels in front of it, Jacob ran his fingers over the rubber, stopping at a spot near the tread. She could hear the hiss of air against them. He cursed under his breath. "Looks like they got you for two."

This time it was more than casual frustration she could shrug off. This time, the hurt, the plain and simple isolation that had been hovering all night overwhelmed her. She pressed the heels of her hands against her eyes. Jacob had already been way too nice. He didn't deserve an overwrought female.

"It's okay." She heard the quick concern in his voice. "We can get this tire off, too, and take both of them to get fixed."

It was the kindness that did it. Suddenly, Celie couldn't stop the tears. Swiping at them furiously, she stood with one arm clutched against her waist, the other covering her face.

Jacob fought back the jump of mild panic as he watched her shoulders shake. Tires, he could take care of. Tears? He didn't know where to start. He knew about being alone, he should respect her obvious desire to get through this herself. And then he uttered a soft oath. Forget alone; he thought and reached out to fold her stiff body against him.

It shocked him, how small she was. There was so much energy to her that even though he'd stood next to her, it had never really registered. He felt the grim anger deepen. Someone had done this to her. He was going to find out who.

And they were going to regret it.

Now, though, he just held her close and stroked her back, feeling the tense muscles relax as she let herself weep. "It'll be okay," Jacob leaned down to murmur to her, his face close enough to the top of her head that he could have pressed a kiss on the dark curls of her hair. He could smell the faint scent of her, so subtle it was barely there, something that had him thinking of sunlit clearings. For now, it was just enough to hold her until the storm passed. The minutes slipped by. Neither of them noticed. It didn't matter.

Celie stirred against him and sighed. And suddenly the need to comfort morphed into the utter awareness of the feel of her body in his arms. Despite his efforts to keep her at a distance, she was here, pressed against him and he couldn't help but feel it. His movements hadn't changed but somehow the absent strokes of reassurance had turned into caresses.

She looked up at him, eyes dark, lips inches away from his own. They tempted him to taste, to lean in and find out just how soft and sweet they were. It was her eyes that were the problem, though, so dark and so deep a man could lose his good sense in them. Eyes that could keep him staring down at her like some moony high-school kid. And if he held her against him for one more second, his body was going to embarrass him.

He released her abruptly and moved away. "Come on, it's freezing out here. Let's get you into my truck and home."

Celie blinked. "What about the tires?"

"Give me your keys. Go sit in my truck and I'll take care of them."

She raised her chin at that. "I don't need taking care of."

"Humor me," he said shortly. "You can be a tough guy tomorrow." He held out his hand. After a brief hesitation, she dropped her keys into his palm.

Celie sat in the cab and watched Jacob, her feelings completely jumbled. For a few moments, she'd felt cared for, protected, safe. For a few moments, he'd held all the feelings of isolation at bay. And then comfort had somehow shifted to desire. Nestled against him, she'd felt the hard, rangy strength of his body. She'd felt the change in the touch of his hands. She'd seen the desire in his eyes.

He wasn't going to push her away again, she thought, watching him over by her truck. Not this time….

The work might have kept Jacob's hands busy but it didn't do a thing to distract him. The moment just kept playing over and over again in his mind. If he could just forget the way it had felt to hold her, he could convince his body it was all over. Instead, he thought of the heat of her against him, the look in her eyes. He thought of just how easy it would have been to have bent down just a bit more and kissed her.

He threw down the tire iron bad-temperedly. But when he got into his truck, her scent was the first thing he noticed.

Celie stirred. "Where are we going to take the tires?"

"There's a twenty-four-hour truck stop on the highway through Montpelier. It's not far." He started his engine, trying not to look at her.

"Jacob, it's nine-thirty at night."

He let out his parking brake. "Then I guess we'd better get going."

She'd forgotten to leave on the outside light, Celie realized as Jacob pulled into Marce's drive.

He eyed the dark house. "So is your porch light burned out or do you just like a challenge?"

"I spaced on it. This is my friend Marce's house. She usually turns on the light and all but she's gone this weekend."

Jacob turned off the truck and opened his door. "I'll walk you up." He reached behind his seat and produced a flashlight.

*Cared for, protected, safe.* There was an intimacy to walking up the narrow path with him. Somehow, not touching made her more aware of him than ever, the measured footfalls, the care he took to reach past her and light their way. When they reached the front steps, he trained the flashlight on the door for her to find the keyhole. It seemed natural that after she'd opened it, he'd step inside to help her with the switches she'd yet to learn. She was sorry when the light came on.

"Looks like you're all set now."

"Do you want some coffee or something?"

Jacob shook his head. "No, I'll get out of your hair." Before he did something he'd regret.

Celie hesitated, then leaned in to give him a quick hug that had him stiffening.

"I can't thank you enough for what you did tonight. I'm sorry I got upset." She looked up at him, eyes sober. "Thank you for being so nice."

"Everyone hits their limit sometime. I'm just glad I could help." And he needed to get out of there and soon because he was looking at her mouth and her eyes and leaning toward her, and he knew he was full of crap with the Good Samaritan stuff because all he'd wanted, all he'd thought about since the first moment he'd seen her was the way she'd feel and the way her lips would taste under his.

And he was damned if he was going to leave without finding out.

The kiss took them both by surprise so that at first there was just the touch of lip to lip. It was contact, but nothing more. Soft, warm even after the night air, there was something inviting about the feel of her mouth. But it wasn't enough. It tantalized more than it satisfied, and as the scent of her rose up around him, he stepped in to pull her against him.

And then her lips parted.

It made him reel, the feel of her mouth alive under his. As elusive as her scent, her flavor kept him tasting. Sweet with a little something more, a hint of spice. Then she made a little noise deep in her throat, and he felt the desire rip through him.

Celie caught her breath. Who'd have guessed that such a rugged-looking man would have lips so soft? He might have kept himself isolated, but he knew how to kiss a woman, oh, he knew how to kiss. The brush of lip, a nip to tease and then the lush stroke of tongue that set up answering demands in her body.

She wanted more. She wanted to get through the layers of heavy winter clothing to find him, really find him. She wanted to get past the distance and down to the essential Jacob, underneath all the layers he used to protect himself.

Impatiently, she stepped back and slipped off her parka. Then she moved in to slide her arms under his open coat to drag them both deeper, feverishly intent on discovering more.

And when his arms tightened around her, she did.

Taste, smell, touch, he was all around her with an immediacy that neither of them could deny. This was Jacob, rough, gruff Jacob who shied from connection with anyone. Jacob, who kept walls around himself to preserve his own private world. But now he'd opened it up to her, and the richness inside was beyond anything she'd imagined.

Jacob groaned softly at the feel of Celie against him. Time had passed since he'd last tasted a woman, but he'd never had his senses overwhelmed like this. A mere touch had never made him drop the barriers. A mere kiss had never dragged him into red-hazed wanting. And all he cared about was more, all he wanted was Celie, naked against him in his bed for long hours while they discovered each other.

All he needed was her.

Blinking in shock, he broke the kiss.

"What's wrong?" Celie asked blankly.

He straightened, not looking at her. "It's late, I should go." It wasn't what you said to a woman when you'd been halfway to ripping her clothes off, but he had no clue what the right words were. Thanks? Let's do it again? He opened the door. "I'll be back over tomorrow morning at seven to get you to your truck," he said, and escaped.

The night air outside was chill. He needed it. He needed to get his equilibrium back because he'd gotten way out of hand. Forget that she'd been kissing him back. Right now, she was feeling vulnerable. It was the wrong time for this. And maybe it would always be the wrong time because it was becoming clear that when it came to Celie Favreau, he was pretty damned vulnerable himself. She'd somehow slashed through the distance he kept himself surrounded with, making him want things he shouldn't want. Making him need her, which was foolish. More than foolish. Dangerous.

Because eventually, inevitably, she was going to be assigned elsewhere.

Eventually, she was going to leave.

## *Chapter Seven*

Celie was a fan of the unpredictable. She liked surprises. She liked different. Different was good.

Usually.

Having a man kiss her senseless out of the blue and then walk away before she'd even caught her breath was certainly different. Good? Not exactly. She'd never use the word *good* to describe the kiss. *Stupendous, mind-blowing, world-rocking,* yes. *Good* didn't quite cover it. And the way he'd left...

The way he'd left, he'd looked downright ticked.

She couldn't figure it out. She couldn't figure *him* out. For a man with a reputation for being a predictable grump, Jacob Trask was full of surprises. Kind about her tires, unexpectedly sweet instead of awkward in the face of her tears. Chivalrous at the house, and then springing that kiss on her. And what a kiss. Even thinking about it still gave her little butterflies.

But why he'd be pissed off after, she hadn't a clue. It had

been his idea, and she knew enough about men to be sure he'd enjoyed it. He'd been as good as his word and shown up at seven to collect her that morning, even if he'd barely said a word to her. Could have been lack of coffee.

Not.

So what was going on?

Celie cleared her throat. "You're chatty this morning."

Jacob just shot her a look from under his brows.

"Everything okay?" she asked.

"Fine."

"I thought maybe you were uncomfortable because we—"

"I'm fine."

"Because if you wanted to talk about it—"

"I don't."

"Okay. I guess you're fine."

He shot her another look.

So maybe she'd take that for the time being, but it certainly wasn't the end of things.

Jacob turned off the highway to the school, and she threw him a sidelong look of her own. "Haven't you forgotten something?"

"Like what?"

"Like oh, say, the tires?"

Then he pulled into the parking lot and stopped beside her truck, which sat there on a pair of gleaming new radials.

Celie stared. "I guess you got the tires. They couldn't fix them, huh?" It had been a long shot, but she'd still hoped for that the previous night even as she'd picked out the just-in-case replacements.

"Nope. I told them to put on the new ones."

And got up early enough to collect the wheels, drive to the school and put them on, all before coming to get her. A person would think he was trying to stay away from her. She felt a little surge of irritation. "Well, thanks, but you didn't need to do that. You should have left it for me."

"I had to pass by on the way to get you. It was more efficient."

"Efficient." She nodded her head meditatively. "And here I thought you were just avoiding me."

He did look at her then, and she caught the glint of humor in his eyes. "You're not that scary."

"Good. Then you'll let me take you to breakfast as a thank-you. What do I owe you, by the way?"

"We can worry about it later." Jacob dug through his pockets, handing her the receipt. "It's on my card."

He'd barely talk to her, but he'd go out of pocket three or four hundred bucks for her. It didn't make sense. "So where do you want to go for breakfast, Hank's?"

His look was pitying. "You've never lived in a small town, have you?"

"Sure I have." But always as an outsider, never as someone who belonged. "What's the problem?"

"Saturday morning. Us. Having breakfast."

"What, are they going to assume we're having deviant sex because we're having breakfast?"

He missed a beat before he answered. "They'll assume something."

And she couldn't really make herself mind, though it would probably give Gavin heartburn. "Are you worried about my reputation?"

"Maybe I'm worried about mine."

"It is a risk. After all, how can you stay on as town curmudgeon if you're seen out on a social occasion?"

"You see the problem."

Celie opened the door. "Well, then, you'll have to come back to Marce's house and let me cook."

"You don't need to feed me breakfast. It's no big deal."

"It is to me. You've spent time on this and fronted me money. I'm not going to feel right unless I say thank you."

"You've just said it."

"You know what I mean."

He folded his arms and looked her up and down. "You really aren't going to let this go, are you?"

"Nope." She folded her arms to mimic him. "It's either Hank's or Marce's, assuming no one's seen us together already, in which case hara-kiri might be the only answer."

"And me with no ceremonial sword."

She grinned. "Then I guess you're stuck."

Celie slid a plate in front of Jacob. "One breakfast special."

"And then some. I would have settled for eggs," Jacob said, looking over the pancakes and bacon.

"They were big tires. I even have genuine Vermont maple syrup, grade A amber."

Jacob scowled as he read the label. "You're serving Franklin County syrup to a Washington County sugar-maker?"

"Don't be so sensitive," Celie told him as she sat down with her own plate. "Marce works at the Institute. She can't play favorites so she has to buy out of the area." She watched Jacob pour some of the syrup into his empty glass and study it. "That was for orange juice, you know."

He glanced up at her. "Sorry. The Franklin County folks always take all the syrup awards." He raised the glass and squinted at it. "I just wanted to get a look at their clarity."

"You sound like you're talking about diamonds," she said, amused.

"I don't make my living from diamonds." He poured the syrup over his pancakes and took a bite.

She watched him. "How is it?"

"Not bad. Pretty good, actually. Could be the pancakes, though." He went through a couple more bites. "Yeah, definitely the pancakes. Are there any more of these?"

Celie raised an eyebrow. "With all that, you want more?"

"Like you said, they were big tires."

"I don't know, if you want more pancakes, it seems like I should get something in return."

"What? If we're going for strict accounting, you're still behind because we've already fed you at the Trask Farm."

"Your mother fed me," she corrected.

"Practically the same thing."

"Nice try. But that's okay. I'm not asking you to cook for me. I want to hear you play guitar."

He rolled his eyes. "Can you pass me the pancakes, please?"

Celie lifted up the platter and held it to one side. "Not until you promise to play for me."

"Forget it. I'll just take the bacon."

"You *are* going to play for me one of these days, you know." She gave up and passed him the platter.

"That sounds like a threat."

"Come on, it would be fun. Don't you get sick of just playing for an empty room all the time?"

"Nope. That's the way I like it."

That she could believe. "Surely you must have done a song or two for your family, at least."

"My mother once or twice when she wouldn't leave me alone. As a kid, I mostly played in one of the top-floor rooms."

"There must be a lot of those in a house that size."

He nodded. "Back in Ethan and Hiram's day, they had three generations living in it. It had to be big."

"It's a lot of space for your mom to rattle around in."

"Yeah. Especially recently."

An empty nest, no husband. And Jacob being Jacob, he was

worried about her. "It probably helps to have you around," Celie said gently.

"I don't know how much it does." He stared into his coffee cup. "I'm not sure what she needs."

"You sound like it's entirely up to you."

"I'm the one who lives here. I'm the oldest."

And he'd always take that responsibility seriously. "Don't your brothers help?"

Jacob shrugged. "Gabe stops by when he can. Nick calls. He's in Boston but he's a firefighter, so sometimes he comes up when he gets a big break. It still lands on me, though." He hesitated. "The anniversary of my father's death is next month."

"That's going to be hard."

"Yeah. We're trying to stick close. But it only helps so much."

"You're doing what you can." Celie's voice was soft.

"I wish I could do more. I wish…" He wished that he could bring back his father but that wasn't possible and there was no use thinking about it.

"I'm sorry." Celie reached out to cover his hand with hers. "You must miss him."

Her fingers were cool and soft against his, dragging him abruptly into memories of the night before, of holding her, the scent of her hair, and her taste, that tantalizing taste that had kept him lying awake for long hours, want settling in his belly like a bag of rocks.

And she'd done it to him again, drawn him into opening up, drawn him into wanting. He lived a simple life, one that his occasional forays into female companionship didn't disturb. He always managed to enjoy himself and give as good as he got without complicating his life in any way.

Celie Favreau was a walking complication. Since he'd stumbled on her in his sugarbush, nothing about his life had stayed the same. Everything about it was changing in ways he was powerless to stop.

And he couldn't stop wanting her.

He moved his hand away from hers before he found himself pressing it to his lips. "Thanks for breakfast." He set his napkin on the table. "I've got to run. Lots to get done today."

"It's Saturday."

"The farm doesn't care." He rose.

She put a hand out to stop him. "Give me a couple more minutes. I didn't just want to say thank you with breakfast. There's something I wanted to talk to you about."

Not the kiss, he prayed. He really didn't want to get into talking about the kiss and why he didn't want to repeat it and why he couldn't stop thinking about doing it again. "What?"

She took the same kind of deep breath she might take before going off a high dive, looking simultaneously excited and uneasy. "Remember the other day I told you nineteen acres of your sugarbush had to come down?"

"Kind of hard to forget, especially since a chunk of it is already gone."

"There might be a way to salvage the rest."

"How? You spent the whole meeting last night telling everyone there wasn't any other way." And he wasn't ready to get his hopes up.

"We have to take out the infested trees and the inner ring. We don't have a choice there. But there might be a way to save the outer ring."

He sat slowly. "Tell me more."

"We've figured out how to distill the chemical the tree produces to battle the maple borer and turned it into an injectable insecticide."

"I've read about it on the Internet but I didn't think it was approved for use here, yet. Just in Canada." He frowned. "And if it is approved, why the hell aren't you using it?"

"I'm not allowed to yet, not broadly, but my contacts tell me the RAL—that's the EPA's regulatory action leader who pulls together all data and recommendations—has given it the thumbs-up. They're just processing the paperwork." She leaned forward, eyes bright. "I can inoculate the trees in the outer ring. If a borer chews into them, it's history. If there are already eggs in them, once the larvae hatch, they'll die."

"What about the people who eat syrup made from the sap of the trees? Will they die too?"

Celie shook her head. "It's a naturally occurring substance, we've just upped the concentration. The chemical makeup of syrup produced from the sap is identical to that pulled from regular trees. Nothing different in the taste, no harmful compounds." She spread her hands. "It's not a panacea but we can use it to save some of your maples."

He gave her a long look. "Why are you doing this? Because I took care of your truck?"

"I'm doing it because I'm sick of watching trees come down," she retorted. "It doesn't need to happen, not if we use Beetlejuice."

"Beetlejuice?"

"The insecticide. The approval's basically a done deal. Once the paperwork's done, you'll be able to buy it off the shelf."

He felt like a man receiving an eleventh-hour reprieve. "So talk to me about the numbers. How many trees would this save?"

"Our tests show the maple borer's range is a hundred yards. We added the fifty-yard cushion to compensate for the limited sampling. If we can inoculate the trees in the outer fifty yards of the circle, they should be safe. With the number of infected trees you have, that'll save about eleven acres."

"And this stuff really works?" Hope warred with suspicion.

"Yes, it really works. My group has been testing it for

seven years, Canada and the U.S. for five. It represents our best bet to get the beetle under control."

"How long does it last?"

"At least a year, maybe more. It actually has a fairly long survival rate in the tree." She paused. "So what do you think?"

He didn't reply right away. He wanted to believe it. He wanted, he desperately wanted to save his trees. But he wanted to be sure. "Where would you get it if it's not out yet?"

"I've got a couple of gallons of the concentrate in the back of my truck, left over from some of the test trials I ran. If you give me the word. I could start tomorrow." She crossed her arms before her. "I need to know by Monday because that's when the rest of the trees come down."

He studied her. "If you were me, would you do it?"

"Yes," she said without hesitation.

"Your judgment's good enough for me."

It wasn't a surprise that Jacob wanted to get to it immediately, but it wasn't as easy as just going into the maples. Celie needed supplies, she needed to mix up jugs of Beetlejuice, but that was only part of it. The truth was that she didn't want him doing the inoculations. That was her risk to take, she thought as she watched him drive away.

She'd told him that the release could come any day. Which, strictly speaking, was true. What she hadn't said was that there was a chance it would take longer, that she was gambling on the probability that by the time anyone found out about her un-authorized use, the insecticide would be released. That was her risk to take and her risk only.

She picked up her cell phone and dialed.

*"Bonjour."*

*"Maman? C'est Celie."*

"Who is calling me in this American-accented French?"

her mother replied, her French, too, laced with the North-American accent that thirty-five years of living in Montreal hadn't erased. "It couldn't be my daughter, who does not come home for Christmas and does not call to tell her poor *maman* she has gone to an assignment heaven knows where."

Celie stuck her tongue in her cheek. "Perhaps it wasn't her fault," she said in English. "Perhaps she's been kidnapped and is waiting for ransom."

"Where was she kidnapped to?"

"Vermont," Celie supplied with a grin.

"Vermont? Why haven't there been any ransom notes?"

"Maybe if you checked your e-mail once in a while."

Her mother cleared her throat. "A truly dedicated kidnapper would have used a better way."

"Carrier pigeon?"

*"C'est qui?"* Celie heard her father boom in the background.

"Someone who sounds very much like our long-lost daughter, accusing me of ignoring my e-mail."

There were sounds of the phone being shuffled and her father came on the line. "Ah, *bébé*, are you coming to visit?"

"I hope so, *Papa*," Celie replied, lapsing back into French. "I am close. I will see you soon."

"We would like that. You could visit us and you could visit the living room."

"The living room?" Celie repeated, mystified.

"Yes, the living room. You could convince her it should be left as is. Your childhood memories, you know, they are delicate. She wishes to change everything."

Now she got it. "Is *Maman* redecorating?"

"Don't listen to him," Celie's mother said in the background. "I just asked him to move some furniture."

"You will not recognize it," he said in English. "You will think you went to the wrong house."

It had been too long since she'd been home, Celie thought, listening to the affectionate sparring. "I'll have to visit to play referee," she told him.

"Please, before it is too late," he said. "And now, I must go open the store."

Of course. Always the store. Celie sighed and tried to think about it the way Jacob would. "How is business?"

"Eh," her father said and she could imagine his shrug. "Business is all right. Quiet after Christmas, you understand, but the High Lights Festival begins soon. You will come for it, perhaps. We will put you to work."

"Just what I've always hoped for." Celie's tone was dry.

"But of course," he said, laughing at his own joke. *"Au revoir."*

*"Au revoir, Papa,"* Celie answered. "Doesn't he have someone to help him?" she asked her mother as she came back on the line.

"He is happiest doing it himself. You know he loves the shop. It's his history."

"I know, his family."

"Exactly," her mother said. "And it's your history, too, whether you want to admit it or not."

Celie opened her mouth and shut it. Legacies. She'd seen from Jacob that they didn't always have to be burdens. "You see too much sometimes."

"I'm a mother. That's what we do. Now tell me about your new home," she said comfortably.

Washington County Maple Supplies was surprisingly busy for so early on a Saturday. Then again, sugar-makers started early, Celie thought, just like any other farmer.

Behind the counter, a gray-haired woman in a sweatshirt smiled at her. "Morning."

"Morning," Celie replied. One of the growers in the store made eye contact. The others went about their business, studiously ignoring her. She ought to be used to it by now; she tried not to let it sting as she set her air canisters down on the counter. "Can you recharge these?"

The woman nodded. "Go ahead and do your shopping. They'll be ready in a couple minutes."

"Thanks," Celie said. She picked up a plastic five-gallon bucket from a display and began wandering the aisles, looking. She'd always loved these kinds of stores, the mix of scents, the variety of gadgets. And yet for someone who'd made forestry her life, she'd never stayed anywhere long enough to have a house and trees of her own. She wondered sometimes what it would be like to really watch a forest grow, to know each individual tree the way Jacob seemed to know his.

She shook it off. It wasn't an option, however appealing it might have been.

Celie walked up to the counter and set down the bucket.

"Find everything you needed?" the woman asked, setting the charged canisters down beside it.

"Actually, I need a couple of needles for an Arborjet injector."

"Oh, we keep them back here." The woman reached below the counter and pulling out a pair of flat, cardboard packages. "You're new around here. I don't recognize you. I'm Muriel Anderson."

"Celie Favreau, APHIS." She put her hand out.

Muriel shook it firmly. "I hear you're working out at Jacob Trask's place. How's that going?"

"I think we've got a handle on it."

"I hope so. Jacob's had his share of trouble, I guess." Muriel began to ring up Celie's purchases. "Good-looking boy," she added. "You're taking down his trees, right?"

"Some of them," Celie said uncomfortably, looking away from the injector needles.

"Well that's a crying shame."

"It has to be done to control the maple borer."

"I suppose I can see that, but it's hard luck."

Celie thought of the gallons of Beetlejuice concentrate in her truck. "I'm doing my best for him."

"Are you?" Muriel put the bottles into a bag. "He could use a woman doing that."

Celie gave her a quick, startled look. "Excuse me?"

"That'll be $23.70," Muriel said smoothly.

Celie tapped the little plastic plug into the hole she'd just drilled in one of Jacob's maples, then set the mallet aside and picked up her injector gun. It looked a little as though it should fire energy bolts instead of doses of insecticide, but she didn't live in a Star Trek world, and firing Beetlejuice suited her just fine.

Trees might appear static to some, but she knew they were in a state of constant change. On the outside, perhaps, the change looked slow except during spring and fall. On the inside, it was rapid and purposeful, fluids traveling, cells multiplying, the whole structure seething with life.

And just like people and animals, the layers that carried fluid could be injected with serums—or in this case, Beetlejuice. Celie punched the gun's needle through the plastic plug and pulled the trigger. Once the fluid was in the little pocket between the plug and the back of the hole, it was up to the tree.

Dabbing the bark with blue paint, she marked the tree and moved on. The holes were tidy and low; unless a person was looking for them, they wouldn't show. Of course, at this hour not much did; the sun wouldn't be up for thirty or forty minutes. It was light enough to see what she was doing, though, barely. She'd managed to put in seven hours the day before. Today, she figured to put in at least ten. That would push her past the halfway point.

Which was important. When Monday hit, she'd be back in the inspection race and any time she put into inoculations would have to be stolen from in the early morning or early evening.

Not that she minded. In a way, the risk and the extra time and effort were her penance for all the trees she'd had taken down. It was a chance to do something genuinely positive for a change, something tangible she could point to.

At least once Beetlejuice was officially released.

"Are you out of your *mind?*" Marce stood at the kitchen sink, the coffeepot dangling from her hand. Outside, the Sunday evening sky purpled to black.

"Why, because I'm trying to avoid taking down trees I don't have to?" Celie asked.

"Because you're doing it with an unreleased pesticide."

"It's practically a done deal."

"It is not," Marce shot back. "Pete told you he didn't know how long it would be bogged down and you know how long it's taken already."

"They're close." Under the table, she crossed her fingers. "The RAL approved it. It's just a matter of time."

Marce eyed her narrowly. "How long have you been working for the government, Pollyanna? Are you going to make me use dumb clichés about fat ladies singing? You can't do this."

"Beetlejuice is under test. I'm just expanding the trials."

"In the field and without authorization. Yeah, that's going to fly. Do you *want* to become unemployed?" Marce demanded. "Because you will be when they find out what you've done. Falsifying reports, use of unapproved chemicals, willful disobedience…" She ticked them off on her fingers. "There are reasons to have those rules in place."

"How are they going to find out?"

Marce gave a humorless laugh. "Oh, a surveyor's transit would be a good start. Or unearthing the disagreement between the number of trees you're ordering removed and your removal report. Celie, you can't do this, you're the head of the program."

"All the more reason I should be able to make an exception."

"Why now? Why him? Wait," Marce raised her hand. "I already know the answer to that. How about this? Can you honestly say that you're being totally objective, here?"

"I'm never objective about any of this, Marce." Wearily, Celie dropped her head into her hands. "It kills me to take down acres of perfectly healthy trees for a safety margin, and in the meantime I've got people slashing my tires because they can't take it out on the maple borer."

"Yeah, well here's one to think about. What happens if Beetlejuice doesn't work and the infestation spreads? How are you going to sleep at night?"

"It's not going to spread," Celie said stubbornly. "Beetlejuice works, we know it does. It's just caught up in interagency politics."

"Yeah, and thalidomide is this really great anti-nausea medication, they just won't release it in the U.S. yet."

Celie set her jaw. "You've made your point."

"I'm not trying to be a hardass." Marce's voice softened. "I just don't want to see you risk everything without being really damned sure you know what you're doing and why. Do you?"

Celie hesitated. "I kissed him, Marce."

"Who, him? Sap Boy?" Marce laughed and then stopped and looked at her more closely. "Oh, good God, you're serious. How was it?"

"The kiss was great. Outside of the fact that he wouldn't talk to me after and he acts now like it never happened."

"Outside of those small details. So what does it mean? Was it a one-time experiment?"

"You've got me. Jacob's not exactly the type for long conversations on the topic. Anyway, it was only a kiss," she said impatiently. "It's not worth dwelling on."

"So why are you?"

"Because. I hate not knowing, you know?"

"Yeah? And?"

"And I wouldn't mind a little more."

## *Chapter Eight*

He'd never been a big fan of washing dishes. Jacob carried a stack of galvanized sap buckets across the snow-covered yard behind the sugarhouse. The idea of spending time cleaning them wasn't even remotely appealing. Still, they needed to be ready to use for the year's sap run, and that meant giving them at least a cursory scrub. All forty-five hundred of them.

He set the stack next to the others sitting by the sugar-house's back door and walked back to the utility cart. Food products were food products and it didn't matter what was acceptable to the state: Molly Trask decreed that all the collecting buckets be washed before the start of each season. And that was what he'd spend the last half of his week doing.

That, and thinking about Celie. Her daily visits to update him on the inoculations were almost enough to make him forget the frustration of being stuck at the sugarhouse instead of helping her. Something about not knowing when she'd appear made her present his whole day. And how pathetic was that?

He reached for another stack of buckets. There were plenty more important things for him to be thinking about, like how much the nine acres they'd lost were going to impact their gross, whether this was the year to start tapping the maples on the northern slope and how the hell he was going to accomplish the work of two people during the sap run.

Minor details like that.

Somehow, though, he found himself thinking instead about a pair of laughing eyes, about the way conversations with Celie never stayed linear but went bounding off in unexpected directions. Somehow, he kept remembering the taste of a pair of cool, soft lips and the way she'd fitted against him.

"Jacob?"

He turned too quickly, and the stack of buckets in his hands knocked a cluster of others off the utility cart, sending them clattering everywhere.

Cursing, Jacob bent to pick them up, turning to see a spare-looking man with a weathered face, hunched into his plaid wool coat. He straightened. "Hey, Deke."

"Sorry about that." Deke leaned over to pick up a few buckets and put them on the cart. "I thought you heard me."

He would have if he hadn't been preoccupied with things that shouldn't have been bothering him. Jacob reached under the axle of the cart to pull out a couple more buckets. "Not a crisis."

"Can I talk with you for a minute?"

Jacob eyed Deke, trying to gauge how much his hands were shaking, which would indicate the purpose of his visit. A loan, maybe, or a favor. Or maybe he was just in the neighborhood. You never knew with Deke. It depended on how much time he'd been spending lately at the tavern. "Sure. What's up?"

Deke shifted a bit and cleared his throat. "I was wondering if you need me to work the sugaring season for you this year."

Jacob wished he had an answer. The sugaring season was about the only time of year Deke worked steadily; the rest of the time he managed to get by with odd jobs and intervals of shiftlessness. Under supervision, the man worked and worked well. On his own, he was erratic at best. Jacob and his father had always traded off—one of them ran the evaporator and the other spent the day in the sugarbush, supervising the gathering crews, keeping Deke on the straight and narrow. This year?

This year Jacob was on his own.

They had storage for about four thousand gallons of sap at the best of times. On a good day, the sugarbush could produce five. That meant that someone had to be boiling sap like mad to make room for it all, or else they'd be letting the precious fluid flow onto the forest floor, and then he really would be in the unemployment line come fall. The problem was, once he fired up the evaporator of a day, he had to stay with it. And that meant leaving Deke and a crew of five or six other guys to roam the sugarbush on their own. If he was lucky, Deke would focus and get the job done. If he wasn't…

"Are you ready to stay dry?"

"That ain't fair, Jacob. I've done some good work for you."

"I know you have. And that's what I need now—you, here, everyday, on time."

"I got it."

"You can't just forget to show up," Jacob said sharply.

"I won't." Deke coughed. "You can trust me, Jacob. Your daddy always did. Floyd and Billy'll work, too."

Floyd and Billy, Deke's brother-in-law and nephew. They'd keep him a little more steady. "I could use all three of you guys, but you're going to have to bust your behinds."

"Billy can only work in the mornings and after school."

Deke's eyes flicked toward him. "He's got a couple of buddies on the wrestling team who want to help out, too."

High-school kids. Not for the first time, Jacob wished he had brothers or cousins around to help, like Charlie Willoughby did. He understood that Gabe and Nick had their own lives. It was just that sometimes he wished thing things could be different.

Sometimes, he wished it didn't all come down to him. But if wishes were horses...

Jacob rested his hands on his hips. "Let's see how it goes."

Deke drew his head between his shoulders, looking a little like a skinny turtle. "You're still gonna need more people on your crew," he said obstinately.

"That's my worry," Jacob snapped. The worrying part he had down; it was the answers that were harder.


Celie pulled up against the post-and-rail fence in the parking lot and turned off her truck. It was break time.

And she wanted to see Jacob.

"Celie!" Molly Trask looked up from folding tea towels to beam at Celie as she walked into the gift shop.

"How are you?"

Molly set the stack aside. "I'm fine. How about you?"

"Keeping busy."

"It looks like it. You look a little tired, if you don't mind me saying. Why don't you come into the café and have something to eat? You can sit down and relax for a bit."

It was nice to be mothered, even if her own was just a few hours away in Montreal. Celie smiled. "Thanks but I don't have a lot of time. I actually need to see Jacob."

"He's out back. You can talk to him in a minute. At least have a bite. How about a maple ice cream? It's quick."

"Aren't you supposed to be offering me a sandwich or something nutritional?"

"'Life is uncertain, eat dessert first.'" Molly quoted, leading her into the café and walking behind the counter. "Sugar cone?" She raised her eyebrows.

Celie surrendered. "No sense in doing things by halves."

"A woman after my own heart." Molly pulled the lever on the machine to send out the pale tan curl of ice cream, whirling it expertly into a tower. "There you are." She handed it over. "Now you can say you've tried our famous maple ice cream."

Celie took the cone from her and sampled. She let out a small moan, closed her eyes briefly and took another taste.

"Well?" Molly raised her eyebrows.

"I'm never eating anything else again." Celie licked up a dollop of the rich, sweet cream and let the flavor spread through her mouth. "This is incredible. I've never had anything like it." She took another taste.

"It's always here. Come on by any time."

"Watch out, I will. And you'll be responsible when my pants don't fit." Celie glanced at her watch. "Jacob's out back?"

Molly nodded. "Take that door to your left just as you go inside the sugarhouse."

Celie stepped through the door that led from the gift shop to the chill of the unheated sugarhouse. Directly ahead of her stood the evaporator, with its pool-table-sized shallow boiling pans. In a few weeks, they'd be full of bubbling sap; for now, the firebox below them was dark and cold, the door at the end of the room that led to the wood supply, closed.

To her left, another door led to the little yard in back. It was partially ajar, sunlight gleaming through the cracks around the frame. Even as Celie put her hand on the handle, she heard voices.

Deke stared down at his feet. "You got a hundred other sugar-makers in the county gonna be hiring people," he said, scuffing his toes in the dirty snow. "You need to decide now. You oughta give Billy's friends a chance."

"I don't need to have a couple of kids looking for an easy buck running around my sugarbush," Jacob responded. "It's my problem and I'll deal with it."

"You need Billy's friends," Deke protested with uncharacteristic force, his breath showing white in the cool air. "You can't do it with just the three of us. Even with Billy's friends we're all gonna be busting our asses. And everyone's gonna be hired by the time you realize it. Who are you going to get?"

"I'll find someone."

"Jacob?"

He turned to see Celie by the door from the sugarhouse. And for just an instant, it seemed everything screamed to a halt. She stood there in her red parka, cheeks rosy against her dark hair, and it was like someone turned up the brightness on his entire world.

"I'm interrupting. I'll go back inside," she said quickly. And licked the maple ice cream cone in her hand.

Ice cream, he thought feverishly, trying not to stare at her mouth. Slick and sweet and way too tempting. "That's okay," he found himself saying. "We're done here."

"Not quite." She pointed at the buckets on the ground.

"Close enough."

She gave one of those smiles that always stunned him. And then he realized that she was looking at Deke. "Oh, uh, Celie, this is Deke," he said. "He works on the gathering crew. Deke, this is Celie Favreau."

"Nice to meet you, Deke."

Deke turned bright red and ducked his head more deeply into the collar of his coat. "'Meetcha," he mumbled.

"Looks like the sugaring season's coming." She gestured at the buckets. "Are you looking forward to it?"

Deke sent Jacob a hunted look. "I gotta go," he muttered and scuttled away. Faster than Jacob had ever seen him move before, now that he thought about it.

"Wait. But…" Celie turned to Jacob. "I didn't mean to run him off," she said helplessly.

A corner of Jacob's mouth tugged up. "Deke's not a big social guy."

"You two must make a great pair." Celie popped the last bite of her cone in her mouth, to Jacob's relief. She bent over to pick up some of the fallen buckets. "You can work together and never say a word. Although he was saying a few from what I overheard."

Jacob shot her a suspicious look and began stacking together buckets. "What did you overhear?"

"That you're going to be in trouble when the sap run starts."

"It's not going to be a problem."

"Really? Working a hundred acres with a crew of four?"

"It's fine." He thumped the buckets down on the cart with unnecessary force.

"So, what, you do the work of three men gathering sap all day and spend the night boiling it down? That works. After all, sleep's for losers, right?"

"It'll be fine."

"There's that word again."

"I'll deal with it."

She put her hands on her hips. "You know, there *are* easier ways to do this."

"I like this way. It works."

"How do you know? The season hasn't started yet. Even you have your limits, Jacob. Oh, I forgot, it's probably fine."

"It will be."

"You know, if you're so obsessed with doing things without help, why don't you join the rest of the sugar-makers in the twenty-first century and link your trees together with tubing? Then you really could do everything yourself."

He spared her a glance. "I don't believe in tubing."

"What is that, a religious conviction?"

He carried a stack of buckets to the sugarhouse door. "Tapping with buckets was good enough for my grandfather and my great-grandfather, and his father before him. It's good enough for me, too."

Celie followed him across the slush with her own stack. "Well, my grandmother and great-grandmother and her mother before her all probably used a washtub and wringer to clean their clothes. Me, I'm smart enough to look for an easier way."

He smiled faintly. "Maybe you're just lazy."

"And you're just stubborn. You can't have it both ways. Either you need more help or you need to go to tubing. Religious convictions or no."

"I'll get it done." He headed back to the cart.

"How?" she demanded, scampering after him. "There are only so many hours of daylight this time of year, in case you hadn't noticed. And even you can't be two places at once."

"So?"

"So why not let modern technology simplify things? If you network your trees with tubing, you'll cut your collection time by a good sixty or seventy percent."

"I'm not going to have my sap running through tubes and maybe picking up trace chemicals and toxins." He slammed the last of the stray buckets together. "I don't trust plastics. They leave a flavor. They might leach out toxins."

"They've tested for all that. It's safe. They've worked out the bugs." She looked out at the sugarbush with calculating eyes. "You could have a tubing system in here in time for this season, if you wanted to."

"Sure, and if we have a couple of bad seasons after I spend all that money, I'm broke. Things are going to be hard enough financially this year as it is." He lifted a stack of buckets. "I don't need any more challenges."

"So do it a piece at a time. It's probably smarter anyway. Technology's not your enemy, Jacob. We're trying to help."

He scowled at her and set the buckets back down. "Do you ever give up? Listen to me, I don't need your help." What he needed was something different entirely.

"But it's the best way." She fisted her hands on her hips. "You'd know that if you weren't being so pigheaded."

"Pigheaded?" His eyes narrowed. "What do you know about it? Have you ever actually worked a maple-sugar farm? Do you have any idea what it's about?"

"Sure I know what it's about. You pound taps into maples and hang buckets on them."

"But you've never actually taken sap from tree to jug."

"Of course not. My specialty is insects, not sugar-making."

"That's what I thought." He turned back to the cart. "That's what you people always do, seize on stuff just because it's new, without ever asking if it's really better or just different."

Irritation flashed in her eyes. "'You people'? What's that supposed to mean?"

"Research types who haven't been around long enough to know how things work."

"And you think that's me?"

"Admit it, you don't know what you're talking about."

"Fine," she snapped, "then show me."

He frowned at her. "I don't do tours."

"And I'm not talking about tours. Take me on your crew. Let me work for you."

"Give me a break."

"Don't you go all superior and start telling me I don't know what I'm talking about when you're not willing to show me. Take me through it," she demanded, "teach me how it's done. I need to know and you obviously need help."

Jacob snorted. "The day I need help from a little bit like you is the day I'm really in trouble."

Celie took three steps forward until she was just inches from him. "Little bit?" she echoed, poking him in the chest in outrage. "Just who are you calling little? I can bench press a hundred pounds."

He took a step back. "Did you have too much coffee this morning?"

"Don't you patronize me." She poked him again.

"Hey."

"You talk so big, back it up."

"You've got to be kidding." He moved to shift away and tripped on one of the deep ridges frozen into the slush and mud of the yard. One minute he was standing, the next he was backpedaling furiously. And tumbling on his back into the three-foot snowbank at the edge.

He sprawled on the snow in his heavy buckskin coat, his feet barely touching the ground. Trying to get purchase and roll over was impossible; he felt like an overturned turtle. Helplessly, he began to laugh.

Celie walked over to stand between his feet and stared down at him. "Want some help?" she asked, sticking out her hand. "Or do you want to do it yourself?"

"This help, I'll take." But she wasn't braced for his weight because when he reached for her hand, she landed on top of him with a surprised *oof.*

Her sherry-colored eyes sparked with irritation, bright and furious on his. But it was her mouth that he couldn't ignore. Full, tempting and he remembered how sweet. So close, so tantalizing, everything he'd been thinking about for days, now here in his arms.

And before he could tell himself not to, he slid one hand around the nape of her neck and pulled her down to him.

Her mouth was soft with surprise, her lips parted. Sweet and addictive as maple cream, warm against his. He could tell himself that he shouldn't want. He could tell himself he had way too many things to worry about. He could tell himself it was the wrong place, the wrong time, the wrong woman. It didn't matter.

He couldn't stop.

This wasn't simple attraction, this razor-sharp need that sliced through him. It wasn't just desire. It was something much more, something elemental, something that struck to the core of who he was. It was raw and heated and all the snow in the world wasn't enough to quench it.

He felt the annoyance fade from her, felt it when her mouth turned avid and questing. And he could taste the maple ice cream, still rich and cool on her tongue. He could taste the earthiness and something else, something that he remembered from the last time because a taste like that stayed with a man.

Celie sighed deep in her throat. For once, she wasn't looking up to him. For once, they were face to face. For once, he wasn't pushing her away but pulling her against him, his hands hard and possessive down the length of her back, over her hips. It didn't matter that the air was freezing, that there was snow beneath them. She couldn't feel it. She couldn't feel anything but Jacob's heat and a driving need for more.

Time had ceased to exist. All that mattered was the feel of his mouth on hers, the heat, the urgency, the faint jolt of pain when he nipped at her lips, the mind-meltingly delightful things he was doing with his tongue. If they stopped, she'd die.

The sharp blast of a horn sounded from the parking lot on the opposite side of the sugarhouse, breaking the moment.

Jacob rolled to his feet and swept the snow off his pants. Here it was again. It was like he got around her and lost all common sense. He cleared his throat. "Okay, look, I need to—"

Celie raised her finger in warning. "Don't start."

"What?"

She shook her head. "You are not going into this routine again."

He glowered at her from beneath his brows. "I don't do routines."

"Then why is this one so familiar?"

"Do we need to have this conversation?"

"What, you kiss my face off for the second time and that's that?"

"No, that's not that. That's a good illustration of why you shouldn't come to work for me."

"Why, because we kissed? Jacob, get over it. We're adults."

"Look, I don't—" He put his hands on his hips and stared down at the slush and sighed. "I've got a lot going on right now with the sugaring season coming and my mom and everything else. I can't afford to get distracted."

"Distracted? Is that what you call this?" She raised an eyebrow at him and he lost a beat just looking at her.

"Uh, yeah, distracted," he said after he'd reminded himself to breathe again. "Look, I appreciate the offer of help, but no thanks."

"You don't have a choice. I am going to be here."

*A match for him in stubbornness.* Jacob sighed. "Are you always this hard to get along with?"

"Sometimes I'm worse. Want me to demonstrate?"

"No. Look, you've got a full-time job. More than."

And she needed one positive thing that wasn't about cutting down trees. "That's nine-to-five. I can put in a couple of hours with you in the morning and as much time in the sugarhouse as you want at night. You need help, I need to learn. It sounds like we can do it together."

He studied her and finally he sighed. "All right, what's the earliest you can get here tomorrow?"

"Whenever you want me here. The inoculations are done."

"Six?"

She traced one finger down his chest. "I'll see you then."

## *Chapter Nine*

He kept his word. If he'd promised to teach her, then teach
her he would. And Celie proved to be better than any hired
help he'd ever had. She worked uncomplainingly, cutting and
stacking wood, sterilizing taps, prepping filters. She helped
him scrub the evaporator pan free of the dust that had coated
it during the long months since it had last been fired up. Together, they cleaned the chimney until she had black smears
on her face like some Dickensian orphan.

Each morning, she arrived at the sugarhouse before dawn
and worked until she had to leave to begin inspections. Each
evening as her workday ended, she returned to work under
his direction.

And each day, he did his damnedest to keep his distance.

He had a plan. If he didn't touch her, if he didn't get close
to her, maybe he wouldn't remember the way it had felt to
hold the length of her body along his, maybe he wouldn't re-

member the silky-soft curls of her hair brushing against his cheeks. And maybe he wouldn't find himself fighting to forget even for a minute that he wanted her.

Keep the chatter to a minimum and keep her across the room. It seemed simple enough but somehow it never worked out. Inevitably she'd get him talking about things he never planned to, wheeling off on some tangent that had nothing to do with sugaring.

And with each day that passed by, he wanted her more, until it drummed through him like some tribal beat, some primitive rhythm that countered every civilized part of him. He'd be in the middle of showing her how to work the valves on the feed tube for the evaporator and suddenly he'd find himself focusing on that soft, barely-there scent of hers that made him want to press his face against her neck and bay like a hound. And that quickly he'd be wondering just what it would be like to peel her out of those clothes, what it would feel like to touch her, wondering what would happen if he—

"Jacob?" She craned her neck to look down at him from where she perched on the stepladder, reaching into the uppermost of the two twelve-hundred-gallon holding tanks that sat outside the back of the sugarhouse. An identical set sat on the opposite side of the sugarhouse door. Jacob stood below her, trying not to think about what lay under her parka. "I dropped the brush. Can you get it?"

He climbed up to peer over her shoulder into the tank where the long-handled scrub brush lay amid soapy water. "Excuse me." He reached past her and snaked his long arm down, groping.

"This would be perfect for a really big bathtub," she observed as his fingers curled around the padded handle. "Fill it up with hot water and bubbles and you could sit out here on a spring evening and enjoy yourself."

And he got an abrupt, vivid image of her naked and wet in the extravagant clawfoot tub Isaac had installed in the master bath, not quite covered by bubbles so that her rosy-tipped breasts bobbed in the water, and he thought of what it would be like to join her and about how reaching around her, holding on to the tub—tank, the *tank* edge with one hand while reaching in with the other was the next best thing to holding her in the circle of his arms, and he thought he smelled burning as his synapses melted from trying to hold on to so many different images and desires at once.

Or not so many desires, because he only really had one—Celie, warm and naked against him….

"Jacob?"

He gave himself a mental shake. "Right." He handed her the scrub brush and hastily climbed down from the ladder, heart hammering as though he'd been running. "Here's the hose," he said and passed it up to her.

"Pesticides lab, Pete Craven."

"You should be." Celie held her cell phone up to her ear with one hand as she drove toward the day's inspection site.

"What?"

"Craven. Crawling. Pleading for forgiveness." She pulled off to the edge of the road.

"Oh, hey, Celie, how are you?" Pete's voice held a forced jollity.

"Puzzled," she said pleasantly, putting on her parking brake. "I must have something wrong with my e-mail because I never got the message you promised me giving me the status of the release. The one you swore you'd send. It must have been caught by my spam filter."

"Well, I've been—"

"Because I know you'd never just blow me off."

"Oh, never," he assured her. "I've been meaning to send an update, I've just been busy. You know how it is, lot going on. And I've been driving the lab carpool so I get home late—"

"Pete."

"And the draft for my fantasy baseball league is next week, lot of action there, you've gotta really be up on the stats and do a lot of research because if—"

*"Pete."*

There was a silence.

"When am I going to see the release? You said two weeks, it's been almost three."

He cleared his throat. "We've run into some delays."

"Try five and a half years' worth. What kind now?"

"You've got the EPA and the USDA and half a dozen state governments involved," he said sarcastically, "what kind do you think?"

"I thought you told me the release was written."

"I did. Right before I told you that didn't mean anything."

She stared out through the windshield as two green Vermont Division of Forestry trucks pulled up. "I'm cutting trees down for no good reason, Pete."

"I know. I'm pushing them."

"Push harder." An edge entered her voice.

"I am. It's getting closer."

"And you can tell that how?"

"The latest version of the release I've seen is on department letterhead," he offered.

"Oh, that's progress."

"It'll happen," he said, all joking gone.

"This century?"

"Maybe."

She got out and rummaged behind her seat for her field kit. "Call me when all systems are go or I'll have to hurt you."

"What, you think you're going to be the first person to use it outside of a field trial?"

She closed her eyes briefly. "Yeah. I do."

It didn't surprise Jacob to find half a dozen people prowling the shelves of Washington County Maple Supplies. The sugaring season was drawing near, and anybody who had any sense was getting ready.

Of course, a few others who had less sense were happy enough to stand by the stove and yap.

Clayton Billings turned to nod at him as he walked to the aisles in the back. "Jacob."

He nodded in return. "Clayton."

"What do you think of all this talk of a thaw? Anything to it?"

Jacob stopped reluctantly. Clayton, Paul Durkin, two other sugar-makers he didn't know well. He shrugged. "Time will tell. I'm getting my taps in."

Clayton laughed. "Never had a tired day in your life, have you?"

"I don't think about it one way or another. The work's got to be done."

"Hear that, Paul?" Clayton said to the redhead. "Work to be done."

Durkin spat into the stove and listened to the pop. "Yeah, well, you can kill yourself getting in a two-day sap run if you want. Me, I'll wait for the real thing."

"You do that." Jacob crossed to the shelf of filter supplies against the far wall. Muriel could talk herself blue in the face about how he should hang out around the hot stove but there were better things to be done. He picked up a box of filters and then turned toward the hardware aisle.

Around the stove, the talk shifted to the scarlet-horned maple borer. "I flat out don't think she knows what she's doing," someone—Clayton, probably—said behind him. "That Rumson fellow from the state says there are other ways to go."

Dick Rumson, living up to his name. Jacob picked up a box of taps and brought them to the counter, along with his filters.

"That do it for you?" Muriel asked.

"Yep. I can do without all the jawing," he said as she scanned in the items.

"That APHIS woman and her crew are going through my trees next week," someone said.

"Her," a voice said in disgust. Durkin, Jacob thought and glanced toward the group at the stove to see that he was right. "I wouldn't let her on my property."

"You heard what she said. She'll get a court order."

"Yeah? She can try all she wants to get in my trees and mess around. I've already been talking to a lawyer in Montpelier who says he'll fix her wagon."

"She seemed pretty sure about it," one of the unfamiliar voices said.

"Big talk," Durkin scoffed. "I'll tell you one thing. If she tries to take down my trees, I'm not going to make it easy for her." He flicked a contemptuous glance at Jacob. "I'm going to let her know she's got a fight on her hands."

"How you going to do that?"

Jacob saw the malicious smile flit across Durkin's face. "I have my ways. I think she already knows she's not wanted here."

Jacob was walking toward the stove before he even realized it. There was a buzzing in his ears. The four men turned to look at him, one by one. What was on his face, he couldn't say, but their self-satisfied grins dropped away. "What was that you were saying, Paul?" His voice was quiet.

Durkin looked at him assessingly. "About what?"

"About showing Celie Favreau she's not wanted here."

"What's it to you?"

"I spent a couple of hours after the meeting the other night taking off her wheels and helping her get her tires to the all-night truck stop. You wouldn't be the one who slashed them, would you?"

"The woman's cutting down your trees and you're playing automobile club for her?"

"That's got nothing to do with what I asked you, Paul." Jacob kept his voice pleasant, but when he took another step, the men at the stove edged away from Durkin warily. "Did you slash her tires?"

"I don't know anything about it," Durkin said with a cocky grin.

Jacob studied him. "You know, I don't really even need to ask you. This is Eastmont. I'll find out. Knowing you, you couldn't resist bragging about it. People will pass it on. It's just a matter of time."

"Don't get any ideas, Trask. Your girlfriend got what she deserved."

"It's the dead of winter, you idiot. You strand someone after everything's closed and they're walking in subzero weather on dark highways with no shoulders because of the snow banks. That's not just being an ass, that's being dangerous."

"You can't—"

"I can." Jacob's voice hardened. "Don't mess with Celie Favreau again."

"Don't come around here telling me what I should and shouldn't do," Durkin blustered. "She's the one who came barging in. If something happens to her, she's got it coming."

Jacob's gaze turned flat and cold. "If something happens to her, I'll know who to come looking for." He took another step forward. "And trust me, Paul," he said softly, "I *will* come looking."

Durkin blanched and backed up. "You stay away from me."

"You focus on your sugar-making, you've got nothing to worry about." And Jacob turned and walked away.

Muriel watched him as he approached the counter. "When I told you that you should talk a little more, threatening people wasn't what I had in mind."

"I didn't threaten him with anything in particular."

"You did worse."

"What does that mean?"

"Guy blusters and rants, you have a pretty good idea he's a little scared underneath and making noise to hide it, or that he's angry but it'll go away. That ice look you've got doesn't. If I were Paul, I'd be worried."

"I just wanted to make an impression on him."

"Oh, I'd say you did."

"Someone slashed four hundred bucks worth of tires. I think that deserves a lasting impression. I want whoever did it to know there are going to be repercussions next time they try it."

"He's a vindictive little bastard." Muriel's tone was conversational. "If I were you, I'd watch my back. Tell your friend to watch hers, too. Paul's not going to do her any favors."

"Paul's just scared," Jacob said contemptuously and picked up his bag.

"And that probably makes him more dangerous, not less."

"I don't really give a damn. Because if anyone tries something like that again, I will personally drop-kick them to Montpelier and back."

"I'll put the word out." Muriel studied him a moment. "So was Paul right, are you and she an item?"

Jacob frowned. "What kind of a question is that?"

"I'll take that as a yes," Muriel said and handed him his change.

\* \* \*

Friday might have been the day to wind down for some, but when Celie arrived that morning, she found Jacob behind the sugarhouse, loading his truck with buckets and a pair of blue supply bins. Nearby, Deke loaded his own truck. A new intensity, a purpose quickened the air.

Jacob glanced across at her and as always it sent something skittering around in her stomach. He hadn't bothered to shave, so his jaw was still dark with the previous day's stubble. Seemingly impervious to the cold, he wore one of his ubiquitous flannel plaids loose and open over a thermal Henley. Then again, it didn't feel all that cold now that she thought about it.

"What's this all about? Is it showtime?" she asked.

"Could be." He set the last bin in the bed of the truck and slammed the tailgate closed. "They're calling for an early thaw in a couple of days. I want to get the taps in place to catch it."

"In February? I thought the sap didn't run until early March."

"The sap runs when it pleases."

"Or doesn't," Deke put in and made a little barking noise that she realized was a laugh.

The corner of Jacob's mouth twitched. "Deke's going to work the upper side of the sugarbush. We'll start at the bottom."

"How long does it take to set the taps?" Celie asked as he grabbed his coat and they headed for the cab of the truck. "Are you going to be able to get it all done in time?"

Jacob got in the driver's side. "We'll finish, if I have to set up lights in the trees."

And he would, she thought, studying him as he drove them along the access road of the sugarbush. She'd never met anyone as determined as Jacob. If he said he was going to do something, nothing was going to stop him.

And if he said he wasn't, he held to that pretty well, too. A week had passed since that mind-melting kiss in the snow, a week during which they'd worked together every morning and every night. And it was there every minute they were together, hovering in the background, giving her those little flutters in her belly whenever she remembered it. She'd talk to him and watch his mouth, remembering what it had felt like.

Wondering when it would happen again.

He'd stayed stubbornly distant, though. She got to him sometimes, she could see it in his eyes. But then he'd find an excuse to move away and the moment would be gone.

He stopped the truck on an access road and Celie felt a little charge of excitement. Jacob or no Jacob, this was the start of it all. Over the days of prep work, she'd felt a steadily sharpening sense of anticipation. Now, the real deal was finally here.

Somehow the maples looked different to her. They were quickening. Slowly, slowly the sap was getting ready to flow, drawn by the heat of a distant sun that sent some nameless, irresistible call to come to life.

She knew how they felt.

"You okay?" Jacob asked.

"Sure. Why wouldn't I be?"

He shrugged and set down the bin of tools he carried before a maple. Running his fingers over a patch of bark where the growth pattern was distorted, he turned to her. "Okay, here's what you do. Find the previous year's tapping scar. Move around the tree about five or six inches and up a couple of inches. The idea is that we want to tap on a rising spiral over the years to spread out the injury."

"Planning for the long term?"

"Makes sense, doesn't it?"

It did, and it was one of the many things she admired about Jacob—he took the long view, understood that the process was about more than just the money he could make today.

Of course, there were other things she admired about him, she thought as she watched his intent, unsmiling face. "Aim to keep all the taps between three and four feet above the ground," he continued. "That makes the buckets easier to lift when they're full."

"How often does that happen?"

"In a good season, every day." He opened the bin and took out a cordless drill.

She picked up one of the iron taps and studied it. "Speaking of planning for the long term, why haven't you switched to narrow-bore taps? There's a lot of talk about them at the Institute—less damage."

A corner of his mouth tugged up. "You're just not going to stop until you get me to change something, are you? I have a different shirt on, today. Isn't that enough?"

She raised her eyebrows at him.

"What?"

"It's plaid."

"So? You got a problem with plaid?"

"No. Not any of the thirty-some-odd versions of it I've seen you wear." Her lips twitched. "I just always thought Trask was an English name, not Scottish."

"Can we please stop discussing my wardrobe?"

"You brought it up. It's not like I suggested you change it. I think they suit you."

He shifted his feet and she could have sworn he looked bashful. "The tapping?" he reminded her.

"I'm sorry, am I distracting you?" Celie touched her tongue to her upper lip. "I know how you hate that."

She was rewarded by seeing his eyes darken for just a moment. "We've got a job to do here," he growled.

"Then I guess you'd better show me how to do it."

He gave her a sharp look, then hefted the drill. "Okay, you

want to go in at a slight upward angle. Increases the sap flow. You want the hole nice and tight, so make sure you hold the drill steady." He sank a hole to demonstrate.

There was something about a man with a power tool in his hands that always made her knees weak. And Jacob's hands were strong and broad and capable, with just a sprinkling of black hair on the back of the wrist. Hypnotized, she stared at them, imagining them on her skin, imagining what they could do.

Then she realized that he was watching her and she raised her eyes deliberately to meet his. He swallowed. "Now place the tap. Use the mallet to knock it in. Then hang your bucket." It took him a couple of tries to get the hole in the bucket's rim over the curling hook on the tap. He dropped the metal bucket cover in the snow and they both bent down for it. And for a thudding instant, Celie's breath backed up in her lungs as they froze, face to face, inches apart.

Jacob moved first, grabbing the cover and standing. "Snap it in place and you're in business," he said, a little hoarsely. "You want to try?"

She wanted to try everything, preferably things that involved the two of them and very few clothes. Celie gave her head a brisk shake to dislodge the image. "Sure."

"Now this guy is twenty inches, so we can put another tap on the opposite side." He handed her the drill. "Go to town."

Knowing he was watching made her extra aware of her every motion. "Like this?"

"The angle's not right," Jacob said gruffly and reached around her to grip the drill. "Here, see? Hold it like this and keep the slant gradual. Okay, now sink it."

But her fingers held no strength and all she could think about was the feel of his body behind hers. How could he expect her to focus on drilling the damned tree when the heat of him standing behind her was turning her mind to mush?

She glanced back at him and found his mouth right at her eye level. And it undid her. She could only stare helplessly, breath shuddering out as she watched his eyes turn slowly to indigo.

And with a muttered curse, he tossed the drill into the bin and dragged her to him, clamping his mouth over hers.

Desire slammed through her. The kiss was hard and furious, all heat and flash amid the frozen silence. She half expected to look down and see a circle of melted snow surrounding them. His mouth didn't tempt, it demanded. Her vision blurred. She closed her eyes to immerse herself in sensation, in taste, in touch. In Jacob. She could feel his body pressed against her, feel him erect even through their winter clothing.

He wanted, she thought giddily, he wanted even as she did.

And he was going to take.

This wasn't the careful, controlled Jacob she knew. Heedless, he plundered, ravished her with lips and teeth and tongue. All she could do was moan helplessly as he worked his way down her throat, stopping where her sweatshirt began. But she wanted more, craved for him to touch her, really touch her the way he never had. And as he caught at the front of her parka, she chuckled low in her throat.

Jacob was lost in a red-tinted haze of carnality, ravenous. Day after day, she'd lingered in his mind. Night after night, she'd crept into his dreams, leaving him wanting, always wanting. And now, finally, he gave himself up to it and found himself nearly overwhelmed. Her lips moved against his, clever, teasing, promising even more than they gave until he was half wild with it. The flavor, the scent of her skin wound into his senses.

And desire pushed him past the edge of control.

Impatiently he stripped off his gloves and slowly drew down the zipper of her parka. Celie's lips were fevered under his. He could feel her tremble and wondered how she would move when she was naked under him, on top of him. Around him.

When her jacket was open, he slid his hands inside and pulled her against him so that they were surrounded in a warm cocoon. And then he slid his fingers beneath to feel the silky skin of her back.

Desire exploded through him. He wanted his hands on her breasts, wanted to have her naked, to drive himself into her until they were both out of their heads with it. He slipped his fingers around her waist and felt her flinch from the cold, heard her involuntary gasp.

It was that, finally, that brought him to his senses. And he forced himself to drop his hands and move away.

Celie only looked at him with dazed eyes and licked her lips. "What's wrong?"

He wasn't a novice when it came to women or to passion. He didn't fancy that he had Gabe's style but then he'd never believed that every woman wanted that. What he did believe was that a woman deserved to be treated with respect. For long moments, though, this hadn't been about respect. Something dark and uncivilized and completely carnal had come out in him, something he barely recognized.

And it lurked there now, waiting. He cursed again. "It's twenty-eight degrees out and I'm pawing you in broad daylight and you have to ask what's wrong?" he demanded, dragging his hands through his hair. "This is exactly what I was talking about. This is not okay."

"No, it's not," she murmured. "It's fabulous."

"Stop joking," he snapped.

And she moved up against him and slid her arms around his neck. "I like the fact that you were pawing me. I like the fact that you lost control." She gave a humming laugh deep in her throat. "I like the fact that I drove you to it. Why don't you just give up, Jacob? This is going to happen between us sooner or later."

The knee-jerk protest died on his lips and all he could do was nod. "Not here, though, not now."

"But soon, I think."

"You are stubborn."

"Determined," she corrected.

He stared at her from under his brows. "Are you going to help me tap these trees or not?"

## Chapter Ten

"What are you doing here?" a voice demanded. "Who are you?"

Celie looked up from the morning paper to see Marce standing on the kitchen threshold in a ratty yellow bathrobe. "Your temporary roomie."

"You're not my temporary roomie. My temporary roomie leaves every morning at five-thirty. You're an alien. You've kidnapped Celie and put someone else in her place."

Celie took a drink of her orange juice. "Your point?"

"It's eight o'clock on a Sunday and you're still here. Bad enough you aliens used to take over my boyfriends. I strenuously object to you taking over my best friend."

"Hey, don't blame aliens for the way Kyle behaved at the end of your relationship. He deserves all the credit himself."

Marce gave a brisk nod and crossed to the cupboards. "You're right. Want some more coffee?"

"Nah, I'm set."

"So why the day off?" Marce poured herself some coffee and pulled a bowl of grapes out of the refrigerator. "Aren't you supposed to be off doing your apprentice sugar-maker thing?"

"Nothing left to do," Celie answered a little too quickly. "Jacob told me to take the day off. The taps are all in and we're just waiting to see if the thaw hits."

Marce picked up a grape. "So you've got a day to actually relax for a change."

"Yeah."

"You don't look exactly relaxed."

"Well, you know, I—"

"In fact, you look a little worried. Is it Jacob?"

"Not exactly."

"Jacob's trees?" Marce asked, watching her closely.

"No, they're—"

"Jacob's inoculated trees?"

"They're fine. It's just…" Celie let out a sigh. "I talked to Pete. Beetlejuice is still held up."

"Beetlejuice. You mean the insecticide that you used illegally."

"Yeah, that one."

"And all those trees sitting out there with Arborplugs."

Celie nodded miserably. "And Dick Rumson's out there just looking for a way to nail me."

"So go over the reason why you did the inoculations again?"

"To keep from cutting down trees."

"Jacob Trask's trees."

Celie glared at her. "Anyone's trees. I figured it was a no-brainer, that it would be released by now. Pete said two weeks, it's been almost three, for God's sakes."

"Any time you've got multiple government agencies trying to agree you're going to have delays."

"That's what Pete said." Celie fell silent, staring broodingly out the window.

"They'll get around to it eventually."

"Hopefully before I drive myself nuts worrying about it. Now's your chance to say I told you so."

"I almost never say I told you so," Marce said with dignity.

"I'm sorry I gave you reason to." Celie sipped her coffee glumly.

They sat in silence, staring at nothing. "You know what I think?" Marce asked suddenly, setting her coffee cup down.

"What?"

"I think sitting around here and worrying about it isn't going to do a thing except maybe give you an ulcer. Let's get you out of here and get your mind off of it. The sun's out and it's a perfect day for skiing. What do you say?"

Celie rose. "I say you're on."

"So how is Sap Boy?" Marce asked as they schussed along the side-by-side tracks of a cross-country trail. "Still playing kiss and run?"

"I don't know. I think he might be playing kiss and hang around now."

Marce gave her a startled look. "You guys didn't—"

"No," Celie said hastily. "But I think he's getting used to the idea."

"No, no, no. Guys are *born* used to the idea. It's the women who have to get warmed up."

"Jacob's his own bad self." Celie slowed to a stop at the branch of two trails and stopped to take off her parka.

"Ain't that the truth. Although I saw him the other day without his beard, finally."

"Nice, huh?"

"Doesn't begin to cover it. Like night and day compared to before. I'd cut a guy who looked like that a lot of slack."

"Especially if he kissed like a god?"

"Especially then," Marce agreed, leaning on her poles. "Do you think it'll really happen for you guys?"

Celie tied her jacket around her waist. "Define 'happen.'"

"You define 'happen.' What do you want? I mean, what do you think about this guy?"

"Truth?"

"No, lie to me, please."

Celie was silent for a long moment, staring at the snow. "I like him, Marce," she said slowly. "A lot. I mean, he's got this rough thing going but he's a good man. Down deep, you know? Where it counts. He makes me feel, I don't know, safe, I guess. Steady in a way I haven't felt in a long, long time. Does that sound goofy?" She looked up to find Marce staring at her.

"Wow."

"What?"

"Just…wow. You've never sounded like that about a guy."

"How do I usually sound?"

"Oh, he's fun, he's sexy, he's great in the sack, he makes me laugh."

"He does make me laugh. The man's gorgeous and his body…I don't know what he's like in the sack but if the way he kisses is any indication, he won't disappoint. If we ever get there."

"Somehow, I don't think that's in doubt."

"And Beetlejuice will be approved next week." Celie slapped Marce's arm. "Come on, let's get going."

"Good idea." Marce made a face. "I've been getting dripped on the entire time we've been standing here."

"Dripped on?" Celie looked up at the branches overhead and felt a drop hit her forehead. Out of a cloudless sky.

*Snow melt.*

"We have to go back," she said.

\* \* \*

Sap-collecting was nothing like she'd imagined. She'd figured on hard, boring labor. She hadn't thought it would be peaceful. The woods had always been her favorite place but there was something almost hypnotic about the process of going from tree to tree, pulling off the bucket covers to find what was beneath. There was something about the grace of the maples, each tree hung with its pail, each spout quietly dripping sap. The rate of a heart beat, Jacob had said.

Celie unhooked a bucket and lifted it off, emptying it into the four-gallon container she carried. Three-quarters full. Time to take it to the cylindrical gathering tank that sat on the trailer behind the tractor. One of the first things she'd learned that day was that a full bucket was awkward to carry far. Three-quarters full, she could manage. She might have made a few more trips to the tank than Jacob and Deke and the rest of the crew, but she was doing her share.

And after three hours, she was starting to feel it. Wiry Deke had to be stronger than he looked. Jacob, not surprisingly, was like an automaton, going from tree to tank with barely a pause. And as the day wore on, they found the sap buckets steadily more full.

Celie carried her gathering bucket over to the tractor. The clear sap swirled in the container like water. Suddenly curious, she took off her glove and dipped a finger in, then raised it to her mouth. Nearly tasteless, with just a hint of sweet.

"The Indians called it sweetwater," Jacob said from behind her. "They used to boil it over a campfire for hours."

"Like you do."

"I do it a little more efficiently, I hope." He lifted her bucket and poured it into the gathering tank. "Well, this gets us to the fill line. Deke, you want to take it down to the sugarhouse and empty it?"

"Sure." Deke climbed into the driver's seat.

"Time for a break," Jacob said to Celie, nodding toward his truck. "I've got some sandwiches here if you want them."

"You're going to feed me?" she asked as Deke started up the tractor.

"Even up for breakfast."

"You trying to pay off blueberry pancakes with sandwiches?"

"They're good sandwiches," he said, opening the door for her. "Besides, if you're nice I'll turn on the heater."

She gazed at him under her lashes as she got in. "Just how nice do you want me to be?" she purred.

"We've got work to do." He closed the door firmly on her and crossed around to the driver's side. "Sandwiches or nothin'."

She gave him a resigned look. "Sandwich, please."

He was right, she discovered as she unwrapped it to take a bite. The sandwiches were pretty good. For a few moments, they munched in silence. Celie stared out at the quiet trees stretching out into the distance. "Okay, I get it," she said suddenly.

"What?"

"I get why you hate the tubing. There really is something about the old-fashioned way."

He gave her a startled look. "Why the epiphany?"

"I don't know." She waved her hand at the trees. "Something about the way it feels. I can see why you would look forward to this every year. Being out in the woods. Doing it the way it's always been done. Even Deke with the tractor. Tubing just wouldn't be the same."

"A lot of people think I'm just being sentimental."

"And you aren't?"

"Partly, I suppose. I grew up doing it this way. Something

about the rhythm of it fits me." Jacob dug out a thermos and some cups. "But converting is also a major investment."

"Which you'd recoup over time."

"We talked about this before. Out of every five years you've got to figure you'll have two great years, two that suck, and one that's average. A sugar-maker who times the switch wrong can wind up going broke. That's just being practical."

"Of course, you could switch over a piece at a time, like you were talking about with taps. Reduce the capital outlay."

He poured the coffee. "I like buckets, even if it is more work. It's work I like."

"That's being sentimental."

"So maybe I'm sentimental. The same as you with your truck and your gloves and your jacket. It's important to stick with things."

"So when you find something you like, you stick with it?" she asked. The glance they exchanged lasted longer than it should have. Suddenly it was hard to breathe, impossible to look away.

"When I find something I really like," he said, "I'm sunk."

The late-afternoon sun shone through the windows of the sugarhouse. Jacob walked over to the wall by the holding tanks and opened the valve to let in the sap. Celie listened to the gurgle as it ran through the zigzagging partitions of the upper pan of the evaporator to a depth of just inches. The fire was already laid; it took only a match to start the flames leaping through the entire firebox.

For long minutes, nothing happened. The first sign of progress was when the sap began to bubble in small patches here and there. Gradually, the bubbles spread until the whole pan was boiling. Jacob stoked the flames in the firebox. And the scent began to rise.

Celie sniffed, trying to identify it. She'd expected a smell like a pancake house but there was no heavy maple odor. Instead, it smelled light, faintly sweet, almost woody. Jacob leaned over the pan and inhaled. "That's what spring smells like," he said, grinning. "I don't care if it is February."

And Celie felt the euphoria like some sort of a contact high.

The steam began to stream upward, flowing up through the plastic-shrouded flue to the high peak of the roof to escape into the evening sky. The boiling sap darkened like caramelizing sugar as it thickened, wending its way from the upper pan to the partitioned syrup pan that sat directly over the firebox. At the end of the last partition lay the outflow spout where Jacob would eventually draw off the finished syrup.

For now, it just flowed slowly, the bubbles forming on top growing larger and larger. Jacob picked up a short butter knife and plastic dish with half a cube of butter in it.

"What are you doing?" Celie asked.

"Watch." He touched the end of the knife to the butter and dotted it among the bubbles. Instantly, they subsided. "It makes the syrup boil down faster."

"Clever."

"Oh, I'm a smart guy."

Steam swirled in the air. The door from the gift shop opened and Molly walked in, a beatific smile on her face. "Oh, I thought I smelled something."

"One batch of Vermont Fancy coming up," Jacob said.

The front door jingled and Molly looked around. "I should get back out there." She took another deep breath and turned to walk out.

Celie couldn't stop marveling at the luscious scent of the sugarhouse. She'd worked side by side with sugar-makers for years and yet there was so much she'd never understood. She'd never understood this, the magic of watching hard work translate into something as tangible as a jug of syrup. There was a closed-circle completeness to it that was like nothing else she'd ever done. Her work was important, she knew that. But work of this kind made a person feel complete, connected, whole.

She walked over to Jacob and crooked her finger to him. "Hmmm?"

He bent down toward her and she gave him a kiss on the cheek. "Thank you," she said, watching the steam billow up through the roof vent.

"For what?"

"For letting me be a part of this."

He leaned down and pressed a quick kiss on her mouth. "Thank you for wanting to."

And he walked away, leaving her dumbfounded.

She was still riding the high into the next day as she put on her APHIS hat and inspected yet another stand of maples. Somehow it all had more purpose now. And it felt more crucial than ever.

But she was tired and it was a relief to have the day over. Another day, another sugarbush, she thought as she headed toward her truck. After a while, they all blended together. She'd have had no sense of advancing at all except for the squares she marked off on the giant county map spread out over one wall of the conference room at the Institute. The reality was, she was making progress, if not a whole lot of friends.

Celie glanced ahead at the edge of the access road and blinked. The passenger door of her truck stood open and someone leaned inside.

She felt a flare of irritation as she walked up. "Want to tell me what you're doing in my property?" she asked. The person straightened and turned.

It was Paul Durkin.

He squinted at her. "You've just been poking around my property. Turnabout's fair play, right?" In his hands, he held her tree injector. He glanced down at it. "Nice piece of equipment."

It sent a chill through her. "I'm glad you think so. I'll take that back now," she added crisply.

"It's all yours," he said, handing it to her and stepping aside.

Celie leaned in the truck to put the injector back into its case, thanking her lucky stars that the bottles of Beetlejuice were safely locked up. When she turned around, Durkin was directly behind her.

"I'm glad I ran into you," she said. *Take the offensive.* "Can we go sit down somewhere? I want to bring you up to date with the results of the inspection."

He folded his arms. "We can talk here. Why? You think you found something?"

"An infested tree, unfortunately. I'll confirm with tests this afternoon. Right now we've only found one and we're just about done. We'll have to do some cutting, but not much."

"No way."

"You don't have a choice."

He gave a short, humorless laugh. "Bet me. You think I don't have a choice, you can talk to my lawyer."

"Your lawyer?"

He fished a card out of his pocket. "I phoned him last week. He's in the process of putting through an injunction that's going to block any tree-cutting until there's been a court hearing."

"It won't stand."

"Oh, I think it will."

"We've beaten them in three other states."

"Yeah, well, I bet they didn't have a state forestry expert testifying on behalf of the plaintiffs, did they?"

Dick Rumson, it had to be.

Durkin's tone was rich with enjoyment. "You try to take out any trees once I get that paperwork and I'll have your ass in court so fast it'll make your head spin. I'll take you for everything you've got."

"Is that a threat, Mr. Durkin?"

"I think you'll need to talk to my lawyer about that. Let's just call it a statement of intent. You want any further details, you can call him."

"Let's hope it doesn't come to that."

"I hope for your sake it doesn't."

She gave him a bright, hard smile. "Not me, Mr. Durkin. The government."

"Not the state government. Dick Rumson's all set to testify for me if I need."

She clamped down hard on her anger. "Those trees are going to come down by mid March, Mr. Durkin," she said coolly. "If they don't, we could have a county-wide infestation."

"Even if they do come down, you could still have one. Why don't you admit that you people don't know what you're doing? You just make assumptions and cross your fingers."

"It's working."

"That's not what I heard. I heard you got another outbreak in Minnesota last year."

"And you'll find it was because of some firewood that got transported from the infested area to another county." She turned from him to walk around to the driver's-side door.

"Or one of your beetles flew farther than you thought it could." He followed her.

"I'll mail you the paperwork. Those trees are *going* to come down."

"In your dreams."

"Do you really understand what you're taking on, here, Mr. Durkin?" she snapped, anger flaring for the first time. "I suggest you tell your lawyer to take a look at the case books and tell me if you still want to do this. I'll give you a week before things start to get ugly."

"Now who's threatening?"

"It's not a threat, Mr. Durkin, it's a promise."

Durkin took hold of the door as she opened it and got in. "Funny thing about that injector," he said conversationally. "It looks like it was used recently. I thought you told us you don't have anything approved for the maple-borer program."

"We don't." Celie reached out to close the door.

"You doing some kind of tests?" Durkin held on to it.

Celie gave a hard tug. "Focus on your trees, Mr. Durkin, leave the rest to us." She slammed the door and backed up.

And Paul Durkin stood, watching her thoughtfully.

## Chapter Eleven

"Hey, there you are."

Celie emerged from the stall in the women's room to see Marce washing her hands. "Hey."

"So do you think as much socializing goes on in the men's room as the women's room?" Marce asked as she dried her hands.

"I don't know. You tell me if you could have a serious conversation while holding on to your tallywhacker."

"Or an unserious conversation, for that matter."

"And you definitely wouldn't want to make eye contact." Celie laughed and squeezed out some soap.

"God forbid. So what's the plan for tonight?"

"Tonight?" Celie echoed.

"Valentine's Day? Ever heard of it? I was thinking we could be each other's valentine and go out for dinner and drinks in Montpelier. You know, get dressed up? Treat ourselves?"

Celie rinsed her hands. "Sorry, I've got to go to Jacob's as soon as I'm done here."

"Ooh, hot times with Sap Boy?"

"Real hot. And sweaty."

"Oh yeah?" Marce's eyes brightened.

Celie grinned. "We're running the evaporator, Marce."

"On Valentine's Day? Oh come on. If he's not going to take you out, he could at least give you the night off."

"Right now's when he needs help the most," Celie reminded her, reaching for a paper towel.

Marce snorted. "Jacob Trask never needed anyone's help in his life. Anyway, he owes you a night out with all you've been doing for him. He owes you something, anyway," she said briskly.

"And what exactly is he supposed to do with the sap in his holding tanks when he's got more coming tomorrow?"

"What am I supposed to do with the sap I'm talking to?" Marce muttered.

"I heard that." Celie turned for the door.

"If I go out and get drunk and wind up flying to Vegas for a quickie wedding, it'll be on your conscience," Marce warned her as she walked opened the door.

"I'll keep that in mind."

Wood smoke from the evaporator streamed up into the darkening sky as Celie pulled up to the Trask sugarhouse. Her lips curved in an unconscious smile as she walked in. Here, she could leave the maple borer and Dick Rumson and the outside world behind. Here, life was simple: sap and fire, wood and syrup. It was a haven.

It was Jacob.

She inhaled the sweet, woody smell and relaxed. Even though it was about twenty-five degrees outside, the inside of the room felt like the tropics, thanks to the giant furnace of the evaporator. Hastily, she unzipped her parka and stripped it off. Her experience of the day before had taught her to expect warmth. She hadn't figured on a sauna. Then again, that had been a run of a few hours; here, it had been fired up all day.

Then, through the steam, Jacob appeared and her jaw dropped.

She'd known men who worked out in gyms, sculpting their bodies obsessively. She'd bet money that Jacob Trask had never been near a weight machine, but he'd make every personal trainer at those fancy gyms weep. He wore only jeans and a sweat-damp Henley with the sleeves pushed up. And even through the thick waffled material, she was conscious only of the lines and masses of the body beneath. He'd shoved the cuffs of the shirt up to his elbows, unbuttoned the deep placket as far as it would go. For coolness, she imagined, trying to ignore the sight of the hard muscles of his chest and forearms. In the dim light and steam, his skin looked coppery.

He studied her, wiping the sweat off his forehead with the back of one wrist. "Do you have anything on under that?"

"Huh?" Celie blinked.

"Do you have anything on under your sweatshirt? You stay dressed like that you're going to die."

If she had to look at him standing there like that without touching him, she was going to die. "Can you open a window?" she asked faintly.

"Sure, but it's not going to help much with the heat."

"Boy, ain't that the truth."

Jacob watched as she reached for the bottom of her sweatshirt. Just for a moment, he let himself imagine that she was truly undressing for him. And what would a woman like Celie wear against her skin? Black lace? Silk?

When he saw, he smiled at himself. He should have expected the obvious: A flowered thermal undershirt, practical yet disarmingly sexy, and snug enough to show every curve. As to what she wore below that, well, it was a mystery.

For now.

"So how'd the day go?" She walked over to stare into the evaporator pan at the boil.

And Jacob watched her. "Busy. How about yours?"

"Long." She yawned.

"No reason you have to stick around, then." Except that boiling sap on his own suddenly seemed like the makings of a long, dull night after the sight of her pretty little shirt with its tiny little ribbon flower gleaming at the neckline, just below the hollow of her throat.

"I want to be here. So what did you do today?"

"Made syrup, mostly. The sap flow's slowed way down. We might get a few hundred gallons tomorrow, plus the couple thousand gallons we've got to get through tonight."

"Tonight?" she repeated.

"Welcome to sugar-making. When it rains, it pours. So to speak." He gave a brief smile. "I should finish up by two or three. Don't worry, you don't have to stay for all of it."

"I want to. It's part of the bargain."

"You already look tired," he objected.

"I'll drink coffee."

"All right." He tried to ignore the quick flick of pleasure he felt at the prospect of her company.

He walked to the far end of the evaporator and opened the doors of the firebox with a metal hook. Immediately behind him, the door in the wall opened out to the area where they'd stacked the firewood a couple of weeks before. The fire subdued any cold air that blew in.

And with Celie there, it had gotten hotter than ever.

Bubbles began to appear by the outflow spout. "Want me to take care of it?" Celie asked, lifting up the butter dish.

"I'll do it," Jacob said. He was the first to admit, he was finicky about running the boils. Then again, so was every sugarmaker he knew. Making syrup was an art, learned over the course of years. It wasn't something you could teach overnight.

Besides, he could think of far better things to do overnight with Celie.

She was disappointed, though, he saw. "I want to help."

"You will." He picked up chunks of wood two at a time and stuffed them into the firebox, then closed the doors. "Tell you what. There's a bag of sandwiches in the café refrigerator. If you can bring them in here along with some water, you'll definitely be helping."

"More sandwiches?"

"This time of year, I live on them."

"Oh boy." She disappeared out to the café, though, and reappeared, bag in hand. "I brought some napkins," she said, handing him a bottle of water. "So let's see what we've got here." She dug through the bag and unwrapped one of the turkey sandwiches he'd slapped together that morning. "Who's your caterer, Dagwood Bumstead?"

"It's not a beauty contest. I was in a hurry." Jacob knocked down the bubbles and crossed to the table where she'd laid out the sandwiches on napkins. "What do we have here, a picnic?"

"Enjoy it. It's about as domestic as I get."

"Outside of breakfast?"

"Outside of breakfast. The one meal I do well."

"I'll drink to that," he said. There was a quiet pleasure to sitting down to eat with her. It felt natural, as though they'd done it many times before.

And then she raised a finger to mop a bit of mustard off

her lip and it wasn't a quiet pleasure at all. "You're not stingy with the hot stuff, are you?"

"More is more."

"I guess," she said, licking her fingers. He lost long seconds as she sucked on the tips, flicked her tongue up to search out the rest of the mustard on her lip. Her eyes glimmered with fun. "Don't you need to check your boil?" she asked him, and he realized she'd been playing him intentionally.

"You're bad," he told her and rose to go to the evaporator. Her response was a laugh.

And the hours slipped by. Gradually, they fell into a rhythm born of complete awareness of one another. Sometimes Jacob fed the fire, sometimes Celie. Jacob would be studying the bubbles and before he could reach for the butter cup and the knife, Celie would hand it to him. He'd be thinking the pile of firewood by the back door was getting low, and he'd discover that she'd already replenished it from the surrounding piles.

And with each minute that passed, each hour, life became bounded more completely by the four walls of the sugarhouse, by the flow of the evaporator. Time was marked not by the clock but by Jacob's periodic draws of finished syrup. And the sap flowed in until their world consisted of just the two of them in steam and heat, fire and the sweet, woody smell of boiling sap.

In the hour that lies between night and morning, Jacob watched the flow of sap near its end. He glanced at Celie. "I don't know if I ever thanked you properly for what you did with my trees. The inoculations, I mean." He gave a brief smile as he walked back around the evaporator to the center of the room. "You'll have to forgive me. I was still kind of in shock at the time."

"You had reason to be," Celie said. "I know what it means when trees come down. To you, especially."

"No, you don't." He stared for a long moment at the bubbling sap then turned to her. "My father died in that ring of trees."

The words stopped her. "The part we cleared?"

"The part you saved. I've found myself out there a lot the past year. Just walking the sugarbush and thinking about him. It made it easier somehow, you know? Like they were his memorial. Cutting them down would have…" He stopped for a moment. "It would have seemed like…defiling his memory."

And she'd almost done it. "Why didn't you say something?"

"How? You couldn't leave trees that were at risk just to make me feel better. We've got to get rid of this bug and if trees have to come down to make it happen, that's what we do." He moved impatiently to the firebox. "I know my dad's not in those trees. If he's here anywhere, he's all around us. He's with my mom." He opened the firebox doors.

"What happened?"

Jacob moved his shoulders. "Heart attack. Last spring. We were gathering sap and then I turned around and he was just down." He stared into the flames. "I tried to get him to the hospital but it was too late. Massive damage. They said it would have been too late even if he'd been right outside the hospital when it happened." He poked at the embers with unnecessary force.

She ached for him. "You did your best," she said softly.

He looked around the room and shook his head. "All this… We always shared the work. It seems wrong to be running a boil without him. It seems wrong to be doing any of it. He should be here." Jacob tested the boil, then brought a bucket to the outflow tap at the outside wall of the evaporator. Syrup rushed out, thin as water at that temperature.

"Is there anybody else in the family to work on the farm, apart from your mother?"

Jacob carried the bucket over to the filter unit and lifted it as though it were a loaf of bread. She saw his arms bulge with the effort, but his voice never wavered. "Nick and Gabe can't exactly come back and work on the farm. They have other jobs, other careers. It's my job to keep it going."

"A hundred acres? That's a lot of responsibility for one person. Who stuck you in the hot seat?"

He looked as though it was a question he'd never been asked before, as though she'd questioned gravity. "I guess I did," Jacob said slowly. "I love this work. Always have."

The others moved on, she thought; he was left.

He sat down on the heavy wooden table that sat against the wall beneath the window overlooking the parking lot and she realized that even Jacob, finally, got tired. "I always figured I'd run the farm someday. But when my dad retired. I never thought we'd lose him like that. No one did." He stared at the sap, stirring only when she handed him the butter cup.

"It must be hard doing it all yourself."

His jaw tightened. "I don't mind hard work. But I guess that's not what you meant." He rose to flatten out the bubbles, but his actions were jerky, as though he were angry. "Yeah, it gets to me sometimes, feeling like I'm the one responsible for it all. Sometimes it's the loneliest feeling in the world. Is that what you wanted to hear?"

For an instant, the sarcasm vibrated in the air. "No," she replied carefully, "not really."

He was silent for a long time. "A hundred and thirty years we've been running this farm," he said slowly. "Five generations. Now Dad is gone, Gabe is gone, Nick. We all made our choices, back when we thought we had a lot of choices we could make. And now it's too late to go back. So that means it's up to me to tough it out." He rose to draw out the last of the syrup and at his nod she pulled open the doors on the firebox. "But that's Trask family drama. Forget I mentioned it."

"No. I won't." Celie straightened up and looked full into his face. "I know more about this sort of thing than you think. You're not the only one with a family legacy."

It stopped him for a moment.

"My parents run a bookstore in Montreal," she said. "It's called the Cité de L'Ile. It's been in our family since my great-grandfather's time. I grew up with that damned store, working there weekends, every day after school." Sitting behind the counter inside the yellowed windows until she felt as musty and old as the books themselves. "We lived in an apartment above it. It was too small, but it was close to the bookstore, and anyway it was all we could afford." She gave a faint smile. "Prestige doesn't necessarily translate into receipts."

"Where are they now?"

"They're still running it, still living in the little apartment. My sister helps them. Margaux loves the place. She's got her lit degrees. She writes. Books are her life. I'm sure she'll keep it going after they're gone. Me, all I ever wanted was to get out."

"Why?"

"It ran our lives. We could never leave for a vacation because someone had to run the store. We couldn't move because we needed to be right there. And we were always so broke because it never made much money, but my father would never dream of selling it. It was like we were locked into not having anything because of that damned legacy. And yes, I got out as soon as I could and never looked back."

"And you think that's how Gabe and Nick feel?"

"I don't have any idea how Gabe and Nick feel. The point is, my parents let me go off to a different career. They didn't understand it, but they let me go. All I'm trying to say is that you have to let people be who they are. You have to let them change if they need to."

Jacob leaned his hands on the table and stared at his reflection in the steam-covered glass. "I've never tried to stop them."

"It's not them I'm talking about," Celie said gently, coming up behind him to rest a hand on his back. "Maybe you need to give yourself the same freedom. Maybe you need to go forward with your life just like they have with theirs."

"That's what I'm doing," he said, trying to ignore the heat from her palm flowing through him.

"Are you? When you spend all your time pushing people away?"

Her whisper vibrated in his ears. He turned to see her staring at him, her eyes large and dark against the ruddy glow from the firebox. Bit by bit, she'd slipped inside his barriers, penetrated his isolation, filled an emptiness he hadn't known he had. And now, in this moment, they'd come too far to turn away.

*Go forward with your life.*

She stepped up against him and slipped her arms around his neck. "Take a chance, Jacob," she breathed. "You've already let me in this much."

"You didn't leave me any choice," he muttered even as he slid his hands into her hair.

"You're not the only one who knows what he wants."

"Thank God." And he bent his head to hers and dragged them both into the kiss

Her heat blazed up around him. It snatched the breath from his lungs, it left him reeling. She was luscious and lush, she was madness, magical. He wanted to touch her everywhere at once, as her taste flowed through him and the insatiable hunger stirred.

Oh, he'd done his best to push her away. He'd done everything he could to remind himself of why he should keep his distance from her, but she'd kept coming back, refusing to take no for an answer until he couldn't make himself say no anymore. And even though he knew he was a fool to let her in, even though he knew that she was going to leave, he just didn't give a damn.

Tonight, he'd let himself have. Tonight, they'd discover what they could be.

This time when he reached under her shirt to feel the soft, smooth skin beneath, she didn't flinch at the cold. This time she moaned and stretched against him and he lost track of time just running his hand over the smooth lines of her back, the soft dip of her waist where the skin stopped and her jeans began.

When she pulled her shirt over her head, he curved his hands around her sides, running them up until his thumbs slid up over the soft rises of her breasts, covered in some silky, skin-colored fabric and he swore he could feel his heart hammering against his ribs. Finally, finally, finally the coats and gloves were all gone, finally it was just them, just his hands on her bare skin.

It was more than he'd dreamed of. It was achingly far from enough. He traced his fingers along her sides, around the front of her flat belly, feeling her tremble.

Then he traced them higher, and heard her helpless gasp.

Big warm hands, sliding over her. The sensation had her twisting against him, nearly delirious with pleasure. Even through the silken fabric she could feel the heat of his hands, feel the sizzle of his touch against her nipples, so intense that she didn't know if she could endure it. So tantalizing she was going to scream if she didn't have more. She wanted him naked, wanted them both naked, together, touching, taking, tasting, driving each other to the edge.

Impatient, she yanked his shirt out of his jeans and ran hands shaking with desire over the hard ridges of his torso, almost giddy at the feel. When she rubbed her fingers over the pebbled dots of his nipples, he caught his breath. "Mmmm, that does something for you," she whispered.

"You do something for me," he growled and dragged her against him before pulling his shirt off over his head. His skin was smooth and beautiful in the firelight, his arms cabled, shoulders nearly round with muscle. He was muscle and sinew, tendon and bone like some anatomy drawing. Anatomy of life, here in her hands. With his jaw dark and his hair tousled, he looked like some primitive god.

And she wanted more.

Celie reached for his belt, fumbled for his zipper. Before he knew what she was about, she'd dropped to her knees before him and slid him into her mouth. Jacob groaned at the rush of wet warmth and reached out blindly for the table. The slick touch of lip and tongue had him almost mindless, sliding along the length of him again and again until he swore he'd turned into a solid mass of nerve endings, until every stroke had him straining for control. And then he caught at her shoulders, desperate to stop her because he was coming too close and he had to be inside her or he was going to lose his mind.

And the last vestiges of civilization slipped away.

He dragged her to her feet and pressed her back against the table, stripping off her bra, pulling down her jeans as she lifted her hips to help him. He stroked his hands down over her quivering belly, along the sweet curves of her hips and the long stretch of her thighs, back up the tender inner flesh until he heard her gasp, felt her arch as he touched her where she was already hot and wet and ready.

Then he gave in and bent over her to press his mouth to her breast, drawing the tender flesh inside to torment himself and her with tongue and light scrapes of his teeth. She twisted against him. "Now," she gasped, clutching at his shoulders, his hair, wrapping her legs around his waist.

And he shifted and drove himself into her in a slick rush that threatened to blow the top of his head off.

Nothing had ever felt this intense, nothing ever could. For a moment he just froze, embedded in her, awash in aftershock of more sensation than he'd ever known. Then he began to move and they were both gasping, rocking, letting the good friction take them up and up, and she was so tight and so wet and so incredibly hot wrapped around him that it made his head spin.

There would be time later for finesse, Jacob thought hazily. There would be time, but now, with her hands urging him on, her legs tightened around him, the moment and the madness spun out and took over. He could only surge against her over and over, listening to her cry out as she made the climb and tumbled over, shaking and clenching around him and thrusting him into the gather and the rise of his own climax. And when he spilled himself, it felt as if it came from the very center of him.

And it was as though some part of his soul went with it.

## Chapter Twelve

Sleep, Celie decided, was overrated. So what if the best she'd been able to manage was a light doze in Jacob's arms once they'd made their way back to his house?

And his bed.

Of course, they hadn't gotten there right away. Delays, she recalled with a smile she couldn't suppress. There had been the delay in the entryway and the one in the living room. She had some good memories of the carpet.

She didn't need sleep to feel whole, though, not right now. She was half drunk on the energy of lovemaking. All she could think was that in a few hours, work would be over and she could go to him again. She thought of the way he'd rested his hands on her hips as he'd kissed her goodbye beside her truck and her stomach gave a lazy flip-flop.

"Hey." Marce bounced into her cubicle. "How was your Valentine's Day?"

"Mine was great, how about yours?"

"Fun, actually. I wound up going out for drinks with Phil and Gary. We walked through the door and I thought I was going to die laugh—" Marce stopped, looking closely at Celie for the first time. "Or maybe you're the one who should be telling me about your night."

"My night? What do you mean?" Celie asked innocently, but the thousand-watt grin that spread across her face gave her away.

"Don't give me that. How was it?" Marce hissed in a low voice, pulling a chair up close.

"Died and gone to heaven."

"That good?"

"Better." Celie let a beat pass. "Every time."

"Gawd. Does he have any brothers?"

"Taken, sorry."

Marce made an annoyed noise. "I always miss out."

"I can ask about cousins."

"Never mind. The good ones are taken. So how was it after? Weird?"

Celie moved her shoulders. "There wasn't really time for it to get weird. We fell asleep and when I woke up I was already late so I just blasted out of there. We didn't really talk."

"At all? That would definitely be weird." Marce leaned her elbows on her knees. "So you don't even know what he's thinking. I mean whether he's cool or freaked out, whether it's a one-time thing or if he's going to turn into Damien or whatever."

Celie frowned. "It's Jacob."

"Right. He's already Damien. So you're really not weirded out?"

"I wasn't until you showed up," Celie said with an edge.

Marce gave a guilty grin. "Sorry. That's just me. I obsess

from the minute the orgasms are over. Gives me something to do until the next one. So has he called?"

"No, but he never does. I doubt he even knows the number. Anyway, I'm usually out in the sugarbush, not here," she reminded herself as much as Marce.

"I'm just asking. So are you going to call him?"

"No way. That *would* get weird." Celie gave an impatient sniff. "Jeez, now you've got me doing it. Look, it's simple. I'll just show up."

Marce looked at her from under her brows. "You had sex for the first time and you didn't talk about it? Trust me, that's never simple. You can't just show up."

"I show up every day. Why should today be different?"

"I suppose you have a point."

"Thank you. Now that you've gotten me completely paranoid, can you give me some peace?"

Marce grinned. "What are girlfriends for?"

The phone rang as Marce walked out of the cubicle. Jacob, Celie thought in relief and lifted the receiver, grinning. "Celie Favreau."

"What are you up to?" a voice demanded.

Definitely not Jacob. "Who is this?" She knew it was Rumson, she recognized his voice, but she was damned if she was going to give him the satisfaction.

"Dick Rumson," he snapped. "Just what do you think you're doing?"

She took his question literally to buy time. "Well, Dick, I'm flattered that you're so concerned. Right now I'm completing some paperwork and in a few minutes I'm going to drive to Charlie Willoughby's sugarbush and inspect his trees."

"Don't play cute with me. You're up to something. What are you doing with an injector in your truck?"

Her fingers tightened on the phone. "I'm a plant health specialist," Celie said calmly. "I always travel with an injector."

"You've got something new and you're using it, and I don't think you're doing volunteer work in the neighborhood."

"I see you've been talking with Paul Durkin again."

"I talk to lots of people."

"Don't I know it."

"What's that supposed to mean?" he snapped.

She put down her pen. "Stop getting distracted by what doesn't matter. The maple borer is the enemy, not me."

"The guys whose trees you're cutting down might not agree."

"They will if it wipes out their sugarbushes."

"It doesn't have to. You're doing a damn fine job of that yourself."

She struggled to keep her slippery grasp on her temper. "Dick, I don't give a damn about taking over your territory or your position or your job. Once this is over, you can go back to playing king of the forest, so you can stop putting so much energy into getting people stirred up. Just let me take care of the infestation and I'll be gone."

"Oh, you'll be gone all right," he said ominously. "You can be sure of that."

She felt cold. "What is that supposed to mean?"

"I think you know. Have a real good day."

And he disconnected with a click.

Jacob lifted the bucket off the tree and emptied it into the gathering container. Sap splashed onto his fingers. He raised his hand and licked it off, tasting the light underlying sweetness. Like Celie. The thought popped into his head unbidden, and with an irritated noise he hung the bucket back on the tree.

He could be ticked at himself but it wouldn't do any good. He'd made the decision the night before to throw caution to the winds. Except he was full of it, he thought impatiently. He'd been working his way edgewise to that particular decision for weeks. Now, he had to live with it. Complications? Life had gotten so far beyond complicated it didn't even bear discussing.

Like he didn't have enough to worry about trying to get through his first sugar-making season on his own while a plague on six legs might be working its way through the trees he had left. Now, when he could least afford the distraction, he'd stumbled deep into the middle of something. Because there was no kidding himself that this was some one-time fling he could shrug off. She'd gotten into his blood and he was well and truly hooked. He couldn't stop missing her. He couldn't stop wondering about her.

And he couldn't stop needing her, not then, not with the memory of her flavor still saturating him.

Sunlight streamed through the maples, but all he could think about was the dimness and firelight of the sugarhouse. All he could think about was the feel of Celie's skin, the warm promise in her eyes.

He didn't need any more complications, but he didn't think he had a choice anymore. The time for backing away had been weeks ago, when he'd first laid eyes on her. It had been too late by the time they'd kissed, and it had definitely been too late by the time he'd turned to see her in the light of the firebox the night before.

And everything he'd tried to tell himself about distance and solitude and safety was a lie, because he'd known in the early-morning hours when he lay holding her, feeling her breathe as she slept, that he was in as deep as a man could get. And if he could snap his fingers that instant and make life go back to normal he wouldn't, because it was that singular, that astonishing. That extraordinary.

Even though he could already see the end.

\* \* \*

The close of the day came as a relief. The upside of dealing with Rumson was that he'd taken her mind off Jacob. Now, seeing the sugarhouse dark as she drove up, she frowned. Granted, it was nearly six and past closing, but Jacob should have been at work running a boil. Instead, for the first time in days, there was no steam rising from the peak.

And she wasn't sure what to think.

Well, if he wasn't at the sugarhouse, she had a pretty good idea where to find him, she thought, and swung the wheel.

There were lights behind the windows of his house as she drove down through the lane of oaks. He was in there, making dinner, perhaps, or reading a book. Or sleeping. She'd show up and they could talk. So he'd shut down the sugarhouse without warning her. It wasn't a big deal. It didn't mean anything.

She didn't think.

Her boots thumped on the porch boards as she came to a stop at the front door. Before she could knock, frenzied barking broke out. Murphy, of course, she thought with a grin. Dark shapes moved behind the etched glass and the door opened to reveal Jacob, with Murphy lunging to get past his legs.

Celie smiled widely and reached out for the dog. "Hi gorgeous. Hey Murph, how you doing? How's this doggie doing?"

Murphy wriggled deliriously as she dove her hands into his black fur and began scratching where she knew he liked it best.

Jacob wore a denim shirt loose over jeans. His hair was slicked back from a shower. His eyes were very blue. Celie looked up at him, feeling suddenly awkward. "Well, it looks like your dog's happy to see me, anyway."

A slow smile spread across his face. "He's not the only one. Come in."

Celie stamped the snow off her boots and stepped inside. She wanted to touch him.

She resisted the urge.

"I stopped at the sugarhouse but all the lights were out. I'd never seen it that way before. I mean, you're always working. So I wasn't sure if something had happened or something." She was babbling, she knew she was babbling, but she was powerless to stop. "I figured I'd come back and check on you."

"Smart thinking. You found me."

Looking good enough to eat, but he still hadn't kissed her or even so much as brushed her hand. "Why aren't you boiling? Too beat?"

"The run petered out today. I finished up around five."

"I noticed things were freezing back up."

"It usually happens like this when we get an early run," Jacob said, rubbing Murphy's ears. "Thaws don't last too long."

Which kind of thaws, the winter kind or the personal kind? "So is that it or do you expect more?"

"Oh, we'll definitely get a run in March that'll last longer. With luck." There was a sudden flash of mischief in his eyes. "Why, did you like it?"

She caught her lip in her teeth. "The tapping was fun but I liked boiling the best."

"That was my favorite part, too."

"It was pretty hot in that sugarhouse." Oddly breathless, she stepped toward him.

"It's never gotten that hot in there before." His hands settled on her hips.

"There's a first time for everything."

"I hope it's not the last."

And the next thing she knew his mouth was on hers, her hands were in his hair and everything was right again.

\* \* \*

"It must be something about this carpet," Celie said after, as they lay on the living-room rug looking up at the ceiling. "We got stalled out here last night, too."

"Maybe Isaac had a spell cast on it," Jacob said lazily, stroking his fingers over her ribs.

"That must be it. Good thing he designed a nice ceiling."

"True. I'm getting pretty fond of this ceiling."

"That makes two of us."

"So how about food?"

"I'm in favor of it."

He chuckled. "Any ideas?"

"I dunno. Whatcha got?"

"Oh, eggs, frozen pizza, bread…"

"…sandwich meat," she finished for him.

"Hey, if I'd known you were coming I'd have gotten premium cold cuts." He rose, sliding on his jeans. Celie rolled to her feet and pulled on his shirt. He looked her up and down. "That looks better on you than it does on me."

"Oh, goody. Can I have it?" Her throat gleamed, white and strong against the denim. Her lips looked soft and bruised from his. But there was something more, a kind of strain bracketing her mouth. He'd seen it when she'd walked in but he'd chalked it up to the same awkwardness he'd been feeling himself. Given that it was still there, he figured it was safe to assume it had nothing to do with the two of them.

So what was it about?

"How'd your day go?" he asked.

Her gaze skated off to one side. "As well as could be expected. We finished the inspection at Charlie Willoughby's and didn't find anything."

"That's good news."

"It is."

But not good enough. "So, let's see…. Inspections, lab tests, paperwork, reports… Did I miss anything?"

"No."

"So what's bugging you?"

"What's bugging…" She met his gaze then. "Nothing's bugging me. I'm just tired. It was a long day on no sleep."

"Tell me about it."

"Nothing to tell. I wrote a status report for my boss. Did some lab testing, confirmed the infestation of Durkin's trees."

"Paul Durkin?"

"Yeah, why?"

He shook his head. "Nothing." And that was where the strain came in, he guessed. "I assume he's not taking it well."

"Well, if Rumson would—" She broke off.

"If Rumson would what?" Jacob watched her shrug, saw the shadows deepen in her eyes and waited for an answer.

"He's just being a pest," she said instead.

"In the usual way or something new?"

"A variation on a theme. He's got Durkin all stirred up to where he's getting a lawyer to block the tree-felling on his property."

"Idiot." Jacob drew her down to sit on the couch. "Can you beat it?"

"I'm confident we can, but it'll take time we don't have. If he ties this thing up in court for three or four months, we're in trouble. We could get a couple dozen adult borers out of each infested tree, and once they get loose, well…" She turned her hands up, helpless.

Catastrophe.

The tension was back in her shoulders, worse than ever. He wanted it gone. Rumson, he had no control over. Durkin, he couldn't fix. There was something he could do, though.

Jacob reached out to wrap his fingers around the neck of his guitar. "So did you still want that command performance?"

Her eyes lit and he knew he'd figured it right. "Of course." She rose to open the French doors to let Murphy in from the hallway. When she sank back down on the couch, the dog settled his head in her lap with an expression of bliss.

"What do you want to hear?"

"What do you want to play?"

He gave a quick smile and broke into a handful of chords and Celie raised an eyebrow at him. "'Don't Worry, Be Happy'?" she asked dryly.

"Seems appropriate," he said. "Okay, you don't like that, how about this?" This time, it took only two chords before she laughed out loud.

"'We Shall Overcome'? What are you, the aural version of Successories?"

"Everybody's a critic," he complained and segued into a song she didn't recognize. The notes were fluid but it was his hands she couldn't get enough of. She'd seen them at work, she'd felt them on her skin, but the quick, sure grace of his fingers on the strings was a revelation. He coaxed a pure, sweet tone from the guitar that looked effortless, the same way he'd coaxed pure, sweet pleasure from her.

And then he began to sing, a slow folk ballad. His voice was true, a little rough, a little smoky. His blue gaze snared hers as he sang of joy and pain, of lovers meeting, lovers parting. It was beautiful enough to make her ache. And she understood, finally, how much more he was than she'd ever guessed, this guarded man, this solitary man, at once steadfast, loyal, unexpectedly generous, deeply kind.

His hair fell down over his forehead and she reached out to push it back. When he flashed her a quick, crooked grin before starting the chorus, it made her heart squeeze painfully in her chest.

And when she thought of leaving, it made her want to weep.

## Chapter Thirteen

Celie stood on the edge of the road that ran along Paul Durkin's sugarbush, listening to the rumble of diesel engines. She felt the familiar depression at the prospect of taking down acres of trees. Even if Durkin hadn't been difficult, it would have been unpleasant. His combativeness made it more distasteful than usual.

Joe Doluca, the head arborist, walked up to her, consulting his clipboard. "Looks like everything's in order. All the trees look marked. I just need your signature and we can get started."

Feeling vaguely sick, Celie signed the sheet.

Then Joe waved his hand and the driver of the Caterpillar with the grappler claw revved his engine and prepared to drive forward.

"You'd better stop that right now," said a voice behind them.

Celie and Joe turned to see a Washington County sheriff's deputy standing behind them, an envelope in his hand.

"Hi Roy," the arborist said to him.

"Hey Joe. How's Emily?"

"She's good. What have you got there?"

"Depends." He turned to Celie. "Are you Cecilia Favreau?"

"Yes."

Lines networked his face. He looked like he'd seen enough that nothing would ever surprise him. "I have here a court order to stop all cutting on Paul Durkin's property." He handed it to her even as Joe Doluca's arm shot up to signal the Caterpillar driver to halt.

Celie tore into the envelope, fighting down fury. Durkin had been as good as his word. He and his Montpelier lawyer had managed to get to a judge and put through an injunction. The whole time-wasting case was in court and until they beat it, no clearing could go forward. Of course, the scarlet-horned maple borer didn't know from court documents. When it hatched, it would merrily chomp its way through the host tree and emerge to infest others.

While the lawyers were busy with dueling motions.

Celie stifled the urge to curse. She knew who was behind it. She knew it wouldn't stand.

And she knew the last afternoon of her week wouldn't be spent doing anything productive; instead, she'd be on the phone with legal trying to find a way to shut down the lawsuit before it ever really got started.

There had to be something better to do on a Saturday afternoon, Jacob thought, than standing around a fancy hotel feeding people maple sugar. Still, he'd made a promise, and in his book that was as good as done.

He walked into the gift shop to see Kelly at the register. Shiny, blond Kelly, the spookily precocious teen. "Hey, Kelly, you seen my mother?"

"Hey, Jacob," she purred. "What are you all dressed up for?"

He'd put on one of the outfits he'd been given during the makeover. Soft wool slacks, some kind of thin black sweater and a sport jacket over the top. At the time, he'd brought the clothes home and tossed them in the back of the closet, figuring they'd never see the light of day. He still wasn't sure what had possessed him to dig them out instead of his usual pressed khakis and twill shirt. He definitely hadn't bargained for running into Kelly, who spent way too much time staring at him these days for his comfort. "Oh, gotta go over to the Hotel Mount Jefferson," he muttered.

"Your collar's all messed up." She stepped out from behind the counter. "Here, let me fix it for you."

"I've got it," he said hastily, checking it himself and wishing desperately for his beard. When he'd had it, his life hadn't been in chaos. Life maybe hadn't been as interesting, he thought, his mind turning to Celie, but at just that moment, interesting was overrated. "Look, what I really need is to find my mother. We've got to get rolling."

"I think she went into the sugarhouse," Kelly said, patting his shoulders proprietarily before walking back to the cash register.

"Thanks." He hurried down the passageway to the sugarhouse door, hoping it didn't look like flight. "Hey Ma, we gotta go," he called as he opened the door. "I told Gabe—" He stopped. "Ma?"

She stood at the evaporator, staring into the partitions. When she turned, he saw the marks of tears on her cheeks.

Oh no, he thought, stomach sinking. "You okay?"

She wiped her cheeks. "I'm fine. It just hits me out of the blue sometimes."

Jacob didn't need to ask what "it" was. Instead he crossed to her and pulled her to him.

"A couple of newlyweds came in on their way up to Montreal," she said, her voice muffled. "You know we'd have celebrated our fortieth anniversary next year?"

"I know," Jacob said helplessly. "I'd give anything if I could bring him back."

She pressed her cheek to his chest for a moment and then he felt her shoulders rise as she took a breath. "I do, too. You can't go backward, though. But I miss him every single minute of every day. Lately I feel like we got cheated of time."

"I wish I could make it stop hurting you so much." He wished he could believe that that hurt would ever go away.

"Those were wonderful years there. If he'd been a sonofagun, I might be happy he was gone, but I'd have nothing good to look back at. I guess I should call it a good tradeoff."

He drew her to a bench along the wall. And when they were seated, he put his arm around her, not knowing what else to do. He could fix his mother's leaky faucets and work every day to earn a living for them both from the sugarbush. He could climb up to take down hornets' nests from the eaves, risking stings to save her pain. There wasn't a damned thing he could do to help her with this pain, though, except sit beside her and feel useless.

"I don't know what's wrong with me today," she said with an apologetic laugh. "I can't stop the waterworks." She exhaled and looked up at him with a forced smile. "So, where's your helper?"

"Celie?"

"Of course, Celie. Who else?"

"She had to catch up on some work this morning. She was going to try to stop by and say hi before we left." Celie would know what to do, he thought in a rush of relief. She'd know how to make things better. She understood people that way.

"You know, she really is one of the good ones. It's important to me to see you with someone like her."

"I don't know that we're *with* each other," he hedged.

"Well I don't know what you'd call it, but if you let her slip away you're a fool." Her voice was sharp. "You need her, Jacob. You need the extra pair of hands, and not just in the sugar-making. Don't think I haven't noticed the change in you."

He looked away and sighed. "Well don't get your heart set on it. It's strictly short-term."

"Oh, don't say that."

"But it is. With her job, her life, this is just a temporary stop. She'll be leaving in a month or two, chasing that bug, and that'll be the end of it." If he were smart, he'd pull away now, get a head start on the grief instead of getting himself in deeper by the day. Get used to an empty house at night again, instead of one ringing with her laughter. "It was never something that was meant to last."

"You know, lasting and not lasting is a funny thing," Molly said gently. "I have a friend who lost her husband a month after they'd married. I have another who got divorced after eighteen years. And then there are your grandparents, who celebrated their golden anniversary and then some before they were through. If you're looking for guarantees in life, you'll be disappointed." She brushed a bit of lint from his knee. "You just have to live it and take your chances. If you care about this woman, then make it happen."

Sure, all he had to do was dig out his magic wand. "I can't follow her around the country, and she can't stay here."

"If you want to badly enough, you'll figure something out," Molly retorted. "I never meant to raise a hermit."

His chin came up at that. "I'm not a hermit."

"My mistake. I thought if you hide out all the time and refuse to let anyone into your life, then you're a hermit."

"There are people in my life."

"Name six."

"You, Gabe, Nick. Lainie." He thought. "Hadley and Sloane."

"Your brothers' girlfriends and fiancées don't count yet. You've only met them twice."

"Deke."

She snorted. "Will you listen to yourself?"

"Muriel."

"Why not mention the postman?" Molly sighed and put a hand to her son's cheek. "Oh, Jacob. Somewhere along the line you started closing all the doors, and I don't know how that happened. At first I thought it was that Marjorie Butler going off the way she did after she left for college. You started growing your beard out, hiding in the sugarbush—"

Jacob stared. "Jesus, Ma, that was sixteen, seventeen years ago. I'm not hung up on a girl I dated before I could even drink."

"I'm sorry."

"You should be." He folded his arms grumpily. "That's insulting. I mean, what about René and Ellen and Brenda and…" Christ, what was her name? Blond, pretty, allergic to dogs… "I get involved with women," he said.

At least until they started pushing for more than he wanted to give.

"I'd hardly call it involved if you can't even remember their names." Her voice was tart.

"Lorraine," he said triumphantly.

"Well, I don't know, what am I supposed to think? None of them have even stuck around much longer than a season."

"I'm a maple-sugar farmer, Ma. Most women want something more than hauling buckets and sweating over an evaporator." An image of Celie in the glow of the fire came unbidden. He pushed it away and forced a smile, squeezing his mother closer. "Besides, I've got you to take care of and the farm. Losing those trees isn't going to be easy to get around these next couple of years, but we'll make it. I'm not going to let you down."

Molly smiled. "I know you won't," she said with a smile that slowly faded. "I don't know, maybe it's seeing Nick and Gabe so happy. Maybe it's thinking about your father…." She took a shaky breath. "Maybe you look at me and think that you never want to go through what I'm going through right now. Don't think that. Don't think you're better off alone. Because, even now, I wouldn't trade a moment I had with your father for anything in the world." A tear escaped and slid down her cheek.

Jacob felt his throat tighten.

"It's no good to be alone, Jacob. Trust me, I know."

He didn't answer. He didn't know what to say.

She wiped her eyes. "Well, look at me, a fine ambassador for maple sugar on snow. I need some fresh air. Do me a favor. I set out some maple goodies in the basement to take with us. Go on down and get them, please. I'll meet you outside." And she walked out the door, leaving him with his thoughts.

It had taken way too much of the morning to catch up on her lab work after her time-wasting Friday but at least Celie *was* caught up. And if she were lucky, maybe she'd get a few minutes to spend with Jacob. She reached the steps of the gift shop just as Molly came out.

"Oh. Celie," she said blankly. "Jacob's down in the basement getting some boxes."

"Well aren't you all dressed up. You look really…" Celie took a closer look at Molly's face, saw the swollen eyes, the pink nose. "Are you okay? Dumb question. Of course you're not okay." Celie reached out to catch her hands.

Molly's smile wobbled only a little. "Having one of those days, I'm afraid. And Jacob and I are supposed to go over to Gabriel's hotel to do maple sugar on snow."

Not that she seemed in any shape to go. "Stay home," Celie said positively. "Close down the gift shop. Put on your fuzzy slippers and have a good cry."

"Don't tempt me."

"It's what you should do."

Molly's blue-gray gaze was direct as she thought it over. "Only if you can do me a favor," she said at last.

"Sure, what?"

"Go to the hotel with Jacob and take my place."

"But I don't know the first thing about maple sugar on snow," Celie protested. "I'd just be a lump."

"Don't be silly. Jacob and Gabriel can teach you everything you need to know when you get there. Otherwise, I'll just go."

"Don't even think about it," Celie ordered. "Of course I'll fill in. I'm happy to do it." Especially if it was with Jacob. "It'll be a nice break. Besides, I'll get to see what all the fuss is about with Gabe's hotel."

"Oh, it's gorgeous. You'll love it." Molly rummaged in her pocket to pull out a recipe card. "Now give this to Gabriel when you get there. It's directions on how to prepare the syrup. He already knows about the donuts and the dill pickles."

Now that stopped her. "Dill pickles?"

"Of course. You have to have dill pickles for maple sugar on snow."

Celie had been envisioning some kind of maple-flavored snow cone. Clearly she had a learning curve ahead of her.

"Don't look so worried," Molly said. "It's easy enough and Jacob can guide you through it."

"So what am I supposed to do?"

"Oh, answer questions about sugaring and the farm. Make nice with the guests. Mind Jacob."

"That I can do," Celie assured her.

"Really?" Molly seemed to really focus on her for the first time.

And Celie could feel her face heat. It was one thing to sleep with a man, it was another to pass the news on to the mother of the man in question. "You know. I mean, I'll make sure he stays out of trouble."

"I'm sure you will," Molly said but the glance she gave Celie was far too speculative.

"Yes, well." Celie looked down at her jeans and parka and then at Molly's nice slacks. "I guess I should probably change into something nicer."

"If it's not too much trouble?" Molly asked apologetically. "It's kind of a fancy place."

"Not at all. I'm representing the farm. Let Jacob know I'll be back in about twenty minutes will you?"

"My pleasure."

Jacob paced in the parking lot. Granted, he never looked forward to the annual sugar-on-snow trip, but he was always paradoxically anxious to get there, perhaps relying on the theory that the sooner he started, the sooner he'd be done. That worked with most things he did, though regrettably not this particular venture. Still, he had a schedule to meet, which always left him itching to leave.

When he saw Celie's car drive up, it was with a wash of relief. Then she opened the door and got out.

She looked as if she were draped in a column of fog. It was a long, narrow knit skirt and a drapey-necked sweater combo that looked soft as a kitten and blue as smoke. She'd cinched it around her waist with some kind of soft leather belt that matched her high-heeled boots. Silvery ear bobs flashed at her lobes; her lips looked red as sin.

And he was struck dumb.

"Are you ready to go?"

Soon, he told himself. His brain would unfreeze soon. He'd be able to form words and maybe even move. In the meantime, he could only stare.

Celie rolled her eyes. "Oh come on, don't look so paralyzed. It won't be that bad. I'll do the bonding."

"You look amazing," he said slowly.

And now it was her turn to stare. "What?"

"You look amazing."

"I heard what you said. It's just that…" She shook her head. "You've never said anything like that to me before."

"Oh, come on. I've given you compliments." Hadn't he?

She laughed, her face alive with pleasure. "Trust me, I'd have remembered."

"Then I'm an idiot," he said.

"I'll let you off the hook if you say it again." She pirouetted in front of him.

He looked at her from under his eyebrows. "You're amazing."

"I believe it was 'you *look* amazing,'" she corrected. "Although I'll take the variation, too."

"Can we go now?" he muttered.

Celie stepped up and wound her arms around his neck. "You're cute when you get embarrassed," she whispered.

His arms slid around her, he couldn't help it, feeling her body under the impossibly soft sweater and for just a moment, the hell with being in public, he let himself taste her because if he didn't he was going to lose it right there.

"Mmmm. We should probably go," she murmured against his mouth.

He had no desire to go. He had no desire to do anything but get her back to his house and talk her right out of that fuzzy, smoky outfit. But they had places to be and it was about thirty degrees out, so he made himself release her. They got in the truck and he turned the key. "You ready?" he asked hoarsely.

Her eyes flashed with mischief. "I'm ready for anything."

She'd always preferred the wilderness over buildings. Give her a tent on a tree-covered mountainside and she'd be happy. All the same, when she caught sight of the Hotel Mount Jefferson gleaming in the afternoon sun, all she could do was stare. After all the talk, she'd imagined a nice resort but something more modest.

She hadn't imagined a fantasy palace.

At close quarters, it wasn't any less magical. When the doorman in the red greatcoat tipped his hat at them and pushed open the door with its etched-glass panes, she sighed in wonder. When they walked into the frankly opulent lobby, she didn't have any breath left to sigh—she'd lost it all.

"My God, it's beautiful." She turned in a slow circle, staring.

"Jacob!" someone cried.

Celie turned to see a slender, fragile-looking woman with white-blond hair hurrying toward them.

Toward Jacob.

"It's so good to see you." The woman reached out both hands to catch his.

Celie was startled to see a genuine smile on Jacob's face; even more startled when he leaned down and kissed the woman on the cheek. He turned to her. "Celie, I'd like you to meet Hadley Stone. Hadley, this is Celie Favreau, who's out working with the maples. Hadley owns the hotel. She's my brother's boss—in more ways than one."

Hadley grinned and held out her hand. "It's a pleasure to meet you, Celie. Welcome to the Hotel Mount Jefferson."

"It's so gorgeous here. It must be hard to believe it's real."

"Every morning when I wake up I have to pinch myself."

"I thought that was my job," complained a voice behind them. Celie glanced over to see Gabe.

"Hush, you," Hadley said.

He was scrupulously careful not to touch her, Celie noticed, but an almost palpable connection hummed between them. Hadley wore a winter-white jacket over a swirling skirt in tones of blue and green. Something in the way Gabe looked at her made Celie almost certain he was plotting ways to get it off at the first possible moment.

Molly Trask and her husband shared some first-class genes, Celie thought, watching Gabe and Jacob shake hands. Very different and equally gorgeous. Or almost equally gorgeous. Without being the least bit biased, she'd take Jacob in a heartbeat.

Gabe nodded at the box on the ground by Jacob's feet. "So, did you bring the syrup?"

"One thirty-gallon barrel of Vermont Fancy, coming up."

"Is that like extra-fancy ketchup?" Hadley asked.

He smiled. "In this case, it actually means something. It's a really light syrup that comes from the first sap of the year. I'll bring you some Grade A Amber, too, when it comes off in a couple of weeks."

"I'd like that." Hadley glanced at Gabe. "In fact, I think eight hundred gallons would just about take care of it. Right, Mr. Food and Beverage?"

Gabe gave her a surprised glance and one of those high-wattage smiles that would have vaporized a lesser woman's blood. "We'll need at least that much for the year. I could authorize that buy," he studied Jacob impudently, "provided I knew the syrup came from a high-quality operation."

"You'd better start talking nicer if you think you're going to get five percent of my output," Jacob growled.

Gabe grinned. "Where's the barrel?"

"Already on your loading dock, where do you think?"

"I'll get things rolling in the kitchen, then," he said, already pulling out a walkie talkie phone and punching buttons. "Hadley, can you get them settled?"

"Sure." She watched him for a fraction of a second longer than necessary as he strode off, Celie noticed, then turned to Celie and Jacob. "We're set up over in the conservatory," she said briskly, and led them across the lobby.

Colonel Mustard in the conservatory with the rope, Celie thought with amusement. It was quickly supplanted by pleasure the moment she stepped into the airy, glassed-in room. Enormous windows looked out on the vast sweep of the mountains beyond, making her feel as though she could breathe more deeply, as though she was lighter somehow. Guests sat here and there reading newspapers or savoring the view. She wished she could join them.

A long table covered in pale-green linen held ice buckets and a gleaming silver coffee urn. Hadley led them to a white-covered table a bit further along. "This all right?" she asked.

"Perfect." Celie looked around her as Jacob put down the box, admiring the garland-draped pillars and the parabolic cutout in the ceiling. "I think if I worked here this would be my favorite room."

"Oh, it is," Hadley agreed. "At least until I walk into the next one."

"I can see how that would be."

Hadley helped Celie open up the box. "So what do you have in here?"

"Goodies from Molly."

"Oh, maple cream. My favorite," Hadley said as she pulled

it out. "And sugar and maple pepper." A private smile flickered over her face as she looked at it. "Well, let's put them all out so that people can try them."

Celie finished unpacking the box with its various grades of syrup and candies while Hadley hunted up plates and knives and napkins.

"We'll be bringing out everything for the maple sugar on snow shortly. In the meantime, is there anything else you need?"

Celie considered. "Toast fingers, if you have them, or something to put the maple cream on."

"Right. I'm sure we can come up with something. And I'll put out the maple sugar with the coffee so people can try it there." She pulled out a pen and wrote on a little card in surprisingly beautiful calligraphy.

"You're the calligrapher as well as the manager?"

Hadley smiled as she fitted the card into a little metal stand and put it by the maple sugar. "I'm the everything that needs doing. Really. It's in my job description."

"Ask her about filling helium balloons," Gabe put in, walking up with his phone in hand. He checked his watch. "Okay, everything's set back in the kitchen. We should be ready to roll in ten or fifteen minutes. Jacob, we'll want you to stand up and say a few words before we get started, kind of a welcome and maybe a Q and A." A hunted look flashed over Jacob's face and Gabe burst out laughing. "God, that was priceless. Don't worry, we've got you covered."

Jacob gave him a hard look. "You know, I almost pitched you out the window when they brought you home from the hospital. But I didn't. I was feeling generous."

"What a guy."

"I can undo that mistake at any time," Jacob said pleasantly.

Gabe winked at Celie. "Big brothers are all the same. No

sense of humor. All right, all right, I guess Hadley will M.C. and you can do the demos, Celie."

"I could if I knew what I was doing, maybe," she said.

Both Trask men turned to stare at her. "You've never done maple sugar on snow?"

"Never."

"But you grew up in maple country," Jacob said blankly.

"I had an underprivileged childhood."

"Clearly we need an intervention." Gabe put his arm around her. "If you'll just follow me—"

"I think you're needed at the front desk to sort paper clips," Jacob said, neatly turning Gabe to transfer his arm to Hadley. "Guess that means I'll just have to show her myself."

## Chapter Fourteen

The room off the hotel's kitchen had once been a private dining room, since converted to storage. Celie and Jacob sat there at a bare table, amidst the extra chairs and trays and service items. Elegant, no, but it was quiet, at least, and currently empty.

Jacob busied himself setting down plates and bowls and cutlery. Eventually the mix resolved itself as a plate with a plain cake doughnut and a dill spear, next to a bowl of ice and a small dish of maple syrup.

"Now about those pickles," Celie began.

"Critical."

"But it's maple sugar on snow, not dill pickles on snow."

"All part of the process."

"And just where is the maple sugar?"

He shot a look at her. "Okay, so you've got your boiled down syrup and your doughnut and your ice." He held them all up in turn. "The idea is that you drizzle the maple syrup over the ice to harden it."

"Where's the snow?"

"It's shaved ice. Same difference."

"But they call it maple sugar on snow. There's supposed to be snow. There's supposed to be maple sugar."

"You *adapt*."

"Okay, I'm adapting." Fighting a smile, she folded her hands in front of her like an obedient schoolgirl. "What now?"

"Then you eat it."

"That's it?"

"Yeah, that's it."

"But I thought there was some ceremony."

"Ceremony?"

"You know—" she waved her hands "—a maple sugar on snow ceremony. Some special order for doing things, the magic, the flick of the wrist. Instructions."

"Those are the instructions. It's like an ice cream cone. You eat it."

"But what's with the doughnut and all the utensils? And there's still the whole dill pickle thing out there. If you want this to catch on it's going to have to be more organized."

Jacob looked at her from under his brows. "People have been doing it this way for three hundred years. I think it's caught on."

"I still think whoever dreamed this up could have been a little more focused."

"I'll look up their ancestors and tell them," he said with exaggerated patience. "Okay, you want specifics, I'll give you specifics. You can put the maple sugar on the doughnut or you can dip the doughnut in the warm maple syrup—"

"Or you can put the maple syrup on the pickle?"

He stopped.

"Sorry, I was just getting into the spirit of it. So it's a personal freedom thing. I can dig that. What's it like?"

"Well, taste it."

She eyed it. "Demo, please."

He shot a glance up to the ceiling, then looked down and spooned up some maple syrup. "Drizzle," he said, following suit. "Lift." He teased a bit of it loose with the tine of the fork and laid it on a chunk of doughnut and held it up. "Eat." He popped it into his mouth.

"And the pickle?"

He shook his head. "I think we need to keep your mouth busy." He made up a bite of maple and doughnut and pressed the other hand to her cheek. "Open up."

Instantly, her knees went weak. And he fed it to her, his fingers brushing her lips.

Rich sweetness exploded through her mouth. The maple syrup was cool and earthy tasting, the texture soft and bendable as warm wax. But it was the touch of Jacob's fingers that she focused on, even though he'd moved his hand and his touch was only a memory. A memory and a promise.

"And now, drum roll please, the pickle." Jacob held out the dill spear to her. Gaze locked on his, Celie leaned forward and took it in her mouth, wrapping her lips around it until she saw his eyes darken. The tangy bite cut the sweetness of the maple, but it was the touch of it on her mouth that remained long after she'd swallowed.

"So." Jacob cleared his throat. "What do you think?"

What she thought was that it was a very great pity that with all of these rooms and all of these beds, there was no place they could go to be alone. "I think we'd better get back out to the conservatory or I'm going to find myself doing something wholly inappropriate to you."

A corner of his mouth quirked. "Right here?"

"Why don't you test me and find out?"

His eyes were intent on hers. "I think that I—"

"Are you guys going to get out here or what?" Gabe stood in the doorway looking at them. "Come on, bro, we need to get this rolling. You can make goo-goo eyes at each other later."

Celie smothered a giggle.

Jacob eyed Gabe narrowly as he walked past. "Aren't you the master of tact?"

Gabe grinned. "These special moments we share."

"Next time you show up on my doorstep," Jacob growled, "you're sleeping with Murphy."

Only one or two guests still milled about the conservatory as the mountains faded into evening darkness outside the windows. Bow-tied staff cleared up the last of the bowls and melted ice and stale tag ends of doughnuts. Celie rubbed her back.

The maple-sugar-on-snow party had been a zoo. She'd laughed, joked, drizzled syrup, handed around samples and generally had the time of her life. True to form, Jacob hadn't said much and only interacted with the guests when forced, but he'd been there every time she reached for a jar of maple cream or a candy. It was as they'd been in the sugarhouse that night, a team, working together as a single unit. Now, the last guests were drifting off to dinner and she could finally relax.

"We did well," she told Jacob, showing him a handful of order forms for maple products.

"*You* did well," he said, kissing her lightly.

"Two compliments in one day. You're getting positively excessive."

"You want me to show you excessive?" he asked, a predatory glint in his eye.

Gabe and Hadley walked up before she could reply.

"Hooray, we're done," Hadley said. "And a good time was had by all."

"So, were we a success?" Celie asked.

"Unquestionably. In fact, we'd love to do it again come the March sap run. I think our guests really got a kick out of it. You know, old New England stuff and all that."

"You want quaint, we got quaint," Jacob said.

"Thank you so much for taking the time to come over. I'm sorry Molly couldn't be here, but, Celie, it was such a pleasure to meet you. If you ever decide to change careers, you could have a real future in hospitality."

Celie gave a mock bow. "You want schmoozing, we got schmoozing."

"Well, you're both wonderful."

"Hey, don't lay it on too thick or he'll start thinking he's got a choice," Gabe complained.

"Well, he does."

"No he doesn't. He's family. He has to do it or my mom will beat up on him."

Hadley rolled her eyes. "I can hardly imagine that."

"You haven't seen her," Gabe said seriously.

"It's true," Jacob confirmed. "She could put the fear of God in an atheist."

Hadley's lips twitched. "Are you two big strong men really afraid of your mother?"

"Yes," they chorused.

"Wow. In stereo, even." Celie looked at Hadley. "We've got to find out how to inspire that."

"I think it has something to do with going through labor and midnight feedings," Hadley said. "It makes you ruthless. We don't quite have it yet."

"Definitely don't have it," Celie agreed. "Look, they're just ignoring us and walking away."

Hadley crossed her arms and watched them. "Yep. Makes for some nice scenery, though."

"You and Gabe make quite a pair," Celie said.

Hadley's face lit up like a spotlight. "He's great, isn't he? I can't believe how lucky I am."

Celie raised an eyebrow. "I'd say he's the one who's lucky."

"Maybe we both are. He's so wonderful. Of course," she gave Celie a sidelong look, "Jacob's pretty wonderful too. He comes off all gruff when you first meet him, but there's someone very special in there."

"I think you're right," Celie said, studying the two brothers as they talked.

"Now if this were a Trask family gathering, you'd have one of the cousins pinning you into a corner and demanding to know your intentions."

Celie gave her an amused look. "And are you going to be the stand-in?"

Hadley snorted. "Gad, no. First, I've been on the other end and I'd never do that to anyone. Second, I'm not part of the family."

It was Celie's turn to snort as Gabe and Jacob walked back toward them. "I'd say that's just a matter of time."

"What's a matter of time?" Gabe asked.

Celie smiled. "Ask Hadley."

"Like she'd ever break down and tell a secret. However, I will have a chance because, Ms. Manager, we've got to get to the Chamber of Commerce dinner. So make nice and say bye bye."

Hadley hugged Jacob and kissed Celie on the cheek. "I'd rather say 'see you later.'"

"And I'll be waiting to say 'I told you so'," Celie whispered.

When Hadley burst into laughter, both men stared. "What?" Celie blinked innocently. "Go to your meeting."

Jacob watched them walk off. "Want to tell me what that was all about?"

"Absolutely not. Girl talk." Celie glanced around. "So, is our work here done?"

"More than. You were something else today."

"That could be taken a number of ways."

"How about if I clarify?" he offered and swept her in for a lingering kiss.

"Wow, um, okay, that works," she said, taking a hasty look around the empty conservatory once he'd released her. "Maybe we should get going somewhere more private." She threaded her arm through his.

"Maybe we should."

They headed out of the conservatory. "So I was thinking, these parties would be a great way to sell things, if Gabe and Hadley are up for it. Bring a couple of cases of syrups and maple cream and stuff. I bet they'd go like hotcakes. We'd clean up. I mean, you would," Celie hurried to amend.

"Sure. I would."

"Well, maybe not you, you, but someone like you," she clarified as they ambled slowly across the lobby.

"Yeah."

"Or not someone like you. Probably someone different."

"No doubt."

"More chatty."

"I got it."

"And isn't the door that way?"

Jacob followed the line of her pointing finger. "Yup."

"So why aren't we going out it? Aren't we going home?"

He led her past the front desk and down a wide hall. "Eventually. Are you hungry?"

"Starving, actually. Those pickles don't stay with you."

"Then it's a good thing we're here." He stopped at the maître d's stand at the wide doorway to the dining room. "Party of two for Trask," he said.

"Very good, sir." The maître d' picked up two menus. "Right this way."

"Good lord." Celie clutched Jacob's arm and goggled as they walked across the octagonal room with its pillars and picture windows. "Have you ever seen a place this beautiful?"

And Jacob knew he'd guessed right yet again. He'd been there a number of times over the years and it still made an impact with its soaring arches, Victorian glass chandeliers and ornate plasterwork. The lines satisfied the builder in Jacob, the graceful ornamentation complementing without overwhelming. It was true to the original plan, right down to the string combo playing soft music in the corner.

The maître d' led them to a table by the window. Candles flickered, throwing reflections in the glass. Outside the window, lights shone out from the conservatory and the back galleries of the hotel. And Celie, he realized, was uncharacteristically quiet.

He looked at her closely. "Are you all right?"

In the soft lighting, her eyes looked enormous. "Of course I am…it's…Jacob, this is beautiful."

"You like it?" Relief swept through him.

"What are you, nuts? Of course I like it. I'd have to be crazy not to. But I—" She subsided as the waiter appeared to pour wine for them.

"Compliments of the managers," the waiter said and showed them what Gabe had told Jacob was the 1997 Wine of the Year.

"Gabe offered champagne but I thought you might like this better."

"You thought right."

He raised his glass. "Happy late Valentine's Day."

Celie laughed. "Is that what this is about?"

"Partly. Valentine's Day is the big date night and you spent it working with me instead of going out."

"I recall doing a few other things," she said with a wicked smile and tapped her glass to his.

Jacob drank and put his glass down, studying it intently. "I haven't done enough for you," he said abruptly. "I realized that today. The past year has been...all over the place. Everything's changing and there's a lot I'm juggling. I get busy and get thinking about the farm and sometimes I forget about the important stuff." He hesitated and made eye contact with her for the first time. "I haven't ever really said thank you. I've been a jerk that way. But I want you to know I appreciate everything you've done. All the work, how great you've been with my family—"

"And your dog."

"And my dog," he added with a smile. He toyed with the cork, studying it as though he'd never seen one before. "Things have been easier the last month and a half and that's been because of you. And this isn't much of a way of saying thank you, but it's the best I could come up with."

She should say something, Celie thought, but she couldn't speak past the lump in her throat. How had he become so dear to her in such a short time? How had he come to feel like home? She didn't have a home, it wasn't a part of her life. And yet when she was with this man who was so deeply rooted in his world and his convictions, when she looked into his eyes, she could see herself getting rooted, too.

She rose and pressed a soft kiss on his lips. "That was one of the sweetest things anyone's ever said to me," she told him as she sat back down.

And something glowed in his eyes, something for her alone.

"So let's try another toast with this wonderful wine," Celie said. "Here's to you."

"Here's to you," he said.

"Okay, here's to you and to me."

The crystal of his glass rang against hers as he tapped them together. "Here's to us."

"Oh, that was incredible," Celie said lazily as they walked out of the restaurant. "I've never had such good food in my life. I feel like I could float home." She stifled a yawn.

"I can do better than that," Jacob said, coming to a stop at the front desk. He nodded at the clerk. "My name's Jacob Trask. I believe there's something waiting for me?"

The young, auburn-haired woman checked her file and her brows shot up. "Why, yes, sir, there is." She brought out a key on a heavy brass disk and passed it across to him. "You're in the Presidential Suite, on the top floor." She handed him a room folio. "I know you'll enjoy it. Have a lovely stay."

Celie stared. "We're staying here?"

He held out his arms to her. "Why not?"

"You're not missing a trick tonight, are you?" Celie asked as they turned to the elevator, next to the broad grand staircase with its gold-twined scarlet carpeting.

Jacob shrugged. "I figure when in Rome…"

"Do as the Romans do?"

"Do as the Sybarites do and get a really great hotel room." She laughed.

She didn't laugh when he unlocked the door to the suite and guided her inside. He didn't turn on the light.

He didn't have to.

Moonlight streamed into the octagonal room from every angle. All around them rose mountain and forest in a vast sweep of grandeur. In the room, graceful antique sofas sat grouped around polished tables. In the center, a curving staircase led to the upper floor.

It felt like a dream, like something that wasn't real because nothing could be as special as this night had been, or promised to be. But when she followed him up, the treads were solid under her feet and they stepped out into a room of pale moonlight, a rosewood bed with bands of sheer, white fabric streaming to either side of the half tester. There was no wind, yet somehow it felt like a summer night with the nearly transparent fabric at the windows moving in some magical breeze.

Celie didn't speak, feeling that to say a word would be to break the spell. Instead, in dreamy silence and moonlight, she turned to him. In dreamy silence and moonlight, they came together. With mouth and hand, they touched in the familiar ways and yet somehow it was new, as though they'd shed an extra layer of skin with their clothing, and lay now more naked with each other than they'd ever been.

And he was beautiful in the pale wash of light, his face pure, his body strong, his hands gentle on her as he took her someplace they'd never quite been before. This time it wasn't about frantic passion but about quiet caresses that seemed all the more intense for the lack of flash. No roaring fire this time but a deep, powerful heat greater than any she'd known. And when he slid inside her, it was inevitable, overwhelming, as though they fused together in some elemental way. And when he caught his breath and tightened, she felt the climax flow into her body and carry her along.

And she knew she'd found love.

## Chapter Fifteen

Feet crunching in the snow, Celie walked around the maple, looking for the tell-tale holes. Nearby, the rest of her team worked their way through that day's territory.

Footsteps sounded behind her and she turned to see Dean Almeda, the burly gray-haired property owner. "How's it going?" he asked. "You find anything?"

He looked a little strained, she thought, like a man waiting for the results of a biopsy. "So far everything looks clean." She was glad of the chance to pass on some good news. "We should be done here in an hour or so."

"Good. We need to start putting in taps. All right if we're working while you're here?"

"As long as you stick with the areas we've already marked."

He gave a sharp nod and she watched while he stumped away. The real sugaring season was about to start. She couldn't believe it was nearly spring. Somehow, when she hadn't been noticing, January had slid into February, and February had become March. Meanwhile, she and her teams had somehow managed to work their way through nearly all the squares on the map back at the Institute. The project was approaching its end.

It didn't bring the usual satisfaction but a low-grade anxiety. Decisions loomed ahead of her, in a situation without choice.

Her cell phone rang. "Celie Favreau."

"How much do you love me?"

Celie frowned. "Is this Colin Farrell again? Because I've told you—"

"It's Pete, for chrissakes. How can you not recognize my voice?"

The aggrieved tone brought a smile to her face. "Oh, maybe because we haven't been housemates in over seven years?"

"That's no excuse. So? Don't you want to know why I'm calling?"

She felt a little stirring of nerves in her stomach. "Your horoscope today was really good and you want to read it to me?"

"It's out," he said triumphantly. "Happened today. Broad, immediate release. You could go down to your local ag supply and order Beetlejuice right now."

She whooped and jumped in the air, letting the phone go. The other inspectors stared but she didn't care. It was the most deserved happy dance she'd ever done, and dammit she was going to savor it. The cell phone squawked. It took several seconds before she noticed.

"Celie? Are you there? Did you just drop your phone?"

She snatched it up. "Pete, I love you. I want to have your baby. I want to lie around in a Princess Leia bikini and feed you grapes. You're fabulous."

"Could you back up to the Princess Leia part?"

"Oh, you have no idea how happy this makes me. What kind of use is it rated for?"

"In conjunction with removal, but only to fifty yards. Annual inoculations for three years and you're home clear."

Cutting a circle of fifty yards, not a hundred and fifty. Clearing less than two acres, compared to fifteen. She felt like a soap bubble, like she was floating on air, everything shimmering around her. "This is incredible. Look, next time I'm in Maryland, I am taking you out for a drink."

"Lots of drinks," he suggested.

"Lots of drinks. And the biggest steak you can eat. We are going to celebrate."

"Wait a minute, what happened to the Princess Leia part? Hello? Celie?"

Jacob stood on the ladder and leaned in under the overhang to check the upper holding tank. The spring sugaring season was going to start any day. He felt the familiar sense of anticipation, like a runner at the starting line awaiting the sound of the gun, the chance to go from poised readiness to all out effort. He had no illusions about how relentlessly hard he was going to have to drive himself, and for how long. It didn't matter. He'd get through it.

Someone burst out of the sugarhouse door behind him. "They released it!"

"What?" He tried to turn too quickly and knocked his head on the overhang. "Celie," he said, wincing.

She hurried over to him. "Oh my God, are you all right?"

"It's only a minor fracture," he said, touching his head gingerly. "I'll be fine." He hopped down from the ladder and kissed her. "So what's going on?"

"They registered Beetlejuice." She threw her arms around

his neck and gave him a smacking kiss. He added a few of his own, just to get into the spirit of things.

And then the words penetrated.

"Registered it?" He pulled away with a little frown.

"Released it. Approved it for commercial use."

"Wait a minute. I thought it was already approved. Wasn't that what you said a couple of weeks ago?"

"It *was* approved by the RAL but now the paperwork's through." She stuck her hands in her pockets and walked over to peer into the holding tank. "Everything's official."

"So it wasn't really a done deal."

"Everything but." She shrugged. "Now the *but* has happened."

"Back up. What about before?"

"What before?"

"When you were putting it into my trees, before." An edge entered his voice.

"I told you, the paperwork had been generated and was being circulated for approval."

"So it could have been turned down at any time?"

"No, the usage documents could have been turned back because someone didn't like a comma. The RAL gave the okay," she reminded him. "The release was a technicality. And one that doesn't matter now. It's history. Beetlejuice is out. You could get Muriel to order it today. Everything's okay. In fact, it's better than okay. It's great." She gave him one of those brilliant smiles and suddenly he didn't care a whole hell of a lot about Beetlejuice anyway.

"So what's our friend the weatherman saying?" she asked.

"The temperature's supposed to start rising and hit the mid thirties in three or four days. Assuming you can believe the forecast that far out."

"Do you?"

He shrugged. "It doesn't matter. I'm ready."

"Do you want me to come tonight to help clean anything up?"

Jacob thought of Isaac's bathtub. "Yeah, I think you should come tonight and help me clean something up," he said, sliding his hands into her hair and browsing on her mouth. "And after you're all nice and clean, we'll have dinner."

"Mmmm. I like the sound of that. Besides, we can celebrate."

"Beetlejuice?"

"Yep. And the fact that we've been through almost ninety percent of the sugarbushes in Washington County and only found the maple borer in two places."

Almost ninety percent. Meaning she only had ten percent left. "That's good news," he said, and gave himself credit for sounding normal. "So I guess you're nearly done."

Her rueful laugh didn't quite ring true. "Oh, there's still lots to do. We've got a few more inspections, and we need to look at the band of trees that overlaps the neighboring counties. And I've got to close on Durkin's lawsuit."

"What's going on with that?"

"Our legal department has filed the paperwork. With luck, the courts will rescind the injunction within the week. We won't have to take nearly so many of his trees now, though, so he's going to be a lot less ticked off."

Jacob nodded to himself.

"There are weeks' worth of slaving to be done," she said lightly. But her smile didn't quite mask the hollow note in her voice and her words couldn't change the reality.

The time was approaching when she was going to leave.

He thought of it as he kissed her goodbye and shut her truck door. He thought of it as he watched her drive off. And he thought of it as he started cutting more firewood, the hard way, with an ax, because he had to keep busy or he was going to go nuts.

He'd been comfortable in his own skin once. He'd had a life that he'd been perfectly content with before she'd come along. He'd been happy enough being alone. Sure, there were times he'd felt at loose ends, but there were many more during which he was quite content to sit in his living room with his guitar and pass the hours. It had been enough. His work at the farm and Murphy and his occasional involvements had been enough. Now he needed someone.

Now he had something to lose.

Illogically, it made him angry at her. Everything had been fine until he'd found her in his trees. He didn't need complications. He didn't need connections.

But he needed Celie. Oh, he needed Celie.

Never had he had to depend on someone else for his happiness. He'd never allowed it to happen, never allowed himself to care that much. With Celie, it hadn't been a matter of choice. She'd barged into his life, his head and his heart and that had been that.

And now she was about to barge right out.

Facts were facts, but he'd no idea what to do about them. He was rooted in Eastmont and she was in a job that could—and would—take her away at any moment. Worse, there was nothing that could tempt her to stay. What would she do, give up a job, a cause she was committed to, a profession with international status to boil syrup with him?

It was ridiculous. She was going to go and he might as well resign himself to it. It wasn't a matter of if, it was a matter of when.

And all he could do was watch it happen.

"You know what I don't understand?" Celie asked Jacob as the steam from the evaporator billowed around them and the clock ticked toward 2:00 a.m. "Why don't you have a cot in here? Then a person could lie down for a few minutes."

He flicked at glance at her. "Because if a person laid down for a few minutes and fell asleep, they'd have a scorched boil on their hands, three hundred gallons of ruined sap and a five- or six-hour cleaning job. And nowhere to put the new sap in the meantime."

"Okay, so maybe it's not a good idea."

"Trust me, it's not." He walked over to press a kiss on her. "After, however, is another matter. We've got maybe another half hour to go, and I have a very comfortable cot back in my house. I'd be happy to give you a tour."

"I can hardly wait."

He turned to the door. "Can you keep an eye on things? I'll be right back." He gave a brief smile. "Got to go see a man about a dog."

"You got it."

"I just filled the fire box, so everything should be all set." He walked over to give her a kiss. "Don't run away."

"I wouldn't dream of it. Can you bring back coffee?

"Sure."

Celie listened to the door close and wished she could freeze life in this moment of expectation, being here, being part of Jacob's world, knowing that any minute he'd be walking back in the door. Everything was coming together. Beetlejuice was cleared. She'd gotten the news earlier that day that the court had pulled the injunction. Durkin's trees would come down in time, and thanks to Beetlejuice, only a fraction of them. She could do the work she needed, finally eradicate the maple borer, without the destruction. She was on the threshold of accomplishing her goal.

And she had Jacob.

Of course, there was no reason they couldn't keep things going after the project was done. She was worrying over nothing. Planes and cars did exist. Even a man as rooted as Jacob would see that it was worth it to spend some time traveling if they could be together. And maybe she was a nomad now but things could change. Even if she couldn't see how at the moment.

Then again, Jacob didn't like change.

Celie frowned at herself. They'd find a way to make it work. She was worrying about silly things because she was trying to dance around the real issue—when did she tell him how she felt? She knew he cared for her. That much was obvious. So should she take the chance and just blurt it out? Should she test the waters? Should she wait until it was time to leave and tackle it then? But how did she hold it back when the words felt as though they lived constantly in her mouth, like butterflies threatening to flutter out every time she spoke? Every time she looked at him, held him, touched him, she wanted to say it. She wanted him to know.

A hissing sound had her looking at the evaporator. The bubbles had come up, larger than she'd ever seen them. And still no Jacob. The clock ticked by. *They'd have a scorched boil on their hands.* The syrup was darker, she saw. The bubbles were the size of golf balls, even bigger. She walked over to the door. "Jacob?" she called, but there was no answer. Where was he?

She came back to the evaporator, tapping her fingers restlessly, watching the bubbles grow. Finally, when they were verging on baseball-sized, she turned to pick up the dish of butter and the knife. She could at least knock them down. She could do that much. She knew that Jacob didn't want her touching the boil. No matter how much he let her help, he always kept her away from the actual syrup. But she didn't think she had a choice. "Jacob?" she called again but she heard no response.

"All right," she muttered to herself and walked over to the

evaporator. She'd seen him do it a hundred times. You just tapped the knife in the butter and brushed it against the surface of the syrup. How hard could it be?

Cautiously, she stroked the tip of the knife against the butter and reached over the evaporator partitions. The temperature surprised her. She'd never realized how hot it got. It was like putting her hand over a barbecue. She ignored it and touched the knife to the syrup in one spot then another then another and—

"Damn!" Syrup splashed her hand from a large bubble that popped just as she was touching the knife down. Reflexively, she snatched her hand back. And with a plop, the knife dropped down into the syrup. *"Damn!"* she cried. Through the inch and a half of syrup, she could see the knife. Was it her imagination, or was the syrup around it darkening before her eyes? She blinked and looked again.

She wasn't quite sure what it meant but she was reasonably confident it wasn't good.

Jacob reached the top of the stairs with the new box of coffee. He should probably know better than to drink it at this hour, but he was so sleep-deprived he seriously doubted it would do anything to keep him up.

Then he heard Celie call his name. He ran through the gift shop and opened the door to see her at the evaporator.

"Jacob, thank God."

"What's happened? Are you okay?"

"I'm fine. It's the boil."

And he looked into the evaporator and saw the knife lying at the bottom, a rapidly darkening halo of syrup around it. "How the hell did that get in there?"

"I dropped it in. I didn't mean to," she said miserably. "I'm sorry. I was trying to knock down the bubbles."

"Celie, I told you to leave it," he said, snatching up the metal tongs.

"I know. I'm sorry. I was trying to help."

He grabbed for the knife, knowing even as he did that it was too late. "*Dammit.*"

"What?"

He shook his head in frustration. "It's burned to the bottom." While he'd been futzing around with coffee.

"What?"

"It's burned to the bottom. The boil's scorched. It's ruined." Sixty gallons of syrup lost, maybe more. The amount of time he'd lose cleaning the evaporator? Six or eight hours, judging by the look of it. While the holding tanks filled up and sap started running onto the ground. He ran some more sap in to dilute things and then shut off the valve on the inlet tube.

"What do we have to do?" Celie asked.

"Dump the boil," he said, opening up the firebox.

"All of it?"

"Of course all of it. The knife is scorched to the bottom of the evaporator. It's all going to taste burned. I've got to get the syrup out of there and clean the evaporator before I can do anything." He'd been an idiot to lollygag in the basement while he left her there to watch it. Having her there had made him sloppy. Just because you had a partner didn't mean they were enough. Sometimes working alone was the best way. You kept up your guard. You didn't screw up.

And you didn't get hurt.

"I'm sorry," Celie said in a small voice. "I didn't mean to do it."

Jacob grabbed a bucket and started drawing off sap. "I know you didn't. Knocking down the bubbles is trickier than it looks. That's why I asked you not to touch it." He watched the syrup pour out and mastered his frustration. "Forget about it. Look, I need to clean this up. It might be best if you go on home."

"At least let me help you," she protested. "It's a big job."

"I can do it faster myself."

"You don't need help scraping or anything?"

"I can do it alone. Now just go, please." He stopped and took a breath. "Look," he softened his voice with effort. "It was my fault. I went down in the basement for some coffee. I shouldn't have been gone for so long. I'm just too tired to think straight."

"And you say you don't need any help."

"I've had just about all the help I can take right now."

She whitened as though he'd slapped her.

"I'm sorry," he said immediately. "That was an idiotic thing to say. I'm ticked off at myself and I'm taking it out on you." He took a deep breath and scrubbed his hands through his hair. "Okay, we're both really tired and this is a one-person job. Why don't you go home, get some sleep? We'll talk later."

"Will we?" Her voice was bleak.

"Yes. I just have a lot of work to do and I'll do it more quickly if I'm not distracted." His voice softened and he walked over to press a kiss on her forehead. "I'll see you tomorrow."

## Chapter Sixteen

Celie stared at her computer. Of all of her job's many aspects, distilling each month's work into a five-page summary was by far the most challenging. Sitting inside when she should have been inspecting trees made it even more difficult. Every day it grew warmer. They were so close to their goal but soon the maple borers would begin to hatch, and heaven help them if they hadn't uncovered all the infested trees by then.

She sighed and hit the spell-check. Of course, she knew the real reason for her funk and it had little to do with reports. Things were wrong with her and Jacob. It made her whole world feel off. It hadn't really been a fight, but in a way that was almost worse. Nothing had been clear, nothing had been resolved. Somehow, though, invisible walls had gone up.

And she didn't know how to pull them down.

There was a sound at the opening to her cubicle. She turned, expecting to see Marce or Bob Ford. And her jaw dropped.

*"Gavin?* What are you doing here?" She stared at her boss in shock. Gavin, who should have been at APHIS headquarters in Maryland. Gavin, who never did field work. Perhaps he'd made the trip to review her progress with his own eyes. Or maybe he was in the area and just decided to stop by.

Or maybe he was here specifically to talk to her. Her insides clenched. This could be nothing good.

"Good morning, Celie. I see you're hard at work."

"My February status report," she said faintly.

"The one due March first?"

She flushed. "I was inspecting and dealing with the lawsuit all last week. This is the first chance I've had to get to it."

"As project head, it's your responsibility to keep me informed. On all levels," he added. Was it her imagination or was there a hidden emphasis in his comment?

"I do my best."

"Do you? Then perhaps you'll tell me why you saw fit to begin injecting an unapproved insecticide into a ring of trees marked for removal according to the eradication protocols that you yourself helped develop."

Once, during first-grade recess, she'd gotten hit in the face with a softball as she'd run toward the swings. No warning, no shouts. One second she was intent on reaching the last open swing, the next, her world had exploded in white-hot shock.

It had felt a lot like this.

For an instant she couldn't speak, could only search frantically for answers that just weren't there. Gee, sir, I did it because I knew the committee protocols were unnecessarily cautious? I did it because I'm tired of tearing down healthy trees when I know there's a solution that's caught up in red tape? Gee sir, I did it because I couldn't stand the pain in the eyes of the man I love as he watched his way of life destroyed?

She sighed. "I thought it was the right thing at the time."

"The EPA is demanding disciplinary action."

"Gavin, give me a break. They released Beetlejuice last Wednesday. What are you going to do, slap me down for beating the registration date by a few weeks?"

He drew himself up. "This is a very serious infraction. The number of days doesn't matter. At the time you injected those trees, you were in direct violation of federal law and USDA protocol. You're a program head. You're entrusted with a certain responsibility and you violated that trust."

"I'm entrusted with eradicating the maple borer in the most effective way possible. The product is safe and it's released."

"That's not germane."

She stared at him. "What do you mean, it's not germane? Beetlejuice got approved by the RAL in early January. All I did was jump ahead of the paperwork cycle."

"It's called SMB-17 and what's *germane* is that it wasn't registered for use when you applied it a month ago."

"It's paperwork," she protested.

"It's the letter of the law," he shot back. "You can't just run around making your own rules, Celie. There are ways things are supposed to be done and until a pesticide is registered, approval is *not* a given, no matter what the RAL says."

"I was trying to save trees."

"It doesn't matter."

"Doesn't matter?" Her voice rose. "What are we doing here? What's this all about, rules and regulations or preserving the forests? You've been behind a desk for so long you've lost sight of your job, Gavin."

"No, I think you're the one who's lost sight," he snapped. "I know exactly what my job is and right now it's removing you from your position in this program."

And all the words stopped up in her throat. There had been

pain on the heels of shock when she'd gotten hit with the softball, pain that overwhelmed everything. It was that way now.
She felt lightheaded with it. "Are you busting me down?" Her
voice sounded far away to her own ears.

"Four grades. Be glad it's not more. You'll work out of the
offices in Riverdale for the time being until we can find something suitable for you."

Maryland, she thought in a panic. Away from the project.
Away from Eastmont.

Away from Jacob.

She stared at Gavin in alarm. "We're finishing up an eradication operation. Who's going to take over?"

"Dick Rumson from the state will step in for now."

*"Rumson?"*

"He'll be assisted by the inspectors you trained."

"He doesn't know the first thing about what he's doing,"
she burst out.

"And the fact that you did didn't make much of an impact
on your performance, now did it?"

Suddenly, she understood. "So how did you find out about
the inoculations?"

"An anonymous informant," Gavin said stiffly.

"That anonymous informant wouldn't happen to be Dick
Rumson, would it? The guy who directly benefited from making sure I got smacked down so far there was an opening?"

"I fail to see—"

"You need someone in here who's qualified, Gavin. Bust
me down to a desk job. I screwed up and I'll take my lumps.
But don't make the county and the state and the region pay
for it. Put Bob Ford in charge, or at least ask him what he
thinks of Dick before you make the move."

Gavin set his jaw. "This is not your affair, Celie."

It wasn't, she realized numbly. After ten years of building

her life around the scarlet-horned maple borer, it was all over. She moistened her lips. "So what happens now?"

"You're suspended without pay for two weeks. At the end of that time, you report back to Riverdale." Gavin rose. "It's not the end, Celie. People have survived these sorts of career disasters in the past and learned from them. I'm sure you'll do fine." He shook hands with her. "Good luck."

And she sat, shattered.

It was a scene Celie had seen so many times, steam streaming from the vent of the sugarhouse, the sweet, woody scent all around her. But she'd never faced it with desperation before.

Her thoughts kept racing in circles and getting nowhere, like a hamster on a wheel. However much she'd fantasized about Eastmont as home, she'd known she was going to have to leave eventually. She'd known she was going to have to leave, but she hadn't expected it to be so soon. She'd thought there would be time, time to talk with Jacob, time to make things right between them, time to hammer out some type of a future together.

Time to tell him she loved him.

Instead, she was being swept along pell-mell without a chance to figure out what to do. The only thing she knew was that she had to try, she had to convince him.

Or else she was lost.

Squaring her shoulders, she stepped into the sugarhouse. Jacob was bent over the evaporator, his back to her as she walked through the door. For a moment, she just stood and watched him, still unable to comprehend how he'd come to matter so much in such a short time. Unable to comprehend a life without him. She took a breath and crossed to him, trying for casual and breezy and feeling anything but. "It's running."

He turned to her and she could see the lines of fatigue on his face. She stared. "Good Lord, Jacob, you look ready to drop. Did you ever go to bed?"

He shrugged. "I needed to get the evaporator running. Otherwise we'd have to dump sap—not enough storage space."

So he'd stayed up all night after she'd left, draining, scrubbing and rinsing away the scorched syrup—her mess—as the hours rolled by. "I'm so sorry," she said again.

He warded her words off with a jerk of his chin. "Don't worry about it. It's done."

Setting the butter dish down, he went back to feed the fire. Everything was okay, he'd said, but clearly it wasn't. It wasn't for him and it wasn't for her. Especially now. She'd never felt this awkward with him, not even when they'd first known each other. She had to tell him, she knew she had to tell him, but couldn't see how to start.

"How's the sap running?" she asked instead.

"Fine."

"And the evaporator's working all right after last night?"

He didn't look up. "Fine."

Celie jammed her hands in her pockets. *Just do it.* She took a breath. "So I got some news today at work." Jacob didn't respond, just used the poker to break up the hot embers. She bit her lip. "I'm being…I mean, I have to…they're transferring me," she blurted.

The movement of the poker stopped. A particular stillness settled about him, a gathering tension that made it impossible to speak and impossible to look away. And then he straightened and turned to get some wood. "That right?" He began tossing the lengths into the firebox with unnecessary force.

Celie waited for him to say more, but after a while it became clear he wasn't going to. "They're sending me to

Maryland," she offered, trying desperately to sound normal.
The thing she couldn't tell him was why. He couldn't know
it was because of the inoculations. What she'd done, she'd
done of her own free will. It wasn't his burden to carry; obligation was the last thing she wanted from him. "We're just
about finished here. They're moving me to other things."

He looked at her finally. "So you're leaving."

"I have to." She swallowed. "That doesn't mean that I'm
walking away from you and me, though."

But she was. Jacob turned away to get more wood, trying
to forget how it had been to wake up with her, silky and fra-
grant in his arms. She was leaving. He'd known it was coming and still, somehow, it made him feel like he'd been
sucker-punched, weak in the knees, unable to catch his breath.
And he knew it was the beginning of the end. "Kind of hard
to have a relationship from five hundred miles away."

"No it isn't. There are phones, e-mail. It's only a couple
hours by plane. We can stay in touch, see each other all the
time." She paused. "Assuming you want to."

"It's not as easy as it sounds, Celie," he said wearily, shut-
ting the firebox door. "I've been there before. Absence
doesn't make the heart grow fonder. It makes you find ways
to do without."

She stared at him, cheeks pale, eyes dark. "I don't believe
that. I knew married people in grad school who lived on different continents and still kept the relationship going."

"And where you are is always going to be more real than
where you were. Things fade away, don't you understand?"

"Do you really think I'm that fickle?"

He looked at her directly then. "I think you're amazing," he
said softly. "But I also know people." He picked up the hydrom-
eter to test the syrup, grateful for the busy work—and then
he realized he was gripping the sample cylinder so hard his

knuckles were white. "Your life is taking you someplace else and this part is over. And when that assignment's done, you'll go again. You'll just keep going." And he couldn't follow.

"This is only a temporary posting. I could wind up somewhere closer, even, for the longer term."

But she didn't understand that he could feel her slipping away already. And he couldn't stand going through the slow, gradual withdrawal, the inevitable realization that he didn't understand what drove her anymore, that they didn't have a shared life.

"Celie," he said gently, "this isn't temporary. I am never leaving Eastmont, don't you understand that? There's too much holding me here. I can't go where your life is going to take you. And I don't want to." He took a breath. "You told me once that all you ever wanted growing up was new places, new things. Well, that's not Eastmont. That's not me. This place is never going to make you happy." And the thought of it made him want to go outside and howl at the moon.

Instead, he got the sap bucket and began to draw off syrup.

"Is that really what you think?"

"It's what I know. Could you really see spending your life here?"

"What does it matter what I think?" she asked in a rusty voice. "You wouldn't believe me anyway."

"People don't stay in this town, even when they grow up here. They don't stay when they move in to work at places like the Institute."

"Bob Ford's stayed."

"Yeah? Bob Ford was ready to settle down. Ask him how long the rest of his staff has been around. They're like you, Celie. In a year, maybe less, they'll have moved on. It doesn't change here, you know. Things stay the same."

"Well, I'm sorry I have to go, whatever you think. And I

hate that I won't be able to stay and help you through the rest of the sugaring. I've got a few days, that's all."

"It's all right. Just go." Amputations were best performed quickly.

"It's not all right. You need help."

"I don't need help," he said flatly, hoisting the bucket and carrying it over to the filter, stumbling a little on the concrete.

"Look at yourself." She followed him. "You're practically falling down you're so tired."

He upended the bucket into the filter. "I do this all the time, Celie. It's nothing out of the ordinary. I don't need you," he said. And he tried to believe it.

Hurt shimmered in her eyes, making him feel like a clod. "Well. I guess you can't put it any clearer than that, can you?"

"You know what I meant."

"Yeah, I do." An edge entered her voice. "I mean, that's pretty much what it's all about, isn't it? Sure, you like living someplace that never changes. That's because you don't want to change. You want to be alone. You've been trying to push me away since day one."

And he should have kept doing it. If he had, he wouldn't be standing here with her now, trying to pretend that he didn't feel like something had been ripped open inside him and left to bleed. He'd gotten distracted, lost sight of the limits he'd always set, the bounds he'd placed around his life. The bounds that had kept him insulated. "Look, none of this is a surprise," he reminded himself more than her. "Let's not make it bigger than it was." It was over, and now she'd go back to her life and he'd go back to his.

And try to ignore the yawning cavern she'd leave behind.

"If I didn't know better, I'd think you sounded relieved," she said slowly.

"Relieved? Hardly."

"Sure. Now you don't have anyone bugging you. Now you can go back to being on your own. Gotta keep up that image. No room there for anyone else. No room for a partner." She glared at him, inches away. "Do you ever get lonely in there all alone, Jacob? Do you ever wish just once that you had some company?"

He'd had company. And she was leaving. "What do you want me to do?" he demanded. "Beg you to stay? To walk away from a project that's been your life? And what happens the morning you wake up and realize it's not enough?" He moved back to the firebox, picking up the hook to open the fire doors and turning to find her on his heels. "Back off, will you? You're going to get burned."

"I already have," she said quietly.

No kidding, he thought. And it was time to end this. "Come on, Celie." His voice softened. "Let's stop tearing each other up and just call it done. We never said this would last."

Color flared in her cheeks. "You're so damned proud of this loner thing. Well guess what? No one gets by completely alone, Jacob, not even you. And you can blow me off now and you can push everybody else away before they get close but sooner or later you're going to have to realize that you can't get along in this world without people."

"I get along just fine," he retorted.

"Oh, sure. You and that precious legacy. Except what happens now? It all ends with you, the guy who'll go to his grave alone because he can't open up to anyone enough to have a relationship, let alone a family? What happens to the Trask family legacy now?"

The words vibrated there in the room. And then the light of anger in her eyes died. Abruptly, she seemed to sag.

"Celie—"

"No." She held up her hand and pulled herself together, he

watched her do it, scrap by scrap. When she had her composure back, she stirred. "We've done enough talking. I'm going, Jacob. Goodbye."

And then she went.

## *Chapter Seventeen*

Coming into Montreal had always been a game for Celie, with points awarded for each change she spotted. New places to eat and drink, new shops to visit. It was a win-win situation.

Except that this time around she didn't have the heart for it. When she realized the first change was the replacement of her favorite bistro by the glowing colors of a chain restaurant, she decided to boycott the game entirely. Further along, the bones of a skyscraper rose up in the place of a building that had housed her favorite music store, the one that had specialized in hard-to-find imports and World Beat.

She shouldn't have been surprised. She didn't understand why it bothered her so much.

Even Vieux Montréal had changed, here a restaurant, there a tourist shop. The cobblestone streets, the graceful, gray-stone buildings remained, the side streets with their cafés, warmly lit and inviting. But it wasn't the same and it didn't feel like home. Then again, it hadn't for a while, when she really thought about it. Too much was different from what she'd grown up with.

*It doesn't change here, you know. Things stay the same.*

Making a noise of impatience, she turned toward the St. Lawrence River. She was not going to think about Jacob. She refused to let herself fall into weeping. Drivin-n-Cryin was all well and good for the name of an indie band; she didn't need it to describe her life. Jacob had made it clear what he wanted, and it wasn't her. He wouldn't even give them a chance, she thought as frustration billowed up. She knew he cared for her. He'd seen what they could be together but he'd rather play it safe and walk away than find a way to make it work.

For a moment, something inside her twisted and she clenched her hands more tightly on the steering wheel. *Stay angry.* So what if she'd fallen in love with him? She'd make herself fall right back out. She wouldn't let him take up residence in her mind. She'd wipe away every last fingerprint he'd left on her heart. And when she was done, he'd be only a shadow, without the power to hurt.

She concentrated on the road. It was good things were different, because it meant she had to think as she worked her way through the city. She turned on St. Paul and headed to the bookstore.

She caught a glimpse of the Place Jacques Cartier as she passed, with its shops and aged brick. In summer, it would be packed with visitors, the cafés spilling out onto the sidewalks and the flower baskets overflowing with blossoms. On this frigid winter weekday, though, only a lone diehard street musician braved the elements, serenading the thinly populated square with mournful guitar music. The way Jacob had serenaded her.

*Stop it.*

One thing that hadn't changed about Montreal was parking. It took her a good fifteen minutes to search out a spot. Of course, she had an inherent advantage with her truck in that she didn't shrink from a little parking by Braille to get into a tight spot and she wasn't the least afraid of vandals or car thieves. Most would doubtlessly feel themselves far too good to sully their hands with her vehicle.

She sighed and rubbed at the back of her skull, trying to alleviate the tension headache. There was a great shadow looming over her that she was afraid to think about too much, because she knew if she did she'd give it a name and she didn't want to go there. Instead, she opened her truck door.

The front of the Cité de L'Ile bookstore looked the same as always, with its pale-gray stone and its mullioned windows framed in dark wood. The display of five books—three new, one used, one first edition—followed the same configuration it always had. Familiar, certainly. It had been her favorite place to loathe as a teenager.

So why, now, did looking at it make her eyes sting?

She pushed open the door, hearing the jingle of the bell. *"Maman?"* she called, setting down her satchel and duffel bag.

"Celie!" Her mother hurried out from behind the cash register, petite and stylish with her hair in a chestnut-brown chignon. She pulled Celie into her arms. And finally, amidst the scents of ink and paper and age, Celie felt like she'd come home.

"Oh, I can't believe you're here," her mother said, putting a hand to Celie's cheek. "Why didn't you call?"

"It was a spur-of-the-moment thing," Celie evaded. She slung her duffel over her shoulder. "Is it all right if I stay for a week or two?"

"Of course." Her mother frowned in concern. "Is everything all right?"

Celie took a deep breath to ward off the tension and summoned up a smile. "It will be."

* * *

Jacob stood at the sugarhouse door watching Deke stop the tractor behind the holding tanks. He frowned. "What are you doing down here? That tank's not more than three-quarters full."

"We were close enough." Deke defended, turning off the tractor and hopping down.

"A hundred gallons shy of full isn't close enough."

Deke gave him a sullen look. "We needed to use the john."

"You've got the entire sugarbush at your disposal."

"It wasn't that kind of need."

"I don't want to know," Jacob said wearily. "Go while it's pumping and get back on that slope. We're running out of daylight."

As the week had gone on, Deke had gotten progressively sloppier. If he was this bad after four days, how was he going to be after four weeks? Jacob had a nasty feeling that one morning soon, Deke just wasn't going to show up, and then he'd really be in trouble. Muriel's nephews? Maybe. Hell, at this point, he'd happily take on a reliable kindergartner.

He turned to push open the sugarhouse door. There wasn't time to think about it. He had to focus on the boils. All the sap in the world didn't mean a thing if you couldn't turn it into saleable product. Concentrating on making syrup would keep him from thinking about profitless subjects like how much he wished he had better help, how colossally exhausted he was, how worried he was that he was going to let something important slip.

And how, deep down inside, he suspected that he already had.

He moved his head to ward off the thought. He didn't need to be brooding about Celie. The nonstop work might have kept his hands busy, but the repetitive tasks of sugar-making offered far too much time to think. So he struggled to keep her out of his head, to lose the memory of how the soft skin of her throat had tasted, to banish the thought of her laughter. To forget watching her sleep in the moonlight, of how he'd felt awestruck, as though he'd found himself entrusted with something very rare and precious.

And as he drew off syrup, he did his damnedest to forget how she'd looked walking out the door.

He'd done the only thing he could, he reminded himself, pouring the syrup into the filter. That was his mantra, the thing he repeated every time he hit one of his black-dog, howl-at-the-moon moments. He'd done what he had to. It was best for both of them. But it didn't feel like the best thing. It felt like hell and it wasn't getting any better.

He cursed. Ridiculous to go over this again. Profitless to think of what might have been. What was, was. And it was what he had to find a way to live with. Scowling, he pulled apart the firebox doors and stirred up the embers.

The door to the gift shop opened, and he heard the sounds of footsteps and voices.

"Seems cranky," a male voice said.

"Are you surprised? He doesn't exactly look like Mr. Personality," said another.

"You know the saying," replied the first voice. "Laugh and the world laughs with you…."

Jacob straightened. "But be a jackass and you're a jackass alone."

"I couldn't have said it better myself," Gabe said, smiling broadly.

"A wizard with words," agreed Nick.

Jacob slammed the fire doors shut and crossed to where his brothers stood leaning against the door. "Hey."

"You look like hell," Gabe said cheerfully, thumping his shoulder.

Jacob shook hands with Nick and exhaled. "Yeah, well, it's been that kind of week. What brings you two here? Did I know about this?"

"I don't know, did he?" Gabe asked Nick.

"You'd think he would have," Nick said. "I'm hurt."

"Not that it wasn't spontaneous," Gabe pointed out.

"Spur-of-the-moment thing," Nick agreed.

"A couple of months ago, anyway."

Jacob scowled at them. "You two going to quit the Laurel and Hardy routine and tell me what's up? Is this for Ma?"

"Nope," Nick said. "It's for you."

"Meaning?"

"We're here to help."

Jacob blinked. "With the sap run?"

"What else?" Gabe asked.

"I don't get this. You guys work."

"I told you at Thanksgiving I'd take some time," Nick reminded him.

"And I told you the same thing." Gabe looked around the sugarhouse. "You've got Nick for two weeks now and I'll be here for the weekends, then I'm here for two weeks and Nick comes up on weekends. Although we would have shown up a lot sooner if we'd realized you were desperate enough to send Deke out to run gathers," he added, wandering over to the evaporator.

"Yeah well, you do what you've got to do."

"Next time you might put picking up a phone and calling for help on that to-do list." Nick flicked him a glance. "We're in this together, you know?"

"I didn't…"

"You didn't what?"

Jacob shrugged uncomfortably. "I guess I figured you guys were just saying it."

"We're your brothers, Jacob," Nick said, with a hint of an edge. "It's the family business and it supports Ma. What would make you think that we wouldn't take the time to come help?"

It was a reasonable question and it made him feel like an idiot. Which triggered his own flare of irritation. "It's not that unreasonable. You don't live here. You've got your own lives. Hell, Nick, you're supposed to be planning a wedding."

"Already done. Try another one."

He didn't need one more person giving him a hard time on this topic, he really didn't. Jacob scowled. "Look, don't start—"

"Hey guys," Gabe broke in. "I know bitching at each other is your way of bonding but you might want to put it aside and pay attention to the boil. It's been a couple of years but I'm pretty sure I remember giant bubbles are bad."

Jacob and Nick stared at each other. The corner of Nick's mouth twitched. Jacob tried to suppress his own smile and then they were grinning at each other. Jacob slung his arm around Nick's shoulders. "Okay, for the record, I don't care how it happened, I'm just glad to have you both here because you're going to work your behinds off. I am dying for the help."

It was uncanny how quickly Celie fell back into life in Montreal. It took less than a week for her French to come back. One minute, she was concentrating fiercely on interpreting the lightning-fast flow of syllables. The next, she was walking down the street behind a mother and daughter, amused at their strident battle over a navel-piercing only to realize that the entire discussion was taking place in French. Even her mental map reformed itself in her head, so that she again motored around the streets without a thought.

Not that she didn't wind up spending much of her time in the Cité de L'Ile.

She stood in the back room of the store with her mother, helping unpack some new books while her father worked up front. "So where is Margaux again?"

"Visiting a university friend in Vancouver." Her mother sliced open a box with an expert flick of the wrist. "We just got done with inventory and the High Lights Festival is starting soon, so she wanted to take advantage of the window to get a break."

Celie remembered doing inventory, all of them in the closed store, working until they were punchy. They'd played soccer in the aisles with balls of packing paper, she recalled with a smile. "I wish we'd ever been able to take a vacation. I think that was the thing I hated most growing up, that feeling we were always tied here."

Her mother looked at her in surprise. "But we went on vacations, don't you remember? Not often, but we took you kids to Toronto and Niagara Falls. We even rented a summer house on Prince Edward Island one year. You can't have forgotten that. You got stung by the jellyfish, remember?"

"Prince Edward Island?" Celie asked. The words shook loose vague memories of sun-faded and briny days, and of sudden, burning pain and an iron-hard determination not to cry. Somehow, she'd placed it on the Saint Lawrence, although of course that was ridiculous.

"You were young for some of them. It was harder to manage when the three of you grew older. Your father always thought it was important to get away from the store, though."

"He was right about that. I grew up hating this place."

"Do tell," her mother said dryly.

"That bad?"

She rolled her eyes. "Let's just say you weren't very subtle about it. But then, teenagers never are."

"It's just that we were always here, every day, every weekend. Everyone I knew was outside doing stuff and I was in here mildewing with the books, it seemed like. It was miserable."

"You didn't always feel that way. I remember when you were still little, you loved being down in the cashier booth with me. You'd sit on your stool with a picture book and babble away to yourself. We called you our mascot."

"I remember that." Celie smiled.

"So it wasn't all a misery, was it?"

"No," she said slowly, "not then." And somehow this time around, the routines were almost comforting, though she was happy to escape for a few hours each day. It was the nearest thing to a safe haven she had, at a time when she really needed one.

"When are you going to tell me why you're here?" Her mother's voice was gentle.

Celie looked at her with eyes full of misery. The crash she'd been staving off for days was suddenly far too close and she'd run out of strength to fight it. "Oh, Maman," she began, her throat tightening. "Everything's a mess."

And as she leaned against her mother, the tears finally came.

"So you haven't heard from him since?" her mother asked, pouring them coffee in the kitchen upstairs. "Not even a message?"

"I won't," Celie said. "That's not his way. Jacob picks a course and then sticks with it." She felt exhausted from crying but the awful tension she'd been carrying around had finally abated. If only the tearing sadness hidden behind it had gone as well.

"You'll get through this," her mother said fiercely. "All of it. You're a fighter and you'll show them all. Remember the jellyfish? You were such a brave little girl. You wouldn't cry. You insisted on going right back into the water. And you'll do the same thing here. You'll—"

A burbling sound interrupted her. It was Celie's cell phone. Celie pulled it out and stared at the area code.

"Aren't you going to answer it?" her mother asked.

She sighed. "I don't feel like talking to anyone."

"What if it's him?"

"I definitely don't feel like talking to him."

"I do," her mother said tartly and plucked the phone out of her hand. "Celie Favreau's line. Yes? Uh-huh. Just a minute." She put the phone aside. "Bob Ford?"

"Bob Ford?" Celie repeated, perplexed, and reached for the phone. "Hi, Bob."

"Celie. It's good to hear your voice."

"Yours too. How's Marce?"

"At loose ends without you, I think, but she's surviving. How about you?"

*Remember the trees we fed into that chipper, Bob?* "I'm hanging in there."

"I missed you when you left last week. I'm sorry for what happened, Celie. I can't tell you how sorry."

"That's all right, I…" Her throat closed up and for a moment she couldn't speak.

"Look, it's okay. You don't have to talk. I have an idea what this means to you. For the record, I think you did the right thing."

Just hearing the simple vote of confidence meant the world to her. If only Gavin had backed her that way.

Ford cleared his throat. "I don't know what your plans are right now, but I wanted to throw out an idea. I've had an open requisition for a research staffer for the last ten months. I haven't been able to find someone I wanted so I've been stalling, hoping a good candidate would show up. I'd bring you on board here in a heartbeat, if you're interested."

Celie blinked. "You want to hire me on at the Institute?"

"It would mean swimming in a smaller pond than you're used to," he cautioned, "but we'd give you a chance to do whatever kind of research you wanted. You could build on your previous work with the maple borer. Get involved with the state Division of Forestry. I know, I know," he forestalled her protest, "but Rumson's a political appointee and his buddy the governor's leaving office soon. He'll be gone after that."

Two weeks before, it would have been the answer to her dreams. Now? "Bob." She took a breath. "Look, I appreciate the offer but—"

"Hear me out, all right? I know you're used to dealing with issues on a federal and a global level, so maybe this is too small-time for you, but it doesn't sound like life's going to be a whole lot of fun for the next while. I'm just saying you don't need to waste your talents. You've got options."

Options, she thought. Take the job instead of letting Gavin bury her alive. In a town the size of Eastmont, though, there was no way she could avoid running into Jacob or hearing about him at every turn. And she just didn't think she could handle it.

Celie sighed. "Bob, you have no idea what this means to me. All of it, everything you just said. And it's a great opportunity, but I really think I need to get my head straight before I make any sudden changes."

"I understand but will you do me a favor? Don't make a decision now. I can stall another two months before the slot has to be filled. Take the transfer, try it out for a few weeks. If you can live with it, then I'll go to plan B. If you can't, well, you've got a home here."

But Eastmont wasn't her home any more.

She wasn't sure anywhere was.

\* \* \*

The problem, Jacob thought as he lay in bed staring up at the ceiling, was that he needed more sap. Never mind that it was the best sugaring season they'd had in four years. Nick's team was bringing in more than five thousand gallons of sap a day and Jacob was manning the evaporator for eighteen hours at a stretch.

The problem was the other six hours. Oh sure, he could keep himself scrambling well into the night, but somewhere around two or three in the morning he ran dry. And then he was faced with heading back to the house and trying to sleep.

Alone.

Sometimes, he could drift off. More often, he woke after just a few hours. When he did sleep, he dreamed of Celie; when he didn't, it was a constant battle to banish her from his thoughts.

And at times like now, he just didn't have what it took to manage it. If he could have gathered sap in the darkness, he would have, but he was sane enough to realize that even he couldn't drive his body twenty-four hours a day. So he lay there trying to fall back to sleep and they bombarded him: the images, the tactile memories, the sights and sounds and scents and sighs, they came at him until he wanted to pound something because it was unbearable and impossible and unthinkable that he'd let her go.

With a curse, Jacob dragged himself out of bed and downstairs, Murphy padding sleepily after him. He was too tired to read and the television was for crop reports, not passing the time. Instead, he picked up his guitar, because it had been the thing that had always been there for him in the past, engaging his hands and mind, giving him a place to drift away to.

Except that every place he drifted away to Celie was there. Always before, he'd concentrated on the fret work and fingerpicking, on coaxing the clearest tone from the instrument. Now, he could only think of Celie's face as she'd watched him play, of the absolute concentration with which she'd listened. Song after song he started, only to stop partway in and begin another. Concentration was impossible; when he sang, he only remembered the Appalachian ballad he'd played for Celie.

And finally he fell silent, setting the guitar aside. On the floor, Murphy gave a low whine. Jacob sighed. "Sorry, boy, it's not the same anymore."

Why didn't he say what he meant? It wasn't the same without Celie. Nothing was. He could do his damnedest to fill his life up with the farm and sugar-making and his family, but there was no ignoring the ache of emptiness that waited for him every time he let his guard down.

He'd been full of it that day in the sugarhouse. He needed her, needed her more than breath, and he'd been worse than a fool for letting her go. He'd been a coward, so afraid of losing her that he'd pushed her away.

*If you're looking for guarantees in life, you'll be disappointed.*

Something cold nosed against his hand and he heard Murphy's whine. "I know, boy," Jacob said, rubbing the dog's ears. "I miss her, too.

"And I'm going to do everything I can to get her back."

## Chapter Eighteen

Marce stepped out into the morning, pulling on her fleece-lined gloves. It might have been March, but the air smelled of snow. Which was just fine with her. The sugar-makers weren't going to like it, but she'd be happy to have one more good storm out of the year. All this bare ground and mud that was appearing bugged her.

She headed down her walk and stopped at the sight of the green truck sitting in her drive. And at the man who got out of it.

She looked at Jacob as though he was week-old roadkill. "She's not here, if that's what you're thinking," Marce said before he could speak. "And don't even start with me, buddy boy, because I am so not your friend." She walked past him to her car.

"And people say I'm cranky."

Marce rounded on him, eyes hot. "People say you're

cranky when you act this way without a reason. I have a reason. Celie is one of my closest friends. I had my doubts about her seeing you when you first got involved, but you seemed to make her happy so I kept my mouth shut. Well, after that stunt you pulled on her after she got demoted, I am not keeping my mouth shut any more. You are, without a doubt, the biggest piece of—"

"Whoa, whoa, what did you say?"

Her eyes gleamed with hostility. "I didn't get around to saying it yet. You're a—"

"About getting demoted," he cut in. "Celie. What happened?"

"You know what happened, you jerk. And if you weren't—"

"Okay, hold it." Jacob put up both hands. "Look, I'm sure I deserve it all and I'd be happy to make an appointment to listen to you rant at some future time, but right now I need to know what happened to Celie. So can we please just cut to the chase here and call me a jackass and go forward?"

Marce eyed him. "Do I get to do the calling?"

"If it'll make you happy."

Her smile held all the kindness of a shark. "Oh, it will. Jackass."

"Feel better?"

"No, but I'm getting there."

"Hold the buzz and tell me about Celie," he ordered. "How did she get demoted?"

Marce made an impatient noise. "It's not that hard to figure out. She used Beetlejuice on your trees and Rumson blew the whistle on her. They yanked her from the scarlet-horned maple borer program. Knocked her way down in pay grade. She wasn't supposed to use it. It wasn't approved," Marce enunciated as though talking to a child.

Jacob stared at her. "Celie said the RAL gave the thumbs up on it back in January," he protested, but a cold feeling in his gut told him Marce was telling the truth.

"And the paperwork got tied up between agencies. No paperwork, no use. Period." She gave him a contemptuous look. "Don't tell me you didn't figure she was skating close to the edge. You know how strict the EPA is. If you didn't realize the chance she was taking, then you have the brains of a gnat." The shark-like smile flashed again. "And while certainly the word "idiot" comes to mind when I think of you, I'm sure you could figure that one out, bright boy. Then again, if it was going to save your trees, why would you want to?"

Anger surged up, only to be swamped that quickly. Marce was right. He should have asked more questions. He could say that at the time he'd been too preoccupied with everything, but that was a weak excuse. Or a convenient one.

He closed his eyes. "She said she got reassigned to Maryland. She didn't say why." She'd stood there in the sugarhouse saying nothing at all about it. She'd been shattered, she must have been, but she hadn't gone to him for comfort. She'd blocked him out from beginning to end. And at the end, all he'd done was rail at her.

He didn't know who he was more angry at, Celie or himself.

"The only reason she still has a job is because it's easier to replicate Notre Dame Cathedral in gumballs than it is to fire a government employee," Marce continued. "When she comes back from her suspension, she gets the APHIS equivalent of a desk in the basement."

"Suspension?"

"Oh, you didn't know about that, either? So what exactly did you two talk about after she came over? Besides all of her personality failings?"

"That's between Celie and me," he said shortly. "Where is she?"

Marce gave a sharp bark of laughter. "And I should tell you that why?"

"That's between us, too. But it might make you feel more like giving me the information if I tell you that I deserve everything you can stick into your rant and then some. I want to find her and try to make it up to her."

"Maybe I don't know where she is."

"I'll find her anyway, if I have to drive to Maryland and go through the building office by office."

"I might enjoy seeing you go through that," Marce remarked.

"I'm sure you would. But if you really care about Celie, I'd think you'd want her to get the apology I owe her, even if all it does is give her the chance to tell me to go take a flying leap."

She folded her arms. "I might enjoy seeing that, too."

"Sorry, restricted airspace," he told her. "Now are you going to tell me or not?"

Her grin flickered before she could help herself.

Jacob stood on the sidewalk staring at the Cité de L'Ile bookshop and wondering if Celie was inside. He'd driven straight up from Eastmont, his only goal to find her. If he'd had any illusions that the two-and-a-half hour drive would be enough for him to figure things out, though, he'd been sadly mistaken.

He wanted her back. Above all, he wanted her back, but there were things between them they couldn't ignore. And he didn't know if talking about them would only push her further away, but they had to do it. A reconciliation built on a foundation of unfinished business was no reconciliation at all.

So he stood on the sidewalk with his stomach in knots, no idea what he was going to say to her, knowing only that he had to find her. Once he did that, he hoped to God he could persuade her to give him another chance.

The door jingled as he pushed it open and walked inside. It was his dream and his nightmare—linked rooms full of books but so crammed cheek-by-jowl that he was certain he was going to knock something over just by breathing.

A small woman with reddish-brown hair and Celie's eyes looked over at him. "Can I help you?"

"I'm looking for Celie."

She gave him an unfriendly look. "Why do you want her?"

Because she completed his world? Because he needed to know how she could have risked everything she'd worked for just to protect him? Because if he went another day without seeing her, he was going to go nuts? "I want to talk with her."

"I'm not so sure she wants to talk with you."

He didn't bother to ask how she knew who he was. "I'll take my chances."

"You look like the type who would." The woman studied him for a long moment, then nodded. "She's gone walking on the quays in the Old Port." She pointed out the shop window. "Take Bonsecours out here to the water. The Quai de l'Horloge is across the way."

"Is she wearing her red parka?"

"If you want to find her, you'd better hope so."

Celie tightened her scarf against the chill breeze blowing in off the Saint Lawrence and watched the icebreaker make its slow pass of the river. She'd slipped into the habit of walking the quay in the morning. It was a chance to be alone with her thoughts, a chance to get away. However much she'd come to an accommodation with the bookstore, she needed to be out in the open with the wind in her face.

Besides, there was a certain fascination in watching the

ships make their ponderous ways to port, or wondering about their destinations as they left.

As she wondered about hers. The calendar moved just as inexorably as the ships. Her two weeks were nearly gone; as soon as the weekend was over, she had to drive to Maryland and report to work.

Assuming Maryland was where she was going.

Damn Bob Ford anyway. Until he'd called, she'd resigned herself to doing her penance. It would take a couple of years, sure, but she had no doubt she'd work her way back up. Eventually. And then he'd thrown out his offer, and she hadn't had a peaceful moment since. *You have a home here.*

Celie made an impatient noise. No matter how right Eastmont felt, it was impossible to think about going back. After all, it wasn't as if she could live entirely on Institute property. If she took the job, she'd have to live in the town, she'd have to build relationships in the town. Sooner or later, she'd encounter Molly Trask.

And sooner or later, she'd have to deal with Jacob.

It was like steeling herself to test a bad bruise that had faded to purple and saffron. Yes, there was still pain, and loss and regret. But somewhere under there burned a surprising little flicker of determination.

So maybe it wasn't meant to be easy. Maybe that was what she was supposed to learn from all this. After all, there had to be a reason for the days and nights of misery she'd gone through. Maybe there was a time when you grew up, a time when you accepted that enough was enough. And she'd tried and tried with Jacob because she'd kept thinking in the end she'd get through, in the end it would work. But life wasn't a fairytale and happily ever after wasn't always in the cards. And however hard it might have been to accept, maybe the lesson was that sometimes you had to let things go.

For a moment the loss and pain surged up and swamped her as it had so many times, so that she was fighting just to stay afloat, to breathe in and out, to keep from sinking down on her knees and screaming. But she fought it, refusing to give in, and after a while it subsided.

Until the next time.

And she'd fight it the next time, too, she thought grimly. Was she going to let a failed love affair shape her life, then? Was she going to let it keep her away from the kind of opportunity Bob Ford was holding out to her?

*You insisted on going right back into the water.*

Celie reached in her pocket and pulled out her cell phone. It wouldn't hurt to talk with Bob, just talk with him about it. And who knew, maybe in a week she'd—

Footsteps crunched behind her. "Celie?"

She stood there in her red parka at the water's edge, staring at him, her mouth open in utter shock.

"Jacob?"

For a moment, he didn't say anything, just let himself drink her in. In all the sleepless nights, all the long days, he'd never remembered her looking quite as wonderful as she did now, cheeks flushed, hair tossed about by the breeze.

"What are you doing here?" she asked at last.

"Looking for you."

She watched a pair of gulls squabble over a bit of trash at the water's edge. "How did you know where to find me? Marce?"

"I stopped by to see her today."

"That must have been fun." Her lips curved faintly. "She's a big fan."

"We had an interesting conversation. She called me names, I agreed with her. She's very protective of you."

"She's a good friend."

He listened to the grinding sound as a steep-bowed ship made its way through the channel, throwing up slabs of ice before it. He wished they could shove aside all the barriers in their way as easily. "You should have told me," he said softly.

"About wh…" And then she just looked at him. "Oh," she said.

"You should have said something," he repeated. "About Beetlejuice, about the demotion."

"If you'd known, would you have let me do it?"

"There's no way I would have let you risk your job for me."

Celie turned away and looked out over the river. "Maybe I did it for the trees."

"They were still my trees. You should have been straight with me. You don't make that kind of decision yourself, Celie. You don't make me a part of it without giving me a choice. It wasn't fair."

She bristled. "Who are you to say that?"

"The guy who feels like hell because you got smacked down for helping me. The idiot who stood there yapping in the sugarhouse instead of listening. The one who was busy being a jerk while you'd just gone through the worst thing you could go through. That guy."

"So I should have told you about the demotion and that would have made it all better? You think I wanted you to stay with me out of obligation or guilt?" she asked, an edge to her voice. "You think I want you here now because of that?"

"No. But that's not why I'm here." He let out a breath. "You just should have told me what was really going on, both times. That's part of being involved, you know? Letting someone in?"

She snorted. "This is coming from you?"

"Yeah, it's coming from me," he said with a spark of irritation. "I know I'm not the easiest guy to get next to but I'm working on it. You can't go forward in a relationship if you're holding out on one another. It's wrong. Just like I was wrong."

They stared at each other in humming silence. Celie moistened her lips. "Wrong how?"

He gave a humorless laugh. "Pick a way, any way. I got buffaloed when you told me you were leaving. I'd been thinking about it, a lot—all the time, pretty much. And when I heard you say you were going, I just… I jumped to conclusions and I didn't listen." His words were abrupt. "I didn't want to get sucked in and wind up with you walking away."

"So you decided to do it for me."

"Appears so, doesn't it? I should have trusted you. I didn't give you a chance."

"You didn't give *us* a chance," she corrected. "We had something really great, Jacob."

His stomach tightened. "Had?"

Celie stared out at the icebreaker, watching its stern as it moved away. "I've been doing a lot of thinking the past two weeks. You say you didn't come out of guilt and obligation, but there are other wrong reasons. I mean, I've always been the one chasing you. I catch up, you run away. Now I've stopped chasing. So is that why you're here? Because if you are, that's not the basis for a relationship, that's a pathology."

His brows lowered. "That's not why I'm here."

"Then why are you?" she demanded. "A couple of weeks ago you couldn't get rid of me fast enough."

"And I was an idiot. I've been doing a lot of thinking, too, the past couple of weeks." He couldn't find the words, he thought in panic. He couldn't find the words and she was going to turn and walk away and he was going to lose her, this time for good. He felt smothered, desperate, unable to breathe. "Look, I don't know a lot, but I know that I want you in my life somehow, and I don't care what shape that takes. I'll do anything as long as you're there." He swallowed. "I need you, Celie." And if it took begging, he'd do that, too.

She stared at him, eyes huge. "What did you say?" she asked, her voice a thread of a whisper.

And suddenly, he knew the words. "I love you," he said simply. "I've known since Valentine's Day. I've been an idiot and I know I blew it, but I'm hoping you'll give me a chance to prove to you I've changed. I need you in my life, Celie." He looked at her intently. "And I think you need me in yours."

The seconds ticked by and he stood, watching her, his nerves stretched to the breaking point.

And then she flung herself into his arms. "Oh my God, Jacob, do you mean it?"

"More than I've ever meant anything in my life." Suddenly, he was breathing great gulps of air, feeling as though his heart was going to explode with feeling.

Tears were running down Celie's cheeks. "I was standing here trying to tell myself that it just wasn't supposed to happen for us, that it was okay and I needed to accept it when I was just crazy inside. And then you showed up and I didn't know..." she pulled back and looked at him. "I love you so much. It nearly tore me apart to walk out that door."

"It about tore me apart to watch you." He kissed her forehead and then her lips and pulled her close. "I'm sorry I put you in that spot."

"I know you said things fade, but that's not us. This isn't going to fade. I can't imagine this feeling ever changing."

"I can."

She gave him a startled look.

"We've got a lot to learn about each other," he said simply. "I think the way we feel is going to be different in a year and different again in five or ten. And maybe we'll have to do a lot of that learning over the phone and the Internet, but we'll do it."

"But we won't have to," she blurted.

"What do you mean?"

"Bob Ford offered me a job. I was just about to call him when you walked up."

"You're not going to Maryland?"

She shook her head and he swept her up and whirled her around, whooping so loudly that a couple of shore birds near them took flight, looking back reproachfully.

"Okay," Jacob said, "this is real, right? This isn't going to be one of those dreams where you suddenly turn into a sea-gull and fly away and I'm standing here freezing and I wake up and find out the covers have slipped off and everything still sucks, right?"

Her eyes had widened in mixed alarm and amusement as he'd talked. "I don't know. I could pinch you, I suppose. Or I could do this." She leaned in and rose up on her toes to nip him on the neck.

"Hey!"

"Am I looking like a seagull?"

"No."

"Then you're probably not dreaming."

"I think we should be sure," he murmured, and pulled her in for a kiss.

\* \* \* \* \*

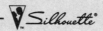

# SPECIAL EDITION™

*USA TODAY* BESTSELLING AUTHOR

# *PATRICIA KAY*

BRINGS YOU THE CONCLUSION OF

## CALLIE'S CORNER CAFÉ

*It's where good friends meet...*

# SHE'S THE ONE

March 2006

After her credit card company called about
suspected identity theft, Susan Pickering
needed police lieutenant Brian Murphy's help.
Was Susan's rebellious sister the culprit?
As the questions mounted, one thing was
certain—identity theft aside, the lieutenant
made Susan feel like a whole new woman.

# Since when did life ever tell you where you were going?

Sometimes you just have to dip your oar
into the water and start to paddle.

# THE
# SUNSHINE
# COAST
# NEWS

## KATE AUSTIN

Available February 2006
TheNextNovel.com

HN32

HARLEQUIN
Next

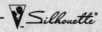

# SPECIAL EDITION™

## HE WASN'T THE RIDE-OFF-INTO-THE-SUNSET TYPE...

T. J. "Cowboy" Whittaker wasn't looking to be anyone's hero, but when sheltered city girl Priscilla Richards turned her tear-filled blue eyes on him and asked if he could help her uncover the secrets in her past...well, how could the sexy P.I. say no?

# CALL ME COWBOY
## *by JUDY DUARTE*
### Available March 2006

Judy Duarte "pulls the reader deeply and satisfyingly into the hearts and minds of [her] characters."
—*Romantic Times BOOKclub*

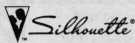

SPECIAL EDITION

**#1741 THE BRAVO FAMILY WAY—Christine Rimmer**
*Bravo Family Ties*
Casino owner Fletcher Bravo wanted Cleo Bliss to open her on-site
preschools at his resorts, and when they met face-to-face, he wanted
Cleo Bliss—*period*. But the last thing this former showgirl needed
was a brash, high-living CEO in her life. Would seeing Fletcher's
soft spot for his adorable daughter open Cleo's heart to the Bravo
family way?

**#1742 THE BABY DEAL—Victoria Pade**
*Family Business*
For Delia McRay, hooking up with younger Chicago playboy
Andrew Hanson on a Tahitian beach was a fantasy come true. But
what happened on the island, didn't stay on the island—for when
Hanson Media met with Delia's company months later to land her
account, there was a pregnant pause…as Andrew took in the result
of their paradise fling.

**#1743 CALL ME COWBOY—Judy Duarte**
When children's book editor Priscilla Richards uncovered evidence
that her father had long ago changed her name, she hired cocksure P.I.
"Cowboy" Whittaker to find out why. Soon they discovered the painful
truth that her father wasn't the man he claimed to be—and Cowboy
rode to the rescue of this prim-and-proper woman's broken heart.

**#1744 SHE'S THE ONE—Patricia Kay**
*Callie's Corner Café*
After her credit card company called about suspected identity theft,
Susan Pickering turned to police lieutenant Brian Murphy for help. Was
Susan's rebellious sister the culprit? Hadn't she turned her life around?
As the questions mounted, one thing was certain—identity theft aside,
the lieutenant made Susan feel like a whole new woman.

**#1745 LUKE'S PROPOSAL—Lois Faye Dyer**
*The McClouds of Montana*
Bad blood between the McClouds and Kerrigans went back to the 1920s.
But when Rachel Kerrigan sought Lucas McCloud's help
to save her family's ranch, he thought of their fleeting high school
kiss and agreed. In return, she made a promise she couldn't keep. Would
her deception renew age-old hatreds…or would a different passion
prevail?

**#1746 A BACHELOR AT THE WEDDING—Kate Little**
The oldest—and singlest—of five sisters in a zany Italian family,
Stephanie Rossi had ditched her boring fiancé, and was too grounded
and professional to let her heartthrob boss, Matt Harding, step into the
breach. But attending her sister's wedding with the rich hotelier seemed
harmless—or was Stephanie setting herself up to be swept
off her feet?

SSECNM0206